Always you, Edina

V G Lee

Ward Wood Publishing
www.wardwoodpublishing.co.uk

Published by Ward Wood Publishing
6 The Drive
Golders Green
London NW11 9SR
www.wardwoodpublishing.co.uk

ISBN 978-0-9568969-9-5

British Library Cataloguing in Publication Data. A CIP record for this book can be obtained from the British Library.

Designed and typeset in Garamond
by Ward Wood Publishing.

Cover design by Mike Fortune-Wood
Artwork: Pretty Retro Blonde Woman With Martini by Creatista
Supplied by agency: Dreamstime

Printed and bound in Great Britain by
Imprint Digital, Seychelles Farm,
Upton Pyne, Exeter EX5 5HY.

Always you, Edina

ONE

Spring

Okay. Here is a revelation passed on to me by my grandmother who is a *very* old woman rather than just old, who has already outlived both her sons and their wives by several years. I believe it to be true although Gran can and could fabricate to please an audience. This afternoon I was her audience – the dutiful granddaughter bearing fresh fruit.

My shoulder-length ash blond hair was tied back with a velvet ribbon. I wore a pea-green linen trouser suit. Around my neck I'd looped a scarf in a silvery thread, one of my own designs. I'm fifty years old but my partner, Jay, tells me I look at least ten years younger. I'd wanted to impress Gran, show her that although I'd never been her favourite grandchild, still I'd done well for myself.

The *Three Elms Residential Home* is a large detached house just outside Bromsgrove, originally belonging to a married couple; Murray and Anne Bristow. In the garden there is a wooden bench dedicated to them both. The weather had turned surprisingly mild; I'd been able to sit on the bench for the first time this year. I'd looked out across the lawn, then over fields as far as the horizon thinking about the Bristows and wondering if they'd been happy. They'd died within a year of each other, Anne in August 1995 then Murray the following June.

'Do you think he died of a broken heart?' I'd asked Gran later.

'Incompetence more likely. Your grandfather wouldn't have lasted five minutes if I'd gone first.'

'He might have re-married.'

'And who would willingly take on a fifty-year-old alcoholic?'

'Another fifty-year-old alcoholic?'

Gran was in bed. I'd pulled up a white plastic chair a nurse had brought in from the conservatory. She'd offered me a cushion but Gran advised against it.

'You never know whose bottom's been sitting on the cushions around here.'

'Are some of the residents incontinent?'

'Doubly.'

'Surely not?'

'Bonnie, you'd argue with your own shadow.'

I didn't want to be seen as a woman who'd argue with her own shadow – my role was of caring and concerned granddaughter. I offered Gran first a grape from the basket of fruit I'd brought with me and then to plump up her pillows. A firm 'no thank you' to both offers.

'Gran, should you be in bed in the afternoon?'

'It's called an afternoon nap.'

Her bed is positioned facing the open door so she can keep an eye on whoever passes by in the corridor and make sure they keep on passing.

'You can't afford to turn your back on 'em for a moment, Bonnie. I have to sleep with one eye open or they'd clean me out of toiletries.' Gran winked at me.

I smiled and tutted sympathetically as if I really believed that the nurses were so desperate for toiletries they'd bother to pinch her 4711 talcum powder or dried out *Helena Rubinstein* lipstick.

'Not just the nurses, the residents as well. *And* their visitors.'

In her latter years my grandmother has developed a sense of humour. There is something of the gabby parrot, something of the gabby pirate about her, and surprisingly if I hadn't known her better I might have imagined she'd come round to liking me at last. She watched me, her eyes alert. Their particular, bright raisin quality had faded; the brown and the black of her iris become two tentative dabs from a water colour palette which made me suddenly, out of my childhood memories, think of Aunt Ed and her blue eyes. Bright blue.

'You loved your Aunt Ed, didn't you?' Gran said, reading my thoughts.

'Yes I did.' I heard the change in my voice. She heard it too. Something uncontrollable even after so many years.

'When your Uncle Brian first brought Ed home I was very taken

6

with her.'

'Were you?' I blinked and sat up straighter. 'But you've always insisted Aunt Ed was impossible to get on with.'

'It was only when I realised your dad was getting silly about her that I changed my mind. Well, he wasn't your dad then. You weren't even a twinkle in anybody's eye.' Gran re-tied the faded ribbons at the neck of her nightdress. 'These damn ribbons are going to strangle me one of these days.'

'I don't suppose they will.' I helped myself to a plum. 'In what way did Dad get silly?'

'Years ago all the women were after him. He had a special quality that your Uncle Brian didn't have. Of course, everyone liked Brian. You couldn't help but like Brian. Your dad was very different, not so easy to fathom but he had...' and here she suddenly looked a little out of her depth, almost embarrassed. 'Well I suppose *you'd* call it sex appeal. Not only did he have it, he knew he had it.'

We were both uneasy. Sex has never been a subject much mentioned in our family, but now here was my dad's sex appeal set free in Gran's small bedroom and he or it couldn't be ignored.

'Dad knew?' I repeated. 'My dad knew he had sex appeal?'

'Of course he knew.'

'And Aunt Ed? Did you think she had sex appeal?'

'You know she did. Oodles of the stuff. It was a bloody nuisance.'

I wanted to ask if she thought I had sex appeal but Gran was settling herself more comfortably against the pillows. She folded her arms as if preparing for a siesta, or possibly a peaceful death, and then closed her eyes.

'Bring in chocolates next time or *Turkish Delight*. Fruit have an adverse reaction.'

'The nurses want you regular.'

'I'll decide whether I'm regular or not.'

It was a long journey back from Bromsgrove; first a taxi to Birmingham New Street Station, then out again to London and Fosters Grove where I live. I had plenty of time to think. Of course I'd known that something was going on between my father and Aunt Ed but, during what I recalled of my childhood, how Aunt Ed saw *me* had been my chief preoccupation.

7

Aunt Ed could light up a room – if there was a man in that room. She adored men; my dad, Uncle Brian and Grandpa to name but three, although she'd swing her hips coming up our path if she saw our neighbour Mr Mallaby in his front garden and Mr Mallaby certainly didn't have sex appeal. And she'd laugh – a lovely, deep laugh.

She was small and skinny which made her breasts seem even larger and more pronounced. They weren't like Gran's or Mum's. Their bosoms, although sizable, slithered away into the fat covering their rib cages. Once when I was very small I overheard Aunt Ed telling my mum, 'You want to invest in a decent brassiere, Eileen. Those droopy things of yours are only fit to carry home the spuds.'

Which didn't go down well – my mother resorting to her chicken impersonation of dipping her head between her shoulders and then bringing it forward in a pecking movement, which meant she was offended and/or embarrassed; even words like 'throat' or 'hip' brought an uneven colour to her cheeks. Even a word like 'cheek' brought out that uneven colour.

Not so Aunt Ed. She let all and sundry know that her body gave her pleasure. Those breasts stormed into the room ahead of her. They were her introduction, Aunt Ed's version of a firm handshake. *Good afternoon. We are so much attached to this desirable young woman!*

Aunt Ed was Gina Lolobrigida and Grace Kelly – fire and ice. In the early 1960s she still had holidays to plan and furniture shops to visit. Brian needed his tie knotted and their kitchen wanted flimsy gingham curtains fluttering at the picture window.

At school I remembered how I daydreamed while doodling wobbly profiles of beautiful women in the margins of my exercise books. Women I would mean everything to, women I would save. There was never any doubt in my mind that I could save them and yet within a few fleeting years Aunt Ed, the first (and maybe only) woman I'd ever love, was dead.

'Good-night, Miss World,' Reg the ticket collector called out at the Fosters Grove barrier. This has become a funnier acknowledgement as I've got older. At the station shop I picked up a pint of milk and walked down Cat Alley towards home. Cat Alley is really too wide to be called an alley; it is more a concrete pavement with shrubs and trees on both sides. It was dark, nearly nine o'clock in the evening. I

8

could have been nervous except I'd walked that route back from the station for over twenty years. There were fewer cats now. Sometimes when it was quiet I saw a fox, once I'd seen a badger. I walked quickly, hoping Jay would be home and the dinner started.

I was still thinking hard, searching my memory for something I sensed I'd missed. I was hot. The warm day had turned into a sultry evening. I took off my linen jacket. Underneath I'd worn a silky vest top and I swung my arms to make a breeze against my skin. Skin, bare flesh – how my mother had hated it. On evenings like this one, our family congregating together in the back yard of our Birmingham terrace, my mother almost angrily peeling off her stockings. Immediately she'd pull her skirt down to cover her knees and slip her feet back into her shoes, never ever wriggle her toes in the cool night air.

And where would my dad be and how would he be dealing with that first spring warmth? Suddenly I had a very clear picture of Dad sitting on grass. Proper grass, not the patchy stubble that my mum had called lawn. But it isn't spring; I believe it is a moment in late summer. He's wearing his old ex-army trousers, his feet are bare and he's in the process of taking off his shirt. Then he pulls his vest over his head. He balls it up and tosses it at someone. Now he relaxes, one forearm resting on his knee. Dad lights a cigarette. He is half-smiling, half-squinting upwards. His fringe flops near his non-squinting eye. Dad's chest is skinny but I'd say attractively so. He's still young.

I tried to listen to this mental picture of mine. No traffic sounds; perhaps birdsong, lapping water and the movement of trees. I believe I hear Aunt Ed's voice transformed into a mock American drawl, 'What are you waiting for?' In my head maybe, I've added her saying, 'Big boy.'

Dad's smile broadens. 'You,' he says. 'Always you, Edina.'

TWO

Spring 1964

My name is Bonnie Benson. I live in Waverley Road, which is about two miles from where the new Bull Ring shopping centre will be opened by Prince Philip in May.

Gran and Mum think 'it's a ruddy eyesore' but dad disagrees.

Dad says that as England's second city 'Birmingham deserves cutting-edge architecture'.

'Cutting-edge be blowed,' says Gran. 'I'll stick with the parade of shops on Golden Hillock Road thank you very much.'

Our house is Victorian. Gran calls it a 'back-to-back' but it isn't. We have a yard and some grass and we are *not* attached to the back of the house that is in Byron Road. Our house is near a pub and a church. Across the road is Small Heath Park which has a boating lake and a wooden pavilion that sells ice cream in the summer.

I don't like my name. If I could change it I would call myself Isobel. I imagine people (which covers anyone I know now or in the future) saying to other people, 'Have you met Bonnie Benson? Ah here she is.' The people who didn't know me look up with expectation in their eyes which fades to disappointment. Not bonny at all.

My Aunt Ed says that at best Bonnie Benson sounds like a music hall turn and why didn't mum choose Ava, Gloria or her personal favourite Sabrina?

I'm named after Scarlett O'Hara's and Rhett Butler's daughter in *Gone with the Wind*. Aunt Ed knows this. It is a family story that my mum read the first half of the novel while expecting me and then stopped. She said she didn't care for its 'sexual connotations' or Scarlett's liking for drink. A few years later she read the rest of the book and came into the kitchen in tears.

'Bonnie dies,' she told Gran.

'Oh I think she'll outlive the lot of us.' Gran didn't even look up from her crossword puzzle.

'Not *our* Bonnie, the Bonnie in *Gone with the Wind*. She gets thrown from her pony. How could Margaret Mitchell let a small child die?'

Gran didn't know how Margaret Mitchell could and Dad said, 'It's not real Eileen. It's not like *All Quiet on the Western Front.*'

'Although in some ways Bonnie is young for her age, she is exceptionally bright,' my form teacher Miss Wozencroft wrote on my school report for the Autumn Term which I think sums me up satisfactorily.

I am eleven years old in five months' time.

At school (St Benedict's) everyone is pony mad, although nobody, not even Joanna Bayliss – the richest and most popular girl in our year – has their own pony or takes riding lessons. Joanna and her two friends, Estelle and Lesley, pretend to be horses in the playground. Joanna's horse is pure white and named Silver Star – Estelle and Lesley make do with a chestnut and a pinto. Nobody dares to be a black horse as that would annoy Linda Portman, who is always Black Beauty and has a nasty temper if another horse tries to drink from the same puddle.

If Linda Portman didn't exist I'd have been a black stallion called Midnight. I'd gallop gracefully up to Joanna, nuzzle her two friends out of the way, and then together we'd gallop through the school gates our hooves striking fire off the rocky terrain.

Joanna Bayliss has a grown-up brother living in New York. He sends her broderie anglaise party dresses, also at least three angora boleros, a rabbit skin coat and a pair of red leather bootees with a small heel. Joanna's clothes never seem to get dirty. She isn't the kind of girl to have a leaky fountain pen and she isn't the kind of girl that boys flick their own leaky pens at.

On my Spring Term report Miss Wozencroft wrote 'Bonnie is a bright likable child who fails to concentrate' which isn't true. I concentrate very hard on Joanna; the length and darkness of her eyelashes, the curve of her cheek, her ringlets. Joanna tosses her ringlets at least a dozen times in every lesson. I've counted, making a pencil mark in the margin of my exercise book. Her highest score for ringlet tossing is twenty-three. Then there are her surprisingly chubby wrists with the silver charm bracelets Miss Wozencroft confiscated but was forced to return after Joanna's mother wrote a letter of complaint to the school governor.

All around the playground is a low wall with iron railings set into the brickwork. There is a wooden bench where I sit and eat my sandwiches during the morning break. Usually I have the bench to myself but to my surprise, one morning last term, Joanna sat down next to me and took her packed lunch from her shiny leather satchel. Sticking out of a side pocket was a recorder. I hadn't known Joanna played an instrument.

I said, 'Are you good at the recorder?'

'Not really,' she said, 'but Mummy thinks it would be nice for me to accompany her on the piano at family parties.'

'I expect you come from a musical family?'

'No.'

Silently she ate her sandwiches.

'What's in your sandwiches?' I asked.

'Ham and pickle,' she said.

She didn't ask me what was in mine. (Corned beef.) At any moment I could see that Joanna would finish her lunch, pick up her satchel and leave me. I said, 'Do you want to play a game?'

She pulled a face. 'What sort of game?'

From my own satchel I took a wooden ruler and pointed to her recorder. 'We run round the playground hitting the boys with these. Not hard but hard enough to get them to take notice. They'll chase us and try to kiss us.'

'Will they?' Joanna looked impressed.

'Yes,' I said firmly.

'Okay.'

We raced up to where a group of boys were playing cricket. I shouted 'Tally-ho' and was pleased when Joanna also shouted 'Tally-ho'. We poked and batted the boys in the ribs or their backs.

'Bet you can't catch me!' we cried. Together we ran across the playground, jumped onto the wall and clung to the railings. The boys did chase us. As we held on tightly they banged us on our shoulders before rushing back to their game. No boy actually tried to kiss us. I was quite glad about that and Joanna didn't seem

12

bothered either.

In the afternoon break we played the same game and at the end of the day Joanna walked arm in arm with me to the school gates. Her mother was leaning against the open door of their two-tone Vauxhall Victor. Joanna waved and her mother waved back. Joanna turned to me. 'That was the best day's play I've ever had,' she said.

I bumped my face into hers and kissed her hard on the cheek, my nose hitting against her eyelid.

'Ouch!' she said laughing. 'You're a complete nutcase.'

Gran was late collecting me. I'm often the last one waiting at the school gate but I didn't mind. I was friends with the most popular girl in our year. I'd made up our play and she'd found it 'the best'.

The next morning I couldn't wait to get to school. I kept telling Gran not to dawdle whereas normally *she* kept telling *me*. As I came into the playground I saw Joanna, surrounded by her usual group of friends. She had her back to me but I knew she knew I'd arrived by the way everyone else looked at me and then at her.

'Hello, Joanna,' I said.

Her head swung round, thick curls brushing my face and then she moved a step away. 'Mummy said I wasn't to play with you anymore,' she said, her expression quite friendly but as if she was speaking politely to someone she didn't like very much.

'But why?'

My face and ears felt boiling hot. The other girls stared at me, their eyes sharp with interest.

'Mummy said your game was most unladylike.'

'But you said you enjoyed it.'

'Not that much,' she answered. 'Anyone going to the canteen?'

They all were.

THREE

When Dad told me my grandpa was dead I said, 'Good-oh.'

My dad is very tall and I'm quite small for nearly eleven; he put one hand on my shoulder and then hunkered down in front of me looking serious.

'Did you understand what I said, Bonnie? Your grandfather, my father has died.'

I nodded.

'And would you say 'good-oh' if I was dead?'

'No.'

'Then you may be thinking 'good-oh' but would you please not say it to anybody else, particularly not to your grandma. She would be very upset.'

I nodded. He stood up and scratched his ear. 'Why aren't you sad?'

'I don't know.'

I do know. Grandpa smelt. I'd overheard Gran telling Mum, 'It was as if I lived with an old decaying Labrador. I was still very fond of him, Eileen, while being aware that he was never the Labrador he should have been.'

The bad thing about Grandpa dying was that my gran would now live with us and I was being shunted up to the attic; but the good thing about him dying was that there would be a funeral with a party at our house afterwards.

For a few days my dad didn't go to work. Each morning he went to help Gran clear the house. The day before the funeral she came back with him.

'That's it. All done,' she told Mum. 'The stuff of a lifetime boxed up and got rid of.'

Dad said, 'Well at least we've got some of your furniture here. That dark oak rather suits the front room, doesn't it Eileen?'

14

Mum looked surprised to be asked for an opinion but agreed that dark oak did rather suit the front room.

'You could have brought anything else you wanted, Mum. We'd have made room for it.'

'There was nothing else. That part of my life is over.'

Dad took Gran gently by the elbow and sat her down in the armchair.

'Bonnie, I think it's time we had a cup of tea, don't you?'

'Yes Dad.'

In the scullery I filled the kettle, put it on the hob and lit the gas with a match. I listened to their conversation.

Dad: 'We should all be proud. He made captain. He was a war hero.'

Gran: 'But he never got over the war.'

Dad: 'He was a good father to me and Brian. We never went short.'

Gran (sounding annoyed): '*I* saw you never went short.'

Mum: 'It broke his heart when they laid him off at *Raleigh Bicycles*.'

Gran: 'He was drunk in charge of a fork lift truck. It wasn't the first time. They had no choice. Is this how it's going to be in the future – waiting hours to get a cup of tea?'

The kettle began to whistle. I called out, 'Minnie Moaner' (my dad's nick-name for the kettle) 'is boiling, Mum.' (I'm allowed to put the kettle on the stove but not take it off.)

Mum: 'Fruit cake anybody?'

I carried in the tea tray while Mum brought the big family tea pot. She put it on a raffia mat and said, 'I'll just let it brew for a moment.'

We all sat down around the table. I felt resentful that Gran was with us, although she'd often stayed for tea in the past. But now she was staying for tea forever and breakfast and dinner as well. Gran would never go home again and allow my mum to breathe a sigh of relief when the front door closed.

Mum started pouring. 'Have you got a special memory? Of Pop in the old days? For Bonnie? She never really knew her grandfather.'

Gran looked at me as if she'd only just noticed I was there. Sometimes I think she thinks I'm a trainee maid and nothing to do with the Benson family at all. She helped herself to the biggest slab of the fruit cake and broke it into pieces. She spoke to the pieces.

'As you all know I love a bit of chocolate. During the war, Pop managed to get me a bar of *Fry's Five Boys* on the Black Market. This might seem like nothing much to you, Bonnie, but chocolate was neither easy to get or cheap to buy. The day he gave me the chocolate I was wearing a green headscarf with a pattern of black and white Scottie dogs around the edges, the ends tied under my chin like the Queen and Queen mother wear their headscarves. Pop said "Shirley, you look so pretty in that scarf. It makes your face quite heart-shaped" and he kissed me on the cheek.'

She raised her eyes and looked straight at me. 'Your grandfather wasn't a man to dish out compliments. He was a man of few words but whatever words he used, he meant them.'

I thought about this while I demolished my own slice of cake in three big bites.

'What happened next then, Gran?'

'What do you mean?'

'How does the story end? Did you eat the chocolate, did you share it with him, or did you save it for later?'

The day of the funeral it poured with rain. Mum complained that her new stockings would be spattered. I complained that my new white knee socks would be spattered. Gran asked us to please have some respect for the dead.

Assembled in the front room Gran checked us over. She brushed invisible dust off the shoulders of my dad's Crombie coat. 'You'll do,' she said.

Through the net curtains we saw the hearse pull up outside.

'Bonnie, put your hat on,' Mum said.

'I don't want to wear my hat. It looks like a jelly mould.'

'It's that or your school beret.'

'I can't wear my beret. Everyone will laugh.'

'Nobody's interested in what you're wearing,' Gran said. 'Do as you're told.'

'If nobody's interested, why must I wear it?'

'We are all wearing hats.' Gran pulled her new black straw hard down on her head. 'Ladies and little girls do not go into church without a hat.'

'Bonnie, put your hat on.'

'But Dad – '

16

'Put it on or you go to your room.'

I put it on. Dad burst out laughing. 'Actually you do look daft in it. Never mind, you can take it off as soon as we leave the church.'

We went outside. Dad opened his umbrella and held it over my gran while they stood in the rain inspecting the flowers on the roof of the hearse.

'They're lovely. He would have loved the flowers,' Gran said.

For a second I wondered who 'he' was and then remembered Grandpa. Had he loved flowers? One year he'd grown stringy runner beans but never flowers.

A black Daimler pulled up behind the hearse with Uncle Brian, Aunt Ed and my cousin Susan in the back. As we walked past them on the way to our funeral car, which wasn't so grand but still black and glossy, I noticed Susan was hatless.

'Mum, Susan isn't wearing a hat.'

'I expect she'll put it on when she gets out of the car.'

'What if she doesn't?'

Gran raised her eyes heavenwards. 'God, give me patience with this infernal child.'

It was a bit of a squash in the car. Dad sat in front next to the driver while I squeezed in between Mum and Gran.

'This is a cortege,' my mum observed as the three cars moved off.

'What is?'

'This. Us. A procession of cars.' Mum rubbed at the condensation on the window and looked out. 'You'd have thought Mrs Mallaby could have pulled her stockings up from around her ankles as a mark of respect. What will Ed think of us having neighbours like that?'

The hearse drew level with Mrs Mallaby. She crossed herself and then dropped an awkward curtsey. Gran said, 'I believe her heart's in the right place. She brought Pop home a couple of times from the pub when he was worse for wear.'

Mum sniffed. Mum has an eloquent sniff. 'That doesn't surprise me in the least. I mean, you couldn't call Mrs Mallaby a lady.'

'Will you shut up?' Dad said.

'I don't see why I should.'

'That's enough you two, here we are. Stand by your beds.' Gran took her black leather gloves from her handbag and put them on.

The hearse pulled up in front of the main entrance to the chapel while our car followed Uncle Brian's into the reserved parking spaces. I peered out at the small crowd feeling suddenly shy. As our car stopped my dad jumped out, nodded to Uncle Brian and then opened the car door on Gran's side. Mum waited for someone to open the door on her side but nobody did.

'Well really.'

She pushed the door open and swung her legs out, knees and ankles pressed together the way her magazine *Woman's Own* advised was approved by debutantes and high fashion models.

I also tried to copy the *Woman's Own* instructions but caught the brim of my jelly mould hat on the door frame and it tipped forward over my eyes. I recognised Susan's snort of laughter. I pushed back my brim. Susan was already walking towards the chapel. Susan is six months younger than me but already taller and her shoes had a small heel. From behind, in her dark coat and a neat, silver grey cloche hat she looked like a grown-up. She walked exactly like a high fashion model might walk; slim handbag tucked under one arm, wearing one leather glove, carrying the other in her gloved hand.

Uncle Brian was helping Aunt Ed out from the back of the Daimler. Mum's mouth dropped open. For the first time in days my dad smiled.

'What the devil – ' Gran exclaimed.

The rain had stopped. A weak sun broke through as Aunt Ed took Uncle Brian's arm and began to walk towards us. I forgot Susan – Aunt Ed eclipsed all thoughts of my cousin. Instead of a coat she'd brought a short fur cape which she wore draped over one shoulder so we could see that her dress was sleeveless. The bouffant skirt was patterned with pink and black roses. Also black satin gloves to above her elbow. Also a picture hat in black stiffened voile. Even with the bells tolling mournfully in the background, the traffic and the murmur of conversation, I heard the swish of Aunt Ed's net petticoats, like the sound of car tyres on a wet road at night.

'Hello, Mum.' Aunt Ed kissed my gran on the cheek.

'If Pop could see you now, he'd be turning in his grave.'

Aunt Ed grinned. 'Give Pop a chance. He's not buried yet. I expect he'd have said, "You look grand Ed".'

18

Gran almost smiled. 'Well yes you do look grand Ed, but there's a time and place. Where's Susan scooted off to?'

Uncle Brian negotiated the brim of Gran's hat to kiss her forehead. 'We sent her into the church to sit with her friend Lucy at the front. I hope you don't mind Mum, we asked Lucy as company for Susan. They are best friends.'

'I damn well do mind. This is a funeral not a tea party. Lucy's nothing to do with this family.'

Dad said, 'I think the vicar's signalling. Better get a move on. Ed, you brighten up a dark day.'

'Well thank you kind sir. TTFN.'

Mum pursed her lips. 'Is it really appropriate that Ed should brighten up a dark day?'

Nobody answered her; all our eyes were on Aunt Ed. In the doorway of the chapel she let go of Uncle Brian's arm and turned back. She puckered her deep red lips and kissed the palm of her gloved hand. She blew the kiss at me.

'Caught it, Aunt Ed,' I shouted.

'Well,' my mum sounded as if she was carrying on a conversation she'd been having with someone for some time, 'wasn't that edifying?'

'Don't start Eileen.' Dad sounded tired.

'Of course I won't start. Ed can say and do what she likes and I'll just keep my mouth shut. We all dress in sombre clothes as a mark of respect to your father, while she turns up looking like a floozy in a bar and gets smiles and admiration.'

'You're like a dog with a bone.'

Mum looked round and appealed to an invisible crowd: 'I'm lost for words.'

'Good. Keep it that way till after the ceremony. Ready, Mother?'

'As I'll ever be. Eileen, give me your arm.' I got a steely look. 'Bonnie, get along inside. Sit with your cousin and her friend.'

I opened my mouth to say, 'Must I?' All three of them looked at me. I closed my mouth and set off along the cobbled path. I'd find Aunt Ed. She'd be sure to want me to sit with her.

'Don't run,' Gran shouted.

I'm not running, I said in my head, *I'm walking fast.*

I liked the feeling of being on my own; away from my mum's anger with my dad and knowing that he would have been happier

19

going in with Uncle Brian and Aunt Ed. Whenever the three of them were together there was always laughter. Aunt Ed said they were the Three Musketeers, all for one and one for all.

I forgot about my horrible hat. I was pleased with my navy blue, double-breasted coat, white knee socks and new black loafer-style shoes from *Saxone*. Unfortunately they were also my best shoes so I wouldn't be allowed to wear them at school to show off in front of Joanna Bayliss. I admired the fashionable chisel toes as they shot out in front of me, my leather soles making a pleasing important sound on the flagstone path.

In the entrance a verger handed me an Order of Service.

'Your name is?'

'Bonnie Benson. I'm to sit with my aunt, Edina Benson.'

'Ah yes, or should I say, ah no?' He laughed. 'Mrs Benson said you're to sit in the front with your cousin Susan Benson and her friend. All the girls together, she said.'

He put his hand on my shoulder and turned me till I was looking down the aisle to the farthest pew, and there were Susan and Lucy looking back at me.

'Off you go.' He gave me a little push.

The front pews formed wooden stalls, a panelled gate at each end. Susan and Lucy had turned away, their heads close together. They were whispering like two conspirators. As I put my hand on the gate of the stall both of them sidled along the seat towards me, resting their feet on the prayer book shelf so I couldn't get in. In a low voice I said, 'Can you move up please, Susan?'

'No. Sit somewhere else.'

I walked along the front of the pew to the other gate. Susan pushed Lucy and they both slithered along so now Lucy blocked the entrance. They looked at each other and giggled.

'Please Susan, Let me into the pew.'

'You've got to take that hat off first.'

'I can't.'

'Why? Is it glued on?' More giggling.

I looked round for Aunt Ed or anyone I knew. The only familiar face was the verger's. He saw me and made an impatient movement with his hand for me to sit. I rushed round to the far end of the pew and tried to get in but again they were too quick for me.

'Please Susan.'

'Just take your hat off and then we'll let you in, cry baby.'

'I'm not a cry baby.'

'Take it off.'

I took my hat off.

'Give it to me.'

'Why?'

Susan said in a sing-song voice, 'Yours is not to reason why, yours is but to do or die.'

I handed her my hat. She balanced the brim on her index finger and twirled it. 'What shall we do with it, Lucy? It doesn't deserve to be called a hat, does it?'

'Let's kill it.'

'Killing's too good for this hat but I don't want it in the pew with us.'

She dropped it onto the stone floor and stood up. In the cramped space she still managed to give it a good kick. My hat disappeared, sent spinning under the pew through all the dirt and dust.

'Now can I come in the pew?'

Susan sat down again and folded her arms. Lucy folded her arms. They both shook their heads. I walked back along the side aisle looking along all the pews for my hat. And then I gave up. I found a row of wooden chairs behind a pillar and sat down. I picked up the *Book of Common Prayer* and began to study it as if it was as absorbing as *Little Women*. My head felt cold without my hat. If I'd had my school beret in my pocket I'd have put it on.

'I thought I told you to sit at the front with Susan. Where's your hat?'

Gran had found me.

'I don't want to sit with Susan and I've lost it.'

'You've lost your hat? Do you realise what a serious, sad day this is for everybody? Everybody except you, apparently.'

'I'm sorry, Gran.'

'Sorry's nowhere near good enough. This is the last time I'm telling you; go and sit with Susan.'

I didn't move. 'I can't, Gran. I just can't.'

Suddenly Dad was with us. He put the palm of his hand against my cheek.

21

'Bonnie's very hot. I hope she's not getting a chill. She's going to sit with us, aren't you Bonnie?'

'But I wanted the girls to sit together.'

'Does it really matter, Mother? I don't think so.'

'Quite a gratifying turn-out,' Gran said with a grim smile. We were back in our house and I was being used to ferry coats up to Mum and Dad's bedroom. Susan had gone off with Lucy and her parents so I was the sole child in the adult gathering, which was how I liked it. The front room where Uncle Brian was in charge of the sherry and beer was full of cheerful, noisy mourners. There were several men from the *Raleigh Bicycles* factory.

'Your grandfather was a card,' a man wearing an emerald green tam-o'-shanter told me.

I was about to say, 'What card? A Happy Families card? A Beat-Your-Neighbours-Out-of-Doors card?' but Mum stepped between us.

'He certainly was that. Bright as a button. Bonnie, take my hat upstairs.'

'But Mum...'

'Oh yes, bless him. Bonnie, right now, if you don't mind.'

'But Mum...'

'But me no buts, the cold buffet's on its way.'

I took the hat upstairs. It was a black flowerpot of a hat, which Mum said was 'the high street version of a Normal Hartnell model', and although 'high street' not easy to come by. I tried it on and it lodged on the flaps of my ears. My reflection in the wardrobe mirror was no surprise.

I left the hat on their bed and went up to my attic room. I stood by the open window. It was dusk. I looked down onto our back yard. There is a laburnum tree and an old bench. When I was little my dad used to stand on the bench with me and say that if I looked hard enough I would see Mount Everest. Mum has tried to plant a lawn but it's patchy. She says it would help if Mrs Mallaby's cat wouldn't keep relieving itself on it.

In the light thrown from the kitchen window I could make out Dad and Aunt Ed, see the firefly glow of their cigarettes.

Dad and Uncle Brian are very tall. Over six foot. Next to my dad Aunt Ed looked tiny, as if a puff of wind might topple her over.

Nothing of interest to report. Dad making small talk. He likes Aunt Ed but often seems quite shy when on his own with her.

'Hopefully we'll get Bonnie's bedroom back eventually,' he said.

'Good-oh,' I thought.

'In your dreams, lover boy. You'll never shift the old lady. She's got her feet well and truly under your table.'

'Oh I don't know. I expect she'll be glad to settle in a little flat. There's a block going up in Hagley Road.'

I heard Aunt Ed sigh in exasperation, the way she sometimes did with Uncle Brian. 'When will you learn, Ken? She claps her hands and you boys jump.'

'That's not such a bad thing, is it Ed? Me responding to a woman's hand clap?'

Aunt Ed laughed. Well done, Dad. He sent his cigarette stub spinning in an orange arc up into the laburnum tree. They seemed to have run out of conversation. Aunt Ed shivered.

'I'm chilly, Ken.' Dad took off his jacket and put it around her shoulders.

'Bonnie,' my mum called from the landing, 'What are you doing up here? Uncle Brian's made you a lemonade shandy.'

'Just coming,' I said, but before I could move away from the window she was already crossing the room. She stood next to me, looking down on Dad and Aunt Ed, two blue figures in the fading light. Only their hair gleamed – his blonde hair almost silver, Aunt Ed's a brilliant gold that even darkness couldn't subdue.

'I wish I had hair like Aunt Ed,' I said.

'It's out of a bottle.'

'What do you mean?' I imagined hair pouring like liquid gold from a fairytale flagon.

'Ed has a hairdresser friend who comes to their house and does it for her but don't tell anyone I said so.'

'Does what for her?'

'Dyes her hair of course. You didn't think it was natural, did you?'

'So could I have hair that colour?'

'Over my dead body.' Mum leant out of the window. 'Kenneth, don't let Ed catch cold out there,' she shouted.

Both of them started as if Mum had woken them from a dream. They looked up at us, their faces two pale ovals. Aunt Ed's red lips

23

turned to a purple crescent.

'Don't worry Eileen. Ken's looking after me.'

'Actually I think your Brian could do with a hand in the front room.'

'Oh Brian can take care of himself.'

Mum turned away from the window. To herself she said, 'She always has to monopolise him. Without fail.'

Grandpa didn't leave anything specific to anybody apart from Dad. He had nothing to leave. And my dad only got a book of poetry with a dusty green cover; *Rupert Brooke, the complete poems*.

Gran said, 'He wanted you to have it Ken. God knows where he got the book. There's nothing for Brian unless he wants the cigarette card collection. It might be worth a bit in about fifty years' time.'

Uncle Brian *did* want the cigarette cards. They were in a dusty shoe box, in sets held together by green rubber bands.

'Good grief, we've got everything in here; footballers, cricketers, ocean liners, tropical flowers. I'm going to have some fun going through these.'

'Not at my kitchen table, you won't,' Aunt Ed said. 'I'd rather you confined box and cards to the garage.'

'Oh Ed.'

'Never mind "Oh Ed". The garage.'

The evening after the funeral my dad sat in his armchair with the poetry book open on his knee. I watched him as he turned the pages, how his eyelids kept blinking and he shielded his face from us with one hand. He read for about twenty minutes then snapped the book shut and took it upstairs.

Mum asked Gran, 'Whatever gave Pop the idea that Ken liked poetry?'

'I expect because he always had his head in a book when he was a boy. Like Bonnie, Ken's a dreamer.'

Mum snorted. 'I wish I had time to dream.'

I thought about what my gran had said. I couldn't tell from her voice whether she'd thought it was a good thing to be a dreamer or a bad.

24

FOUR

Mum has decided to dye her hair which is surprising as she has always been against what she calls 'feminine artifice'. She says (and my gran agrees with her) that there's 'nothing to beat good old fashioned soap and water. There is no need to gild the lily'.

'Is Aunt Ed the lily, Mum?' I ask.

Mum pauses then answers, 'Only in principal. I'm an advocate of natural beauty but your aunt isn't.'

Gran says, 'Stop now Eileen. You're just giving that little tyke more rope to hang yourself with.'

Mum shows me her makeup bag. It is tiny and made of soft, pink plastic with a zip.

'There Bonnie, that's all I need; a powder compact, my orange lipstick and this eyebrow pencil which has lasted years and years.'

I went with Mum to the chemist on Golden Hillock Road. I love the chemist. There are mirrored walls and on the shelf in front of the mirrors, tall glass bottles with pointed, crystal stoppers, full of liquid in beautiful colours; purple, red, green and inky blue.

Mum asks the shop assistant about hair dye in not much more than a whisper because she is embarrassed.

'I'm sorry madam, you'll have to speak up,' he says. 'You want what?'

'I want something to lift my natural hair colour, please.'

'Ah, you want to dye your hair?' he asserts loudly.

'Yes.' Mum's voice is back to a whisper and she looks over her shoulder as if one of our neighbours might be listening in to her conversation, like say Mrs Mallaby. (Mum says Mrs Mallaby sits on her wall and absorbs all the gossip in the neighbourhood and that she is like a fat sponge.)

The assistant places two bottles on the counter. The labels are,

Blonde Mink and *Blonde Bombshell.*

'Most ladies find either one of these successful.'

But there is doubt in his voice which makes me wonder about those other ladies who perhaps haven't found *Blonde Mink* and *Blonde Bombshell* successful. Mum also is wearing a worried frown and rubbing her neck.

'Why don't we go home and check with Aunt Ed?'

'I'm quite capable of making up my own mind without the help of another woman. I'll take the *Blonde Mink* please. It sounds more refined. I expect women like Diana Dors use the equivalent of *Blonde Bombshell.*' Mum shudders.

'I believe they do,' the man says.

Gran and Mum set up their salon in the kitchen. I bring in the bar fire from the front room while Gran unhooks the full-length hall mirror. She leans it against the table so Mum can keep an eye on 'work in progress'. Mum sits on a kitchen chair with her washed hair towelled almost dry.

Apart from the bottle, there is also a tube of paste. Gran mixes their contents together in the bowl we normally use to store dripping. The smell of peroxide is so sharp it makes our eyes water. As Gran drapes another towel around my mum's shoulders she says thoughtfully, 'You know Eileen, this stuff smells like nitric acid.'

Mum is appalled. We imagine the outcome; Mum screaming, her hair sizzling, scalp steaming, Gran and a pan of cold water arriving too late to prevent the worst sort of accident.

'Oh let's stop dithering and give it a go,' Gran says briskly. 'We can always sue.'

She divides Mum's hair into sections and begins to coat the strands with the paste using an old toothbrush. At first Mum squirms and squeals.

'It stings. Mind my eyes.'

'I am minding your eyes. I'm nowhere near your flipping eyes.'

When Gran has finished she wraps Mum's head in tin-foil and sets the alarm clock for twenty minutes.

'We'll have a *Guiness* to calm us down while we're waiting,' she says.

'Shouldn't we keep sober?' Mum asks.

'We've only got to wash the stuff off and put in a few curlers.'

'But in case you have to take me to the hospital.'

'Don't be daft Eileen. All over England women are slapping this stuff on with no adverse effects.'

Gran gets out the bottles of *Guiness* and a box of cheeselets. Weak *Guiness* shandy for me.

'Switch the radio on, Bonnie.'

'Will we hear the alarm?'

'It's only talking.'

We settle down quietly for the afternoon play. Just as someone called Steven is telling his brother's fiancé (called Iris) that he can't possibly live without her, the alarm clock goes off and we all jump.

'Can't we listen to the end?' I plead.

'You are a selfish little girl,' my mum says, pulling off the tin-foil and making for the sink. 'There better be some bloody hot water.'

Gran raises her eyebrows. Mum never swears.

'I'll rinse you, Eileen,' Gran says.

I move closer to the radio.

It is a miracle. Mum's hair had not even been what could be called brown before, more a mix of brown and grey, a sort of slate brown. It dries to a beautiful pale yellow – no grey or brown left. It isn't a natural colour but truly a film star's colour and it suits mum. She looks so much younger. We are all amazed. Gran is gratified. She feels she's had a major hand in the miracle; very little credit due to the *Blonde Mink* formula.

Mum stares at her reflection in the mirror. She turns her head from side to side. I fetch her hand mirror and she admires the back.

'I can't believe it. Oh I look so nice. It couldn't be better if I'd paid a fortune at the hairdressers.'

Of course we all want to know what my dad thinks when he comes in from work.

'You look like a million dollars, Eileen,' he says.

'Do I, Ken?'

Mum looks at him in such a hopeful manner. I've watched enough romance in the cowboy series on television to know the story. Mum loves Dad. Dad quite likes my mum, thinks she is a game gal, but... he can't help but hanker after the sassy new woman in town with the nifty hat and the frilled parasol.

FIVE

Summer

I tried to read; first my book and then the newspaper but I felt guilty. It was early summer and the train was passing through woodland. A haze of pale green covered the branches of birch trees; the ferns on the slopes running down to the track were newly unfurled. I'm an artist yet I couldn't reproduce the burning brilliance of these colours; greens, yellows and deep rich brown that in a matter of weeks will still look terrific but muted. If anyone asked me I'd say that this is my favourite time of year yet I rarely allow for it. Like the train, I rush by.

This was my first visit to see my grandmother in several weeks. I'd only made the decision to go now because she was in hospital. Again just too busy, although if I had to list the top ten favourite people in my life she'd probably be sitting inexorably at number two. I really look forward to seeing her. I always have done. Yet the sum of Gran has never necessarily been as satisfactory as her parts. I was smiling as I thought this because I knew that my gran's sum not being satisfactory was probably the reason I remained so fond of her.

At least she's not in a geriatric or a mixed ward.

'It would have finished me off if I'd had to look at men's dangly bits first thing in the morning,' she'd told me on the telephone. I'd never heard her refer to men's 'dangly bits' before. As far as she was concerned men didn't under normal circumstances, have such things.

I arrived at the hospital at ten-to-two to find Gran slumped in an armchair next to her bed with her eyes shut and her mouth hanging open. She looked awful; hair sticking spikily out from her head at mad angles. I rarely get angry with her; upset, offended, surprised – but not angry. All she had was a urinary infection and yet there she sprawled looking a mere step away from death. I was frightened *and* angry with her for frightening me.

I shook her arm. 'Gran, wake up.'

'What the – '

'Why haven't you combed your hair? Why is your cardigan on inside out? What are you doing, fast asleep in a chair and drooling at this time of the day? Where are your teeth?'

A full thirty seconds passed before she sat up straight.

'I could do with a fag.'

'That's not funny. I'm not amused. You don't smoke. You haven't in years.'

'Bonnie, you have no imagination.'

Silently I handed her the plastic box containing her dentures. Without looking at me she opened it and took out her teeth.

'Don't watch,' she said.

I unpacked my carrier bag of *Marks & Spencer* food; arranging sandwiches for both of us, yoghurts, cakes, sweets, crisps, a jar of honey, on a tray on her bedside cabinet, then I sat down at the foot of the bed. Gran was combing her hair while pulling faces at herself in the hand-mirror. She glanced at my purchases and sniffed. She didn't in any way look pleased or grateful.

'You must be getting good money to shop at *Marks & Spencer.*'

'I am.'

'For knitting?'

'Designing knitwear.'

'Who'd have thought?'

'Yes who would?'

I tore open a packet of sandwiches and laid them on a paper plate for her.

'Plain crisps or salt and vinegar? Come on Gran, you must eat. These are delicious.'

'I'm sure they are, Bonnie. I remember that sandwich you brought in last month was quite appetising. Lucky I don't depend on you and your posh sandwiches to keep body and soul together. What do you think I eat when you're not here?'

'I've no idea, but I am here with sandwiches, so please tuck in.'

She studied the sandwich but made no attempt to touch it. The

29

nurses have told me that my grandmother is a 'red tray patient'. This is because left to herself she won't eat. She pushes her food around her plate then squashes the lot into a smaller shape so it looks as if she's eaten some of it. She folded her arms.

'Gran, I don't want you to die. It would be most inconvenient. I've got several important commissions and a holiday in Portugal planned.'

'I hate the food here. It looks impressive enough on the menus but it's nothing more than slop.'

'It's not slop. I've seen it. I'd say it was the equivalent of school dinners.'

'*You* hated school dinners. Eileen had to make sandwiches for your lunch.'

I smiled at her. 'And I had currant buns.'

'You never had money to buy buns.'

'The dinner ladies gave them to me for free. They saw my sandwiches and thought my mother must be starving me.'

'You little blighter.'

'Shall I bring you in a stock of currant buns?'

She sighed. Refused to smile back at me. 'Don't bother. I've no appetite. I'm hot. There's no fresh air in here. The sheets are heavy. Once they turn down the lights half the ward starts moaning and screaming. It's like living in bedlam.' She pauses, looking wistfully towards a distant closed window. 'Although I could murder a slice of beef Wellington.'

'You're not allowed red meat.'

'I didn't for one minute imagine you'd have a slice of beef Wellington on your person – it was just an idle remark, but at my age if I chose to take a sniff of crack cocaine, I should be allowed the right to choose.'

'I'm not bringing in crack cocaine, Gran.'

'Does your pal, Jay take drugs?'

'Not anymore.'

Gran looked interested. 'What drugs did he take?'

'Speed, cannabis.'

'And what about you?'

'Not really, Gran.'

'I don't know that "not really" is a good enough answer. Will the two of you get engaged?'

'No Gran, we won't be getting engaged.'

'Married? I love a good wedding. You've left it too late for children.'

'We have indeed. Eat your sandwich.'

'You don't like talking about your personal life, do you?'

'Not really. No. Sandwich.'

'What sort of sandwich is it?'

'Fresh salmon and cream cheese.'

She looked so very disappointed.

'Since when did I eat fresh salmon with cream cheese?'

'I remember you liking salmon.'

'That was tinned, mashed up with Salad Cream.'

'Can't Susan bring in sandwiches? I don't suppose she lives as far away as I do.'

'She's working, Bonnie. She visits when she can.'

There was an awkward pause. I wanted to ask more questions; to grill my grandmother. What exactly does Susan do? (I couldn't imagine her having much of a job.) What does she look like now? Has she put on weight, got a partner, husband, children, mortgage, cat, dog, canary?

I stood up, reaching for my shoulder bag. 'If I can find a beef sandwich will you eat it?'

'Yes.'

SIX

Summer 1964

Susan is away at boarding school but it's my half-term. Uncle Brian collects me just after breakfast.

'A visit from you, Bonnie, will cheer Ed up.' He picks up my small suitcase. 'What have you got in here? Bricks?'

'Books.'

'For one night?'

Gran hands me my cardigan.

'She won't need that. It's going to be a scorcher,' Uncle Brian says.

Mum comes out of the scullery carrying a basket of wet washing. 'I hope you're right. I'd like to get these sheets dry today.'

I'm glad to be setting off with Uncle Brian. I hope the Mallabys spot me getting into his car although it's a bit early for Mrs Mallaby. Mr Mallaby often tells us that 'she likes her beauty sleep'. Mum and Gran think this very funny but never laugh in front of him.

Aunt Ed is watching out for us, leaning on the sill of their lounge picture window. She's wearing a black and white gingham frock with cherry red buttons down the front.

'I like your frock, Aunt Ed.'

Aunt Ed looks pleased. She smoothes the material over her hips. 'It's called a shift dress. It's something of a fashion departure for me but I think I'm pleased with it.'

We follow her into the kitchen. It is perfect and nothing like our kitchen at home. There are white wooden shelves with hooks underneath for pale blue and white spotted mugs. On the bottom shelf are blue and white tins with the words Tea, Biscuits, Sugar, Flour printed on the front. Next to them is Aunt Ed's transistor radio. She switches off Jerry and the Pacemakers singing 'Ferry Cross the Mersey'.

'That's enough of them,' she says.

The kitchen walls are painted tangerine. I know this is the shade because there has been much discussion of the colour at home:

Mum: 'Tangerine! Why would she want an orange kitchen?'

Gran: 'Emulsion will show up every stain and splatter.'

It isn't orange at all; it is pale pinky… tangerine.

'Brian, do you need to get off immediately?' Aunt Ed asks, filling up the kettle.

He doesn't. We sit on pine benches at the pine table while Aunt Ed makes a pot of tea and cuts slices of Angel cake. Uncle Brian lights a cigarette and Aunt Ed puts an ashtray next to his elbow.

'Pity it's started raining,' Uncle Brian says, looking at his watch. 'I told Eileen it was going to be a scorcher. Well this won't bring the pennies rolling in.'

'What do you make in your factory Uncle Brian?'

'Small parts for *Vauxhall Motors*.'

'Which small parts?'

'Don't ask me, ask Martin.'

He and Aunt Ed look at each other and laugh.

'That's a family joke, Bonnie. My foreman Martin Rossiter is the font of all wisdom.'

'What's a "font"?'

'A source.'

He kisses Aunt Ed's cheek. 'Don't overdo it, Ed.'

She slaps his arm playfully with the tea towel. I can tell they are fond of each other. Even in love. My mum and dad never behave like that.

'I've put you in the blue room. Brian calls it "a glorified box room" but I think it's charming. There's a view out over the fields and it gets the morning sunlight. You could have had Susan's bedroom but I thought you might prefer somewhere of your own.'

She pushes open the door. There is an immediate impression of blueness; sky blue wallpaper sprinkled with tiny white daisies. The bed has a white painted headboard, a blue eiderdown, white ruffled pillows; a fluffy white bedside mat. Next to it is a circular cane table with a glass top. On the glass sits a grey plastic hippopotamus.

33

'It's a night-light,' Aunt Ed explains.

'It's lovely, Aunt Ed. Everything's lovely.'

Facing the bed, in an alcove, is a shelf full of tiny glass ornaments; elephants, swans, fauns, cats, several spindle-legged poodles. Even though it is raining outside and very grey, they still glitter.

'I'm glad you like the room, Bonnie. Not everyone appreciates the niceties.' She smiles at me and pushes a gold curl back behind her ear.

Because of the wet weather Aunt Ed says we will make ourselves comfortable in the lounge. She switches on the gas fire which has 'radiated bar heat and a log effect fire with flames' behind a glass panel. It's called a 'Richmond'. I like the way that everything in Aunt Ed's house has a name. She sits on the large cushioned sofa which is from the 'Marlborough Range' as are the two matching armchairs. (At home we have a settee but Aunt Ed's settee she refers to as 'the sofa'.)

Aunt Ed kicks off her shoes and puts her stockinged feet up with a cushion under them. 'For my circulation, Bonnie.' She reads several magazines and the newspaper while I bring down my *Daily Mail Annual for Girls,* which I've read from cover to cover at least ten times but still enjoy. My particular favourite section is 'Janet Page – Girl Groom' plus an article about training your own pony, both written by Judith M Berrisford. In my head I make up other stories about Judith M Berrisford. How when I leave school I'll write to her c/o the publisher *Morrison and Gibb* in London and she'll offer me a job in her stables.

Every now and then I look out of the window at Uncle Brian's fruit trees being lashed by wind and rain. In the distance dark clouds rush across a greeny-grey sky. At home when the weather's stormy our house seems part of the storm, the darkness leaks in, the fire smokes because rain comes down the chimney, everywhere smells wet.

'It's nice being indoors,' I tell her.

'Yes. On a day like today, it *is* nice being in.'

At five o'clock Aunt Ed makes me spaghetti on toast with a poached egg. She carries it into the lounge on a tray.

'Aren't you having anything, Aunt Ed?'

'No, I'll eat later on when Brian comes in.'

At six o'clock Aunt Ed goes upstairs to get changed before Uncle Brian gets home, which seems extraordinary. I can't remember my mum ever going upstairs to change because Dad was due in from work. I think of all the extra clothes to wash, but Aunt Ed has a washing machine whereas Mum has the scullery sink. Aunt Ed has a spin dryer while my mum has only a wooden clothes horse and the washing line.

Above me I hear Aunt Ed running the bath. She is actually going to have a bath as well! Will she wash again before she goes to bed?

Ten minutes later I hear her light footsteps crossing the landing. She calls out, 'Bonnie, come on up and keep me company.'

I lay my book aside and go upstairs. Everything in Aunt Ed's bedroom is cream and turquoise blue. The cupboards and bed are cream, the carpet turquoise blue. The walls are cream, the curtains turquoise blue. The lampshades are cream, their china bases turquoise blue. It is the sort of bedroom I imagine Joanna Bayliss's mother might have but perhaps with pink instead of turquoise.

I perch on the edge of the bed while Aunt Ed, wearing a lacy white petticoat, perches on the dressing table stool. Around her head she's wrapped a towel and her face is shiny from the bath. Without make-up her face is different, very pale, only her eyes are the same bright blue colour. She looks much younger than my mum. More like Susan's older sister.

'This is foundation cream, Bonnie,' she holds up a bottle of browny pink liquid. 'I'm going to dot it over my face and then smooth it in for an all-over matt effect. I'm quite pale complexioned so it gives me some colour.'

I watch her. I am mesmerised. Then she takes the lid off a small circular box. A cloud of powder rises from it and there is a smell of rose petals.

'Now I take this brush – it's made of sable – and I brush powder over my face and neck.' She checks the results in her three-way mirror turning her head from side to side.

'What's in the other pots?' I ask.

'Make-up, Bonnie. The small ones are for eye-shadow and definition; the larger ones for powder and tone. In the summer I give myself a little more colour, in winter I rather like to look pale, like a camellia.' She smiles at me reflected in her mirror. 'When I first met your uncle I was in show business. Only in a small way. Just for a few years but you have to learn how to apply make-up correctly.'

'Were you in films?'

'No, I wish I had been. I did a bit of dancing.'

'Ballet?'

'Latin and ballroom. Brian's pretty good as well. This weekend we're going to a dinner followed by dancing to Edmundo Ross and his orchestra.'

Before I can ask who Edmundo Ross is she jumps up and throws open the wardrobe doors. I've never seen so many dresses. Mum has four, my gran more but as they're all the same colour, black, she might as well have just the one. Aunt Ed must have at least twenty dresses – each one hanging from its own padded coat hanger.

'I've got that much again in Brian's room.'

'Uncle Brian's room? Isn't this his room as well?'

'No. He's got his own room across the landing. Come and see.'

I hadn't noticed the door that led to Uncle Brian's bedroom or, if I had, I'd thought it was the door to an airing cupboard because it wasn't a very big door, not high enough for someone who was over six foot tall. He would have to stoop to go in.

'It's been built into the eaves,' Aunt Ed explains, 'a first floor extension. Cost the earth but Brian wanted his own private space.'

Uncle Brian's bedroom is huge but with hardly any furniture in it. There is a single bed over by the window, covered in a brown and beige cotton counterpane, a desk and a leather armchair. A wardrobe is fitted in an alcove, bookshelves cover the other walls.

'Has Uncle Brian read all those books?'

'Most of them. He likes biographies. And historical romances. Don't ask me why, Bonnie.'

I hadn't been going to ask her why. I'd recently read *Jane Eyre* which I'd found very exciting, particularly Mr Rochester's mad wife. I wondered if Uncle Brian had read it as well.

'Whatever are you thinking Bonnie, your eyes are huge?'

'Just that there's so much space. Everyone has a room and nothing's cramped or crowded.'

She shrugs. 'Four bedrooms. That's not so very big.'

'Doesn't Uncle Brian feel lonely on his own?'

'If he does, he's never said so.'

Uncle Brian comes home in a very good mood. He puts a record on the Hi-fi and begins to sing along. The record is Shirley Bassey's 'Kiss Me, Honey, Honey, Kiss Me'. Aunt Ed joins in as well and finishes by kissing Uncle Brian on the nose.

At half past seven I kiss them both and go upstairs to wash and put on my pyjamas. At home I don't go to bed till nine o'clock but although Aunt Ed and I have done nothing much all day, it seems as if we've been very busy and I feel quite sleepy. I get into bed. It isn't quite dark outside, light filters through the curtains. I feel a long way from my family in Waverley Road, in time as well as distance. I don't know if I miss them or not. I hear Aunt Ed come out of the lounge and pause. Then the landing light is switched on and I hear her soft tread on the stairs. She comes into the room. I pretend to be asleep in case she expects me to be asleep. I breathe in the way I think sleeping people might breathe, deep and long. Aunt Ed crosses the room. She is very close to me. Her skirt brushes against the edge of the eiderdown. She is putting something on the glass topped table.

'Bonnie, I know you're awake. Open your eyes.'

I open them. Her face is close to mine. She kisses me lightly on the cheek then switches on the hippopotamus night-light.

'I've chosen these especially for you.'

Next to the hippo she's arranged six of her tiny glass ornaments; two poodles, an elephant, a monkey, a butterfly and, best of all, a swan.

'I love having you here. It won't be the same when you go home. I'll really, really miss you. Try and spare a few thoughts for your old aunty.'

'You're not old, you're young. They're beautiful, Aunt Ed.'

After she's gone I lie on my side looking at the glass figures. I pick up the swan and cradle it in my hand – the chill wears off the glass. I pick up each of the other animals. They all feel cold. I climb out of bed and carefully wrap each ornament in my vest then I put the lumpy package under my pillow. Almost immediately I fall asleep.

It is morning. Aunt Ed opens the curtains to a blue sky. On the

37

table is a cup of tea with two pink wafer biscuits in the saucer.

'A lovely day, Bonnie. No need to rush. Oh, what have you done with your animals? Not packed them away already?'

'They seemed so cold last night that I wrapped them up in my vest.'

Aunt Ed looks perplexed. I take the bundle from under my pillow and as I do the head and neck of the swan falls onto the eiderdown. Gently Aunt Ed takes the vest from me and unwraps the animals. Every single one is broken; a poodle's tail is snapped off, the elephant's trunk is shattered.

'I'm so sorry.' It feels like I've murdered them all.

'There are lots more on the shelf. I'm not angry with you, Bonnie.'

'None of them are as beautiful.'

'Nonsense. Come on. Out of bed. Choose six more and I'll parcel them up properly.'

I get out of bed and make my choices. She takes them downstairs to pack. On the bed, overlooked, I find the swan's head, so perfect in every detail balanced on the fragile curved neck. With great care this time, I wrap it in my handkerchief.

Uncle Brian has already left for work. Aunt Ed makes me boiled egg and toasted soldiers. She has a cup of coffee and several tablets she takes from a tiny enamelled box. She pulls a face at me. 'Heart,' she says.

She washes up and I dry, then from under the sink Aunt Ed takes a large jam jar. We go out into the garden. It's sunny. Yesterday's rain seems to have dried away and only dew twinkles on the lawn.

'Do you remember how this garden used to look, before Brian commandeered it for his vegetables and chrysanthemums?'

I nod although I don't really remember. 'Gran said it used to be a picture.'

'Praise indeed from the old girl.' We both laugh. 'At least he's left me the sweet pea frames.'

The sweet pea frames form a curtain of colour at the end of the lawn. The moment we'd stepped out into the garden I'd smelt their perfume. We walk past the sweet peas, past the leafy chrysanthemum bed to where Uncle Brian grows his vegetables and stop in front of four long rows of cabbages. Aunt Ed hands me the jam jar.

'I want you to pick off any caterpillars you find and pop them in the jar. When the jar's full I'll give you another.'

With my jam jar I hunker down to my task feeling content. Aunt Ed places a glass of *Robinson's Lemon Barley* on a white wooden table in the shade, a crocheted cotton cover trimmed with blue beads over the glass to keep out insects. From down near the stream I can hear voices – the neighbours' children.

While I work Aunt Ed concentrates on her sweet peas, snipping side-shoots, taking off the dead flowers, all the time murmuring words like *darling* and *sweetheart* to them.

After half an hour as the sun grows hotter she brings out one of Susan's sun hats, faded pink cotton, for me to wear.

'I'll be in the kitchen if you want me.' She turns the sun hat brim back and adjusts it. 'It suits you.'

I love the sun hat – I think because it belongs to Susan and everything she has seems special. I have no sun hat of my own. We have no real garden at home for me to sit in the sun to need a sun hat. Time and my gran permitting, Mum would far rather lie down on her bed on a hot afternoon and read the newspaper or a magazine. Only at dusk, in the hour between the finish of tea and the television being switched on, like badger cubs our family come hesitantly outside; a beer and cigarettes for the adults, a bar of chocolate or a handful of crisps for me.

The caterpillars of the Large White butterfly are easy to spot being bright green and going foolhardily about their munching business across the outer leaves of a cabbage. The Small Whites are sneakier. They are cabbage coloured and conceal themselves within the very heart. There is something repulsive but also satisfying about parting the tightly closed buds at the cabbage centres in search of my prey. Some skill is needed not to damage the tender leaves or smear them with squashed caterpillar paste. Ugh, their soft wriggling bodies against my fingers. I imagine them crying out in their own silent language, "Help lads, come and save me", or "Run for it, she can't catch all of us". I try to. Into the jar I drop them to reunite with the rest of their multitudinous family.

Aunt Ed is amazed and admiring.

'Without your help we wouldn't have had a single cabbage left to eat, Bonnie,' she says leaning out of the kitchen window. A spiral of her bright gold hair catches in a fold of the gingham curtain. I would like to put my finger in the spiral. She hands down more jars and I grasp them with hands stained green and black – a mixture of mud and caterpillar. I am proud of my dirty hands. With them I've saved Aunt Ed and Uncle Brian from a cabbageless existence.

'Screw the lids on tightly, don't forget. We don't want the little perishers escaping,' she says.

At one o'clock she calls me in for lunch.

'Do you miss Susan?' I ask her.

'A tiny bit.' She shows me how much by holding her finger and thumb about an eighth of an inch apart. 'But I'd swap her for you any day of the week. Better wash your hands.'

I could live quite happily in Aunt Ed's downstairs lavatory. There are lace curtains at the small window; the toilet seat cover and 'u' shaped surround are of blue candlewick, and the floor – pristine, black and white *Marley* tiles which are the latest fashion. Next to the basin is a china soap dish shaped like a woman's hand holding a bar of *Lux* soap that is always replaced before the etched word '*Lux*' can be smoothed away, and from a chrome ring on the back of the door hangs a white fluffy hand towel. After I've washed my hands I am careful to clean away the marks on the sink and only when certain that all dirt is removed do I dare pat my hands on the towel.

In the middle of the kitchen table Aunt Ed has placed a small glass jug of blue and lilac cornflowers. There is a dish of ham, another of boiled potatoes speckled with mint, and a bowl of salad. On my side plate sits a thick slice of buttered bread. We eat in silence. Somehow I know Aunt Ed prefers silence.

After lunch Aunt Ed puts out a deck chair for me near the sweet peas and brings a shallow dish full of water from the house.

'Bonnie, while I have a siesta, I want you to make me a picture. Pick as many sweet pea flowers as you like and float them on the water. Use the different colours.'

'But won't that spoil your sweet peas?'

'I have so many sweet peas darling, the more you pick, the more will grow. Stop if you get hot and move into the shade.'

In the heat of the afternoon the birds grow quiet, there are only tranquil noises; the rustle of breeze stirring in the top branches of the apple tree, the hot click of crickets.

I make a picture. First I try to create my aunt's face but that is impossible. There is a small likeness but as if I've turned her into a clown. I know she won't be pleased. I take the blossoms out and begin again; mauve and blue flowers for the sky and all the others; pale pink, dark pink, scarlet, purple and white to represent the garden as I imagine it was before Uncle Brian took over.

The blossoms float on the water, the water laps the rim of the plate, the sun moves behind the fruit trees. Uncle Brian is coming home especially early to drive me back into Birmingham before the traffic gets bad. At four o'clock Aunt Ed comes downstairs. I hear her light the gas ring under the kettle, the click of her kitten heels on the path.

'Aunt Ed,' I call out, 'look what I've done.'

Have I said Aunt Ed is pretty? She is so pretty. Her prettiness has nothing to do with me. She isn't *my* mum. She is no true relation. Aunt Ed isn't selfish with it. She scatters it wherever she walks; her prettiness has been in our ham, potatoes and salad. Coats the *Lux* soap and the lace curtains. Her prettiness is in every room of the house.

Aunt Ed kneels beside my deck chair and inspects the plate of flowers. I say, 'It's your garden how Gran said it used to be.'

I can't see her face. It is turned towards the plate. She is very still.

'A picture just like this,' she says.

'What will we do with this picture, Aunt Ed?'.

'Nothing we can do. By this evening the flowers will be dying. They're dying already. But it is lovely. Better come in now, Brian will be home soon.'

I am sent to wash my hands again while Aunt Ed pours me out a cup of tea. There are more pink wafer biscuits and we sit quietly at the table and wait for Uncle Brian.

Suddenly the telephone rings startling us both. Aunt Ed smiles. 'Now I wonder who that is?' She says this in a cheerful voice as if she knows already. She hurries into the lounge and closes the door behind her. I nibble another biscuit. Five minutes later she comes back. There is a change, she is frowning. She looks up at the kitchen clock.

41

'Was that Uncle Brian?' I ask her.

'No. I hope he's not going to be late.'

She begins to clear away the tea things, clattering the cups and plates and sighing.

'Is anything the matter, Aunt Ed?'

Aunt Ed pauses, stares at the tablecloth, then shakes her head as if trying to rid herself of her bad mood.

'Not really. I was looking forward to seeing someone this evening but they've had to change their arrangements.'

'I'm sorry.'

'So am I.' She piles the crockery into the bowl and turns on the tap. Suddenly she says, 'Watch the water doesn't overflow, Bonnie, I've had an idea.'

She hurries out into the garden. Her head bobs past the window and a few seconds later bobs back again. She comes into the kitchen, her good humour restored – Aunt Ed is smiling, carrying one of the jam jars of caterpillars. With her free hand she turns off the tap.

'Now these are a little extra present. A secret between just the two of us. No need to mention them at home. You caught them; you should have some little green pets. They'll turn into beautiful butterflies. I'll tuck them into your bag, on the other side from your glass ornaments.'

'Can I mention my ornaments?'

'Oh, you can certainly mention them.'

'What will you do with the rest of the caterpillars?'

'They'll be fine. Ah, there's your uncle's car. You've got your cardigan. Take another biscuit for the journey.'

Mum must have been watching from the window, because as Uncle Brian pulls up to the kerb she is already in the front garden leaning on the gate.

'Had a nice time?'

'Yes Mum.'

'No kiss for your old mum?'

I kiss her cheek. Her skin smells of cigarettes and coal tar soap.

'Cup of tea, Brian?'

'Can't stop, Eileen.'

'Tea's in the pot. Mother's over with her friend Miss Venables.

Say the traffic was bad. Ken will be in soon. He was going to work overtime but the car's playing up again. He wanted you to take a look at it.'

I go upstairs to my bedroom. On the windowsill I arrange my glass animals. The swan's head I put in the drawer of my little velvet lined jewellery box. Then I take the jam jar out of my case and wedge that between my last year's *Bunty Annual* and *Rupert Bear*. I am unhappy about the caterpillars. They don't make me think of pretty, fragile winged butterflies. I sit on my bed which I'm not allowed to do (Gran says I'll wear out the mattress springs although it's not as if I weigh a lot like, say, Mrs Mallaby), and I look at the jar. From that distance I can't make out the individual caterpillars, just the colours of green and brown. I shiver.

The caterpillar jar is how I feel about my attic bedroom; everything green and brown with dark corners. Nooks and crannies where my mum never ventures with a duster or a mop. My bed is overshadowed by the dark wood wardrobe that squats on claw feet. Sometimes at night I imagine the wardrobe walking, clumping up and down the room. I don't like looking inside the wardrobe either in case I find moths or spiders. And now I've got the caterpillar jar and it is just another thing to feel unhappy about.

I decide to be braver. 'Faint heart never won a fair princess'. I think about Joanna Bayliss at school, how she might be interested in caterpillars. No she wouldn't be but she might be impressed at *my* interest. *I hate to admit it, but that Bonnie Benson is quite fascinating in a weird sort of way.*

Before I go to sleep that night I take down the jar and inspect it. A little movement, not much. Bedtime for caterpillars as well. From my *Junior Miss* manicure set I take out the tiny nail file and puncture two small holes in the jar lid.

'There,' I say soothingly, 'that's better.'

Return the jar to the shelf. Put a postcard from Aunt Ed, Uncle Brian and Susan 'Having a lovely time here in Blackpool. Wish you were here!' in front of it.

SEVEN

My form teacher Miss Wozencroft has grey hair like wire pulled into a bun at the back of her neck. I was going to say 'nape of her neck' but this sounds too nice. Her face is colourless, including her pale grey eyes. Sometimes she puts a spot of rouge high on each cheek but by the end of the morning either one spot or both have rubbed off.

On Friday afternoons Miss Wozencroft teaches us *Practical Work*. We've learnt how to make a sailing boat and Nelson's tricorn hat out of several sheets of newspaper. The Friday after half-term Miss Wozencroft stood on the dais at the front of the class and said, 'Hands up all those who can knit?'

Only three children put up their hands.

'Well, good gracious. At ten years old I could knit a raglan sleeved pullover,' she said. 'Our first project will be a hot water bottle cover.'

John Seton, the tallest boy in the whole school, groaned and said, 'Miss, boys don't knit.'

'But men do,' Miss Wozencroft replied, which was a good reply but left me wondering who these men were who knitted?

I considered what colours I'd choose; pale blue and mauve in soft baby wool. If it turned out really well I'd give it as a Christmas present to Aunt Ed. 'Bonnie you darling child, I'll treasure this.'

'Bonnie, would you like to be knitting monitor?'

'Yes please miss.'

I jumped to my feet. I'd never been a monitor for anything before.

From a cupboard at the back of the classroom Miss Wozencroft took a brown paper bag and a cardboard box and put them on her desk.

'One pair of needles and an ounce of wool per person, please.

44

Remember children, this is not a toy.' She held a knitting needle in front of her. 'Any silly behaviour could result in a serious accident.'

The wool was like string and string coloured. Aunt Ed wouldn't call me a 'darling child' if I gave her a hot water bottle cover made of this. It would have to be for Gran.

Linda Portman put up her hand. 'Can't we use coloured wool, Miss?'

'This is school issue wool, Linda. When you've all learnt to knit properly then your parents can buy you coloured wool, or you can unravel old woollens and wash and skein the wool for yourselves.'

Miss Wozencroft showed us how to knit a square fourteen inches by fourteen inches in plain stitch. At the end of the afternoon the finished squares with our names pinned on them went back in the cardboard box.

'Joanna, have you handed in your square?' Miss Wozencroft asked.

'It's not finished yet, Miss.'

'Well finish it off in your own time, please.'

During the week I checked at home. There were no old woollens waiting to be unravelled.

'We're still wearing our old woollens,' Mum said. 'You could try your gran.'

Gran said, 'I've got a whole bag of navy blue wool from when I started a pullover for your grandpa. You can have that.'

'Only navy blue? Anything in red or pink?'

Gran frowned then said to Mum. 'Is this child never satisfied? She asks for wool. I offer her wool and then she wants red or pink. Who wears red or pink?'

'Doris Day,' I said.

'Never mind wool, you'll get a clip round the ear.'

The following Friday I was knitting monitor again. After handing out the needles and more wool I concentrated on casting-on for my new square while daydreaming of progressing from knitting monitor to class prefect to Head Girl. At first I didn't notice the rustle of movement, heads turning, and then someone giggled. I looked up. Miss Wozencroft's neatly laced brogues stepped smartly off the dais and headed for Joanna sitting two desks back from the front row.

'What is that?' Miss Wozencroft pointed at Joanna's casting-on. Her wool was bright pink.

'Mummy said there's no point me making something that won't be used, Miss Wozencroft.'

From her satchel Joanna took out a finished bright pink square.

Miss Wozencroft's face changed colour. Behind her spots of rouge her skin looked yellow.

'Where is the piece of knitting you failed to finish last week?'

Joanna handed her the half square; all the stitches unravelling. Miss Wozencroft opened and closed her mouth twice, then holding the piece of knitting by one corner as if it were a dead mouse; she carried it back to her desk and dropped it in the waste paper basket.

She said, 'Get on with your knitting. There is merit in completing a task satisfactorily. Next week we will sew up.'

Afterwards in the playground, a crowd gathered around Joanna. Even the frightening Linda Portman joined in, banging Joanna approvingly across her shoulder blades.

'You were so brave,' someone said.

Joanna shrugged, tossing her hair. 'Mummy's right. It would have gone straight in the dustbin.'

Everyone agreed that theirs were going straight in the dustbin. Suddenly Joanna looked at me, standing a little apart from the group. 'Well Bonnie, what will you do with yours?'

I had a brainwave, a memory of a word my gran used. My chest felt as if it would explode.

I said, 'I'm giving it to my gran. She likes things that are robust.'

Joanna looked disconcerted. 'What does "robust" mean?'

I swallowed, a little unsure, and replied, 'Strong, hard wearing.'

Joanna frowned then tossed her curls again. 'Anyway we have electric blankets in our house.'

I left them and made my way back into school. Under my breath I hummed 'To Be a Pilgrim', my favourite hymn. One day, if I can't be a horse or a cowboy, I intend to be a pilgrim and do good works, but not immediately – after all Jesus didn't get going with his miracles till he was thirty.

Our classroom was empty. I hurried across to the waste paper basket and retrieved Joanna's piece of knitting. I held it against my cheek, imagining the wool feeding through her fingers.

'What are you doing?'

Joanna stood in the doorway.

'Nothing.'

'That's mine – give it back.' She held out her hand for the piece of knitting.

'No,' I said and put it in my blazer pocket.

'You *are* a flipping nutcase,' she said.

EIGHT

No butterflies appear. The caterpillars stop moving. They turn into a green, strange smelling sludge. The smell leaks out of the holes I've made. It fills the attic and finally drifts out onto the landing.

The smell of rotting caterpillars is quite particular, not as unpleasant as, say, rotting meat but it is a dirty green smell. Having inhaled it over several days I would recognise it anywhere.

There is a television programme called *Take Your Pick* with 'quiz-inquisitor Michael Miles' as the compere. He isn't at all handsome having a pock marked face and a very large nose which gran says is due to 'immoderate drinking'. One of the games is that a panel member has to put their hand through a hole in a partition to identify an object by sense of touch — or blindfolded do the same by sense of smell. I imagine Michael Miles wafting a jar in front of a blindfolded me. The words 'a jar of rotting caterpillars' appears at the bottom of the television screen. I would sniff deeply and then say with absolute confidence, 'That smell is a jar of rotting caterpillars.' There would be a round of astounded applause from the studio audience. Michael Miles pats me on the back: 'Well done Bonnie, you have won the chance to either take the money or open the box!'

I almost become used to the smell but I can't stop worrying about the caterpillars. My ears strain for any sound. Although I fear they are dead or dying I tell myself that the sludge is a precursor of their butterfly state, similar to my grandpa in his coffin in Witton cemetery. First he'd had to rot down before he could arise in a shaft of golden light to be welcomed into heaven, having not only metamorphosed into an angelic being but also grown a shining white nightshirt.

For a week nobody mentions the smell although Dad has the manhole cover off by the back door and pokes around with a stick.

He checks the u-bend in the kitchen and is quite hopeful when he finds it is full of dripping, hair and unrecognisable but horrible things. Finally they all assemble on the first floor landing. From the top stair of the attic I watch them through the banisters. They check Mum and Dad's bedroom – all clear. Then on to Gran's.

'Have you been emptying the potty, Mother?' my dad asks.

Gran is livid. 'That pong is nothing to do with me.'

Dad goes in anyway and fishes the potty out from under her bed. It contains about half an inch of wee and several *Sharp's Toffee* wrappers. He says, 'It's not on. This has got to be emptied and washed out every day.'

Wordlessly my gran takes the potty from him and carries it into the bathroom. I hear her pull the chain.

Mum says, 'I think the smell's coming from the attic.'

They all look upwards at me looking down at them.

'Bonnie,' my dad says, 'do you know anything about this smell?'

'No Dad.'

'I wouldn't believe a word that critter says,' Gran announces.

'My daughter is not a critter,' Mum replies. 'I expect there's some perfectly satisfactory explanation. Bonnie, we're coming up.'

In a line they advance, Gran at the rear huffing and puffing.

'Oh dear, it really is quite unpleasant,' my mum says.

As they all crowd into my room, the postcard concealing the jam jar flutters down to the floor.

'What's in that jar?' Gran thumps across the room and picks up the jar.

'Don't unscrew it,' my dad shouts but too late.

'Oh my sainted godfather,' Gran says. 'What the heck is that?'

The smell fills the air as if she'd let an evil smelling genie out into the room.

'Bonnie?' Dad looks at me with querying eyebrows. His eyes are kind.

'Caterpillars, Dad.'

They look bewildered. Dad takes the jar from Gran, puts the lid back on then holds it up to the light. 'Yes, once upon a time these were caterpillars. What are they doing up here?'

'They're my pets.'

'Open the window Eileen. Bonnie, I'm afraid your pets are dead. They couldn't breathe properly and so they suffocated.'

'Did I kill them?'

'Well, yes you did although I don't expect you intended to.'

'Aunt Ed said they'd turn into beautiful butterflies.'

They stare at me then at each other. Gran says, 'Ed said what?'

'Obviously Bonnie misunderstood Ed. The important thing is to get these out of the house.' Dad strides towards the door.

'But Ken.'

'Come on Eileen. Leave Bonnie alone.'

They follow him out.

'Ken, it's high time somebody said something...' my mum says.

I don't hear his reply. At my window I wait. A minute later my dad comes out into the back garden making for the end fence that forms a boundary between our house and a strip of waste ground. I'll tell you now what he looks like. He has white blonde hair with a sort of floppy fringe. Most men of dad's age including Uncle Brian have short back and sides. Dad's always had a fringe, long before The Beatles. It makes him look younger than mum and Uncle Brian although he is actually a few years older. His eyes are brown. Exactly the same colour as my gran's eyes.

I watch as his shoulder muscles ripple against the cloth of his shirt. His arm swings back as he lobs the jar as far as he can. Some way off I hear the sound of glass breaking.

Gran has followed him outside. 'That wasn't called for. That's sheer hooliganery!'

Dad takes out his cigarettes. He lights one and blows the smoke up into the sky. Suddenly he starts to laugh, a rich cheery sound, 'Ha-ha, ha-ha', then he kicks a stone and shakes his head.

'There's nothing to laugh about,' my gran says. 'Why the devil did she give Bonnie a jar of caterpillars? Okay, she might have wanted to annoy Eileen or me but even so.'

'Mother, she wanted to annoy me.'

'Then why aren't you annoyed? Is there anything Ed could do to make you angry?'

'I don't think so.'

'Even though she compromised your own daughter?'

'You're over-reacting. Bonnie's fine. She's like her old dad, tough.'

'She's like her old dad in her stupid wilful adoration of someone who just isn't worth it.'

'In your opinion.'

Gran stomps back indoors. Dad finishes his cigarette and then he looks up at my open bedroom window.

'*Rawhide* on tv tonight Bonnie,' he says quietly.

'Good-oh, Dad,' I answer.

NINE

Every year in June 'weather permitting' we have a family picnic in Small Heath Park to celebrate my gran's birthday. Her astrological sign is Cancer which, it says in the horoscopes at the back of Mum's magazine, means that she is changeable, moody, touchy and shrewd. There are some good qualities mentioned but my gran doesn't have these.

This year Gran is fifty-two. She says she feels at least seventy. I can't remember thinking about my gran's age before, but now I have thought about it I think she does look at least seventy. Mum looks forty-two although she's only thirty – I think. It seems to be a rule that most grown-ups excluding Aunt Ed and my dad will look at least ten years older than they are. I wonder when this will happen to me.

Small Heath Park suits both our families as it has a boating lake and a wooden pavilion where we can buy Eldorado ice cream cornets and *Coca-Cola*. Also there are ducks and swans to feed. I love picnics in the park. It makes me feel as if we're all going on an adventure even though we are only crossing Waverley Road at the Belisha beacon opposite the pub and walking through the tall wrought iron park gates. Then we cross the grass towards the lake and it doesn't seem like we live in Birmingham at all, because suddenly we can't see the surrounding houses, only tree tops and sky.

It was a warm and sunny Saturday. The park was crowded but not too crowded. We found a space under a small tree with shade for anyone who needed it. We laid out my dad's old, grey army blanket and sat down. Gran has a canvas chair because she says the damp aggravates her piles, her rheumatism and her temper.

We're always early because my mum insists that punctuality is the sign of good breeding and also we have only got to cross the road.

They're usually late because they live nearly twenty miles away and Uncle Brian has a daily morning meeting with his manager Martin Rossiter that he says 'has to take priority even at weekends'.

Mum said irritably, 'We don't have to sit in silence', but none of us had anything much to say. I waited for Aunt Ed, Gran for Susan, my dad waited for all of them. Through the trees I watched Uncle Brian's car pull into our road and park. It was somehow momentous just the way the big, black car slowed to a stop. I knew that even my mum, who pretended she wasn't interested, knew that they'd arrived without having to first look up and see their car.

'They're here,' I said.

Dad rubbed his chin and his eyes looked like he was ready to start laughing. Mum tugged a daisy head from the grass and began to shred the petals one by one.

And here they really were – stepping off the gravel path and coming towards us through the trees. Aunt Ed hung onto Uncle Brian's arm. She walked carefully so that her spiky heels didn't sink into the grass. She wore a sky blue dress, sleeveless with a scoop neck, fitted bodice, wide white belt and a billowing skirt. And then came Susan struggling with their picnic hamper.

Gran leant forward and patted my mum on her shoulder. 'Eileen, your hair really looks lovely. You look lovely.'

And that transformed Mum's face. She looked up at my gran and smiled, touching her hair as if to reassure herself. Yes she did look different. Even the dash of orange lipstick suited her.

Dad took off his shoes, then his socks. He wiggled his toes in the grass.

'Why do you have to do that, Ken? I don't think it's quite nice.'

He grinned at her. 'It feels quite nice.'

From several yards away Aunt Ed saw my dad's bare feet. She let go of Uncle Brian's arm and slipped off her shoes. Shoes in one hand, handbag in the other, she fox-trotted towards us.

'What a gorgeous day,' she said, taking us all into her smile.

I jumped to my feet. She hugged me fiercely. 'Bonnie, Bonnie, Bonnie,' she said, as if she'd found her long lost child. Susan poked her tongue out at me. I didn't care. Dad was on his feet too. Aunt Ed let me go and my dad took her by the elbows and gave her a loud, smacking kiss on the lips.

'Mind my *Elizabeth Arden*, Ken,' she said but laughingly.

I was proud of my dad in his shirtsleeves and bare feet. He looked so handsome. Much handsomer than Uncle Brian in sensible dark brown trousers and a tweed jacket. I thought, 'My dad is special even if he never does anything special in his whole life.'

Aunt Ed kissed Gran and then turned her attention to my mum still sitting on the blanket.

'Eileen, there's something different about you,' she said. 'Your hair. Of course, Mother said she'd had a go at it. Very unusual. What colour would that be?'

'*Blonde Mink.*'

'Really? How do they come up with these names?' She looked from my dad to Uncle Brian to me, her eyes full of laughter.

'You look like a million dollars,' Uncle Brian said, kissing Mum on the cheek.

Surprised I said, 'That's what Dad said.'

There was a pause broken by Aunt Ed. 'Did he really?'

'Isn't anyone going to wish me a happy birthday?' Gran asked.

We all did although *our* family had already wished her a 'happy birthday' over a special birthday breakfast of boiled eggs and toast. Mum handed Gran our presents.

'Thank you, Eileen. I'll look at them later. I don't want wrapping paper flying all over the park.'

She put them unopened into her leather shopping bag.

I was glad our presents hadn't been unwrapped in front of Susan. They weren't very exciting; stockings and a new hot water bottle from Mum and Dad, my knitted hot water bottle cover and *Woolworth's* hankies from me, with my gran's initial, S for Shirley, in the corner.

Uncle Brian spread out their blanket which was far superior to ours; pure wool (from an Edinburgh Mill Aunt Ed said), in a red, black and yellow tartan. Uncle Brian looked after Aunt Ed in a way Dad wouldn't dream of looking after my mum. He made a bank of cushions for her to rest against and set her cigarettes, matches, tiny enamel ashtray and straw hat within easy reach.

Susan and Gran were a team opening up their picnic hamper. Our family don't have a hamper, we have brown paper bags. Mum got to her feet. 'What a lovely hamper. Can I peek inside? Oh what dinky plates and cutlery. Bonnie, look at these. And the cups. Bakelite. I love Bakelite. Such colours you can get these days.'

54

We settled ourselves on the blankets; Susan sat next to Gran's chair while I tucked in between Aunt Ed and my dad. Uncle Brian lay full length with a cushion under his head, while Mum took charge of handing out food and cups of tea.

'Well, if we've forgotten anything,' she said, 'Bonnie has only got to nip across the road to get it.'

'I might have to use the lavvy,' my gran said. Mum and Aunt Ed wrinkled their noses. They didn't like the word 'lavvy' which I think is why she says it.

'Happy birthday, Mother.' Dad raised his Bakelite tea cup.

'Happy birthday,' we all shouted.

Gran managed a smile. 'Yes, well, don't let the whole park hear you.'

Uncle Brian said he was going to get his cigarettes from the car.

'Have one of mine,' Dad offered.

Uncle Brian winked at him and strolled off.

'More tea, Ed? Another sandwich?'

'I won't, thank-you, Eileen. These new pills are trying to pile the pounds on. It's a constant battle.'

'Ed, there's nothing of you,' Gran said.

'Oh I don't know about that.' Aunt Ed laughed and pushed out her bosom.

Mum's shoulders twitched and she did her chickenny movement then started gathering up the plates.

'What the devil's Brian got there?' Dad said.

Uncle Brian carried two parcels; one very large, one quite small. Aunt Ed grinned. 'We haven't given Mother *our* birthday presents yet. Wait till you see what we've bought.'

'I've told you, I'm not unwrapping till I get home this evening.'

Uncle Brian put the presents at her feet.

'You bloody well are because, if the big one doesn't suit, Ed will have to return it to the shop for a refund on Monday morning. The smaller present is from Susan. She's back at boarding school tomorrow so you won't see her for a couple of months.'

'Well, if you insist.'

'We do insist. It's exciting, isn't it Bonnie?' Aunt Ed was sitting up, her arms hugging her knees. Through her nylons I saw her toe nails were painted bright pink.

'Big or little? Which first?' Gran asked.

'Open mine,' Susan said, speaking for the first time in ages. 'It's with lots of love, Gran. Mum's idea but I chose them myself.'

'Bless you, child' She patted Susan's head.

Susan's present was wrapped in pink tissue paper and tied with a pink ribbon. Inside was a cardboard box patterned with violets.

'That's your lucky flower, Gran.'

'Is it? Whatever next?'

Gran opened the box. 'Susan, they're beautiful.'

We all craned forward to see; handkerchiefs. Out loud I read the writing on the inside of the lid; 'Finest Irish Linen'.

Mum and I exchanged looks.

'They're almost too good to use,' Mum said. 'What's in the big one?'

An electric blanket. It was cream coloured and very soft. You could hardly feel the electric wires running through it.

Gran said, 'It's a magnificent present. Only... aren't electric blankets dangerous? I'm sure I've heard dreadful stories.'

'It's a *Windak*,' Aunt Ed said briskly, 'very reputable. Their slogan is "Safe from electrocution". They aren't cheap, but as a rule I think you get what you pay for. Isn't that right, Brian?'

'You're not wrong.'

Impatiently Aunt Ed snapped, 'I know I'm not wrong, but aren't I right?'

'Yes, of course, darling.'

'Well I'm very pleased,' Gran said. 'You and Ken will be jealous of me come winter with your leaky hot water bottles.'

'Yes, I expect we will. We'll just have to snuggle up, won't we Ken? Fruit cake anybody?' Mum opened the cake tin.

Dad got out his Kodak Brownie 127. 'Come on, Mother – before cake, let's have a snap of you with a smile on your face.'

'No thanks.' Gran covered her face with the newspaper.

Susan put her arm round her shoulders. 'What about a snap of the two of us together?'

'What, beauty and the beast?'

'You've got a lovely face. I hope I look just like you when I'm an old lady.'

'Enough of the "old lady". Go on Ken. Get it over with.'

They turned smiling faces towards him. Dad took the photograph. Nobody seemed to think that the other granddaughter

56

should be in the picture. But then my dad took snaps of us all and one of me arm in arm with Aunt Ed.

Uncle Brian suggested a game of cricket.

'Are you daft?' Aunt Ed demanded. 'Can you imagine me playing cricket at any time, never mind in this heat?'

With much laughter we agreed that we couldn't imagine it.

Dad said, 'How about me and Brian taking you out in a rowing boat? There'll be a bit of breeze on the lake.'

Her face lit up. 'That's a lovely idea, Ken.'

'Suits me,' Uncle Brian said.

'What about the rest of us?' Mum asked.

'You've got your magazine, Mother's got the newspaper. Someone's got to keep their eyes on the girls.'

Dad was on his feet. Aunt Ed held out her hand and he took it and pulled her up.

'Now, take it easy Edina. Don't hurry – and bring your straw hat,' he said. 'I'll go and see about hiring a boat.'

Dad slipped on his shoes and sauntered down towards the lake. Aunt Ed said, 'I'm taking off these bloody stockings.' She looked at my mum. 'You don't mind if I borrow your husband for an hour, do you Eileen?'

'You've never bothered to ask before – why bother now?'

'Well shall I go or shan't I?'

'Do what you want.'

Mum flopped back onto the blanket and covered her face with her magazine.

Aunt Ed bundled up her skirt and net petticoats. There was a glimpse of pale pink lace and the elastic of her suspender belt as she unfastened her stocking tops. She left her nylons on the grass, like two delicate flowers and then barefoot she picked her way slowly after my dad.

'Hang on Ed, wait for me,' Uncle Brian called out but Aunt Ed didn't hang on, she didn't even look round.

'I want to come too,' Susan said.

'There's not enough room. Perhaps Aunty Eileen will take you later.'

'Perhaps Aunty Eileen won't,' my mum said. 'Aunty Eileen's far too hot for rowing a boat on her own.'

Down at the edge of the lake Dad was already paying for the

boat. Aunt Ed had reached him. The breeze whipped her skirts so you could see her white net petticoats.

'Dad,' Susan pleaded.

'No, Susan. Don't make a fuss. You know Mummy's not been well, this is her treat as well.'

'You keep saying she's ill but there's nothing wrong with her. Anyway, why can't Uncle Ken row her about and *you* take me and Bonnie?'

Uncle Brian's shoulders slumped. His big face looked hot and a little disheartened. From under her magazine Mum called out, 'Oh for God's sake Brian, you might just as well take the girls. Let Kenneth and Ed have their damn boat ride.'

Gran said, 'Go on Brian, take the girls.'

'Come on then,' he said dully and marched off down to the lake.

Very slowly I got to my feet. 'I don't know if I want to go in a boat – supposing I fall in and drown?'

'Susan can swim. You'll keep an eye on Bonnie, won't you?'

'Yes Gran.' She grabbed my arm. 'Come on Bonnie. If we don't get a move on my dad will change his mind.'

The lake was smooth, reflecting back the clear blue sky and the trees. Dad's boat was already gliding swiftly across the water towards the small island in the middle. Uncle Brian took off his tweed jacket and laid it next to him on the wooden seat. Susan and I sat facing him. He rolled up his shirt sleeves. His arms were very white whereas my dad's arms are brown. He took the oars and began to row. We shot away from the jetty. Suddenly we were surrounded by water. A gentle breeze ran along the surface of the lake cooling our hot faces. Uncle Brian relaxed. Susan glanced at me. 'Don't worry; you're not going to drown, stupid.'

'I promise you won't fall in,' Uncle Brian said, 'and if you did I am a world-class life saver. Susan, hold Bonnie's hand.'

'I don't want to.'

Firmly he said, 'If you don't do as you're told I'm rowing straight back to the bank.'

She took my hand. Mine was cold, hers was hot. 'Honestly,' she said. 'What a ninny.'

By then Aunt Ed and my dad had reached the island. Behind Uncle Brian's broad shoulders we could see him lifting her out of the boat, swinging her round and setting her down on the grass.

'Can we go to the island, Dad?'

'No, Susan, we'll row round it.'

'But I want to go there. There might be buried treasure.'

'There isn't. You wanted to go in a boat and that's what we're doing. Are you okay with that Bonnie?'

'Yes thank you, Uncle Brian.'

'Yes thank you, Uncle Brian,' Susan jeered.

Uncle Brian concentrated on his rowing while I searched the grassy slope to pick out Mum and Gran and our blankets. Found them. Mum was sitting up shading her eyes against the sun. I waved. She didn't see me waving. Gran waved. I waved back. Mum turned to my gran and said something then she dropped back onto the blanket.

'I can't see Mum and Uncle Ken anymore.'

Uncle Brian said, 'Susan, will you just shut up?'

It wasn't a big island. You could cross from side to side in a couple of minutes. Willow trees dipped their curved branches into the water. Behind them were silver birch saplings and rhododendrons heavy with faded rusty red blossom. As we rowed past I saw that some of the blossom had fallen into dad's empty rowing boat – they looked like splashes of blood. We passed their boat four times before the boatman on the wooden jetty shouted through his loud hailer, 'Number twenty-two, come in please.'

'That's Uncle Ken's boat,' Susan said.

We neared the jetty. The boatman pulled our boat close with a long wooden pole, a hook on the end. Susan leapt out and ran to the end of the jetty. Uncle Brian picked me up and deposited me on dry land.

'Go on back, Bonnie; I'll wait with Sue for Ken and Ed.'

I didn't go back immediately. I watched Susan and Uncle Brian standing together, both of them looking across the water towards the island – and then there was the blue of Aunt Ed's dress and the white of my dad's shirt flickering through the trees. Dad appeared on the bank, Aunt Ed next to him. He held up his hand as if saluting Uncle Brian. Uncle Brian turned away.

'Come on Susan,' he said.

After that the picnic was boring. Susan sulked. Aunt Ed was tired.

She lay on their blanket with her head resting on a cushion and kept her eyes closed, although I don't think she was properly asleep. Uncle Brian took ages over the crossword puzzle in Gran's newspaper. Dad took out a book.

'What are you reading?' Mum asked, which was surprising as she couldn't actually see that he was reading anything because her face was covered with the *Woman's Own*.

'Poetry,' he said.

'What sort of poetry?'

'Just poetry. You wouldn't be interested.'

'Let me guess. Love poetry.'

'No.'

'Ken, read us a poem,' Aunt Ed said dreamily.

'No Ed.'

'Oh come on Ken; why not read Ed a poem? There must surely be some sort of lovey-dovey nonsense in that book of yours.' Mum threw off the magazine and sat up. 'Go on Ed, ask him again. Wheedle a poem out of him. He'd read one for you.'

'Shut up,' Dad said.

Mum made a grab for the book but he held it above his head. 'For God's sake, Eileen, will you leave me alone?'

'Little pitchers have big ears, you two. Cut it out,' Gran said.

Mum lay back down, on her side this time so she faced the lake and had her back to all of us. Dad carried on reading. For twenty minutes nobody spoke, then Gran began to fidget.

'Time the girls fed the ducks. I'm not lugging that bag of crumbs home with me.'

'Can we have ice creams when we've fed them?' I asked.

'If you behave yourselves.'

Susan fished her bag of bread crumbs out of the hamper and I took the left-overs from our sandwiches and some of the fruit cake. Together we walked down to the lake's edge. Ducks paddled towards us, leaving silvery trails in the water.

'No sign of any swans,' I said.

Susan shrugged. 'Big deal.'

Where we were standing, the water was quite shallow. I could see the pebbles and some sharp pieces of green glass. I thought I saw some tiny grey fish. I stirred the water with my fingers. Suddenly I was aware of Susan standing too close. It would be so like her to give me a shove. I stepped away from the water and opened my paper bag and then I realised there were drops of water on Susan's cheeks. Was she crying?

'Is anything the matter?'

Susan wiped her wrist roughly across her face. 'Nothing,' she said.

I tried to think of something to say that might please her.

'You're lucky to have such a pretty mum. Aunt Ed is how I imagine a fairy tale princess would look.'

Susan puffed out her cheeks just like my gran sometimes does and lobbed a crust of bread at a mallard's head. Niftily he caught it in his beak.

I continued, 'Don't *you* think she's like a fairy tale – '

'You are *so* stupid. There is no such thing as a "fairy tale princess". My mum is no prettier than your mum. It's all make-up. And anyway, she's ill and going to die soon.'

'She isn't going to die soon.'

'Yes she is. One day she'll look like a… corpse.'

I didn't want to think of Aunt Ed as a corpse because it made me think of her turning into Grandpa.

'She'll always be beautiful.'

Susan looked at me as if she hated me. 'When you're dead you don't stay looking beautiful. Your face goes like rotten meat and maggots poke their heads out from your eye sockets.'

She gnashed her teeth and pulled a horrible face. 'Whooo, here come maggots,' she yelled and threw the remains of her bag of bread at me.

'Stop it! Stop it! I'm going to tell everyone what you said, Susan Benson, and you're going to be in trouble.'

Crying, I ran back up the slope. Gran struggled up out of her chair. 'Whatever's the matter?'

I hurled myself at her and she put her arms around me and hugged hard. Gran had never hugged me before. I said, 'Susan threw her bread crumbs at me.'

Immediately Gran pushed me away. 'Oh for pity's sake, a few bread crumbs won't hurt you. Whenever are you going to grow up?'

'But she said they were maggots and they poke out of the eyes of corpses. She said Aunt Ed was going to be a corpse soon.'

Everyone went silent, staring at me as if I'd said something awful.

Aunt Ed was the first to speak. More to herself than us, she said, 'That's it. The final straw. She just never learns.'

Gran said, 'Really Ed, it's not serious. Bonnie's far too thin skinned. Ken, Eileen, Bonnie always over-reacts, doesn't she?'

Aunt Ed ignored her. Humming 'America' from *West Side Story* she set off towards Susan.

'Ed, Susan didn't mean anything. She's only a child,' Mum called after her.

Aunt Ed and Susan faced each other. For the first time I realised that Susan was taller than her mum, a good two inches taller than me.

Aunt Ed said, 'Look me in the eye.'

Susan did.

'Mum, I'm sorry.' Susan sounded frightened.

Gracefully Aunt Ed reached behind Susan's neck. I thought she was going to draw Susan's head forward and perhaps kiss her on the forehead. Tell her 'it didn't matter'. But instead, she grasped a handful of Susan's hair and yanked it hard so that Susan's head jerked sideways.

'Ow!' Susan yelled.

'What happens to naughty children?' Aunt Ed asked quite pleasantly as if she really wanted to know.

Susan said, 'They get punished.'

Gran bustled up to them and put a hand on Aunt Ed's shoulder. Aunt Ed didn't even look round; she just shrugged off her hand.

'And do you agree that naughty children deserve to be punished?'

'Yes,' Susan said.

I looked at my dad. He'd taken out his cigarette packet and was offering it to Uncle Brian. Uncle Brian took a cigarette and without speaking they walked a few steps away.

'Okay.' Aunt Ed nodded. 'Don't blot your copy book again. Understand?' Gran reached out and tried to unfasten Aunt Ed's fingers from Susan's hair.

'Don't interfere,' Aunt Ed said.

'It's just a silly quarrel. My boys were always having fights and rows. It's part of growing up.'

'Not in my family, it isn't.'

She let go of Susan. Her shoulders drooped. Her chin suddenly lowered and she placed one hand on her bosom.

'Brian,' she said.

Uncle Brian ran. He ran the short distance to take him to Aunt Ed's side. Dad didn't run. He'd moved further off into a group of trees but he watched. We all watched Aunt Ed. Susan was completely forgotten.

Gran grumbled, 'Ed, you're a bloody idiot getting yourself into such a state. Where are your tablets?'

Aunt Ed was settled back down onto cushions and given the last of the tea. Mum took out her purse and gave me a ten shilling note. She said, 'You and Susan, go and get yourselves a cornet. I'll expect quite a bit of change.'

Aunt Ed looked up. 'Susan's not to have a cornet. I'm not rewarding her for bad behaviour.'

And then Dad came back into our family group. He hunkered down in front of Aunt Ed and took her hands, that were clasped around her bakelite tea cup, in his. 'Ed, let it go. Let the girls have their ice creams. Don't worry about them, worry about getting yourself well.'

'I'm never going to get well,' she said.

'Oh yes you are.'

They smiled at each other. Mum put her hand on my shoulder and gave me a gentle push. 'Go and get the cornets with your cousin.'

TEN

I lie in bed and listen for the sounds of our house settling down for the night. Almost always there is a pattern; first Gran comes upstairs and then ten minutes later I hear my mother's footsteps crossing the hall from the kitchen and know she's on her way. Gran goes into the bathroom and when she's finished she stops outside their bedroom door and taps.

'It's all yours, Eileen,' she says.

When both Mum and Gran have fallen silent, my dad begins to move around downstairs. He locks and bolts the scullery door that leads out onto the garden. Then he fills a plastic beaker with water and pours it on what's left of the fire. Even in summer we have a fire because our house is always cold. Also there is a 'back-boiler' somewhere inside the chimney breast that I've never seen, but has an 'irascible nature' my gran says. Sometimes it agrees to heat our water and sometimes it just can't be bothered.

Dad returns the beaker to the scullery and bolts the inside scullery door from the kitchen side. Often there's a silence once all the bolting is over as if he is looking around the room and wondering if there's anything else he can do.

Finally my dad comes out of the kitchen and into the hall. He'll leave the kitchen door open so 'the residual heat permeates into the rest of the house'. These are my gran's wise words. Not exactly hers. She has read them in a newspaper article. Gran has a scrapbook full of useful household hints, although the 'residual heat' one has been the most impressive. Even Dad, who finds my gran's household hints of no interest, takes note.

It is the night after our picnic in the park. Gran comes upstairs and goes into the bathroom. I wait but there is no sound of my mum crossing the hall. Ten minutes later Gran walks along the landing but doesn't pause at their bedroom door. I am almost asleep but the alteration in her routine wakes me up. Have I heard my mum come up or not?

I watch the luminous green hands of my alarm clock edging past the luminous green numbers. Gran comes out of her room and goes back downstairs. She opens the kitchen door but doesn't go in. I hear her voice because it is quite loud as if she is annoyed. 'I hope you two aren't going to stay down here arguing all night.'

Nobody answers her.

'Please yourself.' She shuts the door. 'A waste of breath.'

After that I can't sleep. When the clock hands show midnight I get up very quietly and peer over the banisters, down to the next landing, to the hall in semi-darkness below. Not a sound. I tiptoe past Gran's room, avoiding the floor board that creaks, and make my way down the stairs.

The stone tiles of the hall feel icy. No 'residual heat' you see. I retreat back to the last few stairs and sit down. I wish I'd put on my slippers and dressing gown. I think, 'Bonnie, you'll catch your death of cold', and feel like I might really catch my death of cold.

Angry muffled voices from the kitchen but no sounds of movement, nobody pokes the fire; the springs of Dad's armchair don't complain as he settles himself more comfortably. I want to go back to bed but keep setting myself to the count of a hundred – surely in that time there will be some reassuring sound? But there isn't. I can't stop shivering. I set another hundred and another and then suddenly the kitchen door opens and light floods into the hall, dazzling me.

Mum stands with her back to me facing into the room. 'It's the disloyalty I can't bear, Ken.'

Then my dad's voice sounding almost bored, 'Eileen, it wasn't disloyalty. I might have mentioned it in passing.'

'In passing what? Ed's bedroom?'

'You're ridiculous. You make yourself look ridiculous.'

'You made me look ridiculous. My hot water bottle against Ed's bloody *Windak*. Bonnie with her cheap handkerchiefs and knitting.'

'I don't want to hear any more.'

'Oh don't you? Well too bad because I'm nowhere near finished.'

She steps back into the kitchen. Dad sees me sitting on the bottom stair and gets up. My mum turns round quickly and gasps, 'Bonnie, what are you doing down here?'

'You didn't come up.'

'I'm coming up now.'

'And Dad?'

'He'll be along in a minute.'

She kneels in front of me, takes my cold hands in her warm ones. 'You're frozen.'

Dad comes out into the hall. She looks up at him. 'See what you've done.'

He twitches his head like a horse shying away from a fly and pushes in front of her. He bends down, bringing his face near to mine, his hands clasping his knees. 'Want a piggy-back, munchkin?'

Which makes me laugh a bit. 'Dad, I'm too big for piggy-backs.'

'Nonsense, you're never too big for a piggy-back from your old dad.'

Dad's arms swing forward and his hands grip me roughly under my armpits.

'No, Dad,' I protest.

I *am* too big. I haven't had a piggy-back in years and years and now I don't want to be that high up on his shoulders with nothing much to hold on to.

'Leave her alone,' Mum says. 'I'll see her to bed.'

'I'm taking her up myself. Come on Bonnie, don't fool around. Let go of the banisters.'

'But I don't want a piggy-back.'

'Of course you do.'

'I don't.'

'She says she doesn't.'

He lifts me off the stairs. Mum tugs at my ankles.

'No, Dad. Put me down.'

They will tear me in half rather than give up the bit of me they are holding.

'What the devil do the two of you think you're playing at?'

We look up to see my gran, her dressing gown tightly belted, face framed by a crown of spiky plastic curlers. Mum lets go of my ankles and my dad lowers me to the floor. Gran says, 'Bonnie, come on up here now, please.'

I run to her. She takes my hand and leads me back up the attic stairs to my bedroom.

'Hop in.'

Gran tucks the blankets tight around me, feeding my arms under the covers as if I am a doll she is putting to bed. I tell her, 'They were arguing about your birthday presents.'

'There is nothing for them to argue over. I'll probably get more use out of the hot water bottle, and the knitted cover is lovely. Whatever Ed says, I wouldn't be happy lying down on wires with electricity running through them and I'm pleased with both sets of handkerchiefs. You can't have too many handkerchiefs in my opinion.'

'Mum thinks Aunt Ed knew that we'd bought you hankies and a hot water bottle and then got the same presents only better versions?'

'Can you imagine your Aunt Ed playing such a mean trick?'

'Never.'

Gran looks at me oddly. 'Well, I suppose that's a good thing.'

The next afternoon, when I get home from school, my mum puts a jam and cream sponge cake on a plate in the centre of the kitchen table

'It's only bought cake. I don't expect it's as fancy as anything you'd get at your aunt's.'

'I don't think they eat much cake. They're watching their figures.'

Gran frowns at me.

'I'm not watching my figure though,' I add quickly.

'And I'm certainly not watching mine. Nor should you be Eileen. There's nothing of you. Come on, my stomach thinks its throat's been cut.'

'That's a horrible phrase, Mother.'

Mum goes back into the scullery for the plates while Gran pulls several different faces at me. I pull several different faces back at her.

'Don't be cheeky,' Gran says.

I eat two slices, nibble at a third. There is not much jam or cream filling but the sponge bit is okay. Mum watches me intently and I make 'yum-yum' sounds so she thinks that I think the whole cake is delicious.

'Get everything done, Eileen?' Gran asks.

'Yes.'

They look at each other across the table. Mum gives her a tiny

67

nod. She gives Mum a tiny shrug. 'Get on with your cake, Bonnie,' Gran says.

'Finished.'

'Well get on with something.'

'I'm glad you enjoyed the cake, darling.'

Mum hardly ever calls me 'darling'. If she does, Gran usually chimes in with, 'I wouldn't go that far Eileen', but on this occasion she says nothing.

Later, when my dad comes home from work, he seems very pleased to see me as well. He's bought me a grown-up paint box made of wood. Inside are a dozen tubes of paint and a choice of brushes, a dainty glass water pot and a palette.

'All you need is a smock and beret.' He ruffles my hair, which I don't normally like people doing.

My head is full of thoughts about them arguing and pulling me about last night but here is Dad wanting me to be pleased with his present and Mum watching like a sad-eyed hawk to see if I still like her. I want to disappear but am not ready to go up to my room in the attic. Instead I go into the front room where I can stand in the bay window and look out onto Waverley Road.

We rarely use our front room except when visitors come, although visitors would really be much happier in the kitchen which is warm and has comfortable chairs. Gran entertains her friend Miss Venables in the front room. If she would only bring Miss Venables into the kitchen I'm sure she'd stay longer. I think that it is so cold in there that after two cups of tea Miss Venables has a desperate need to use the lavatory but is embarrassed to ask to use ours and so hurries back home to Byron Road.

It is quite a scary room once the light begins to fade. On the back of the door hangs Gran's fox fur. If I'm not careful when I go in the head swings round and hits me in the face, or at least startles me. There is a wooden peg attached to its muzzle so you can open and close the fox's jaws. Left to its own devices I believe the fox is quite capable of going for my throat. Mum says this is fanciful but I know she's not fond of it either, although she may be worrying about possible moth infestation.

Most of the furniture comes from my gran's old house. It's all dark carved wood, a settee and two very straight-backed chairs, a gate-legged table in the window covered by a green chenille tablecloth. On the mantelpiece is a dusty Welsh doll wearing a tall black cockleshell hat. Gran told me this is what it is called. She says, 'I have Welsh antecedents going back donkey's years, although they haven't kept up the connection.' The doll has a dress covered by a yellowed apron that is supposed to turn blue if it's about to rain, although nobody has ever seen this happen. Next to her a china lady wearing a pink crinoline curtseys to a gentleman in a powdered wig, and on the shelf underneath stands a marble clock with a loud tick. Every few months Mum changes the crocheted arm rests and chair backs and goes round with her prize possession, the Hoover Junior.

We all refer to Hoover Junior as if he were a member of our family. It is assumed that Hoover is a 'he'. I think Mum imagines Hoover is a very helpful schoolboy while I think he's American and a teenager. He is dusted more often than any of the furniture.

I go straight to the window and lift up the net curtain. There is Mrs Mallaby as always, sitting on her garden wall. Mrs Mallaby is more reliable for predicting the weather than Gran's Welsh doll. If she is on the wall I know that the day is set fair for at least an hour.

She wears her old carpet slippers and her stockings are rolled around her ankles. Her hair is in blue plastic curlers only half concealed under a pink nylon scarf that makes her look as if she has her head bandaged. The only time I ever see Mrs Mallaby on her feet with her stockings pulled up and her hair arranged in sausage curls is at seven thirty in the evening when she sets off to the pub. I'm always asleep before she comes back, although sometimes her singing wakes me up.

Out in the road her son, Donald, is pushing his sister Jenny along in a doll's push-chair. She is miles too big for it but is still screaming with laughter and waving her long legs in the air. Donald is laughing too and veering all over the road as if he is drunk. Mrs Mallaby takes not the slightest notice. Spread out on her fat knees is her pools coupon and she is putting in her crosses with the stub of a pencil.

'What about Aston Villa, Donald?'

'What about Aston Villa?' he shouts back. At that moment the pram tilts sideways and sends Jenny sprawling into the gutter. She scrambles to her feet and starts chasing him. Her skirt is torn and her knees are filthy. 'Mum, he's broken the bloody pram!' she yells.

'You're a big fat lump of lard.' Donald trundles the pram straight at her.

Suddenly they spot me watching them. Jenny pokes out her tongue. 'Butter wouldn't melt in Bonnie Benson's gob.'

Then Mrs Mallaby does look up. 'I'll turn your face back to front if I have any more of that.'

I don't give two hoots what Jenny or Donald Mallaby think of me. Sometimes I envy the fun they have but not enough to want to be allowed to play with them like I want to play with Joanna Bayliss. Quickly I let the curtain drop and step back from the window. And then I notice behind the door a put-u-up bed. I inspect it carefully. It looks brand new. Folded up, the bed resembles a bulky table. From a wire stretched around the table top, or bed head, hangs a pretty piece of material with a sailing boat pattern that conceals the mattress and springs. In a carrier bag next to the bed I find a pillow.

I return to the kitchen. From the window I can see Gran and Dad sitting outside on the bench, smoking cigarettes. Mum is in the scullery peeling potatoes for our dinner. I stand next to her at the sink watching the long, dirty-brown strips of peel fall into the bowl.

'Mum, is that bed for me?'

'What bed?'

'The put-u-up in the front room?'

'Oh that.' As if we have dozens of put-u-up beds. 'It's for your dad.'

'For Dad?'

'That's what I said.'

'So does he sleep in the front room now?'

'Yes. Can we drop the subject Bonnie?'

I've never been asked to drop a subject before. It is a new and quite interesting experience. I leave mum to her peeling and sit down at the kitchen table where I can scrutinise her from behind. Are her shoulders shaking? And if they are, does that mean she is a) crying b) laughing c) chilly?

'You know, Mum,' I call out, 'Aunt Ed and Uncle Brian have their own bedrooms and it seems to work very well for them.'

'Well that is a weight off my mind Bonnie,' she says and kicks the scullery door shut.

ELEVEN

Autumn

My grandmother was out of hospital and back in her room at *Three Elms*. She seemed fragile, whereas I wanted her to return to her robust self immediately. The stay in hospital had frightened her, and my gran being frightened frightens me. Several times she'd said, 'Bonnie, I thought I'd never leave that ward alive', and there had been a tremor within her voice that I hadn't heard since just after Aunt Ed died.

'I wouldn't have left you there, Gran.'

'You wouldn't have had any choice.'

We both know she is right.

I've tried to visit her more often. Jay, who is sentimental about family, said, 'You don't know how long she's going to last, Bonnie, and whatever stories you tell me, the two of you are very fond of each other. Your grandmother is a force of nature and you *will* miss her.'

I want to shout back at Jay, 'Of course I know I'll miss her but I can't afford the time to worry till it happens.' But it must not happen.

Gran doesn't ask why Jay never visits. It's only in the last few years I've even mentioned Jay at all, although we've been together a long time.

In the afternoons, while Gran slept, I'd sketched or read old novels picked from the bookcase in the residents' lounge. So far, over the weeks I'd finished *Of Human Bondage*, given up half way through *Doctor Zhivago,* and was now on the last few pages of a yellowing copy of A J Cronin's *Hatter's Castle.* It was a gripping story of a cruel, megalomaniac father who bullied his family, resulting in the

71

premature death of his wife, his youngest daughter hanging herself from a beam in the kitchen, his son running away with the father's young mistress and the oldest daughter, heroine Mary, losing her illegitimate baby before finding a happy haven with young and kind hearted Doctor Renwick.

Gran snoozed in the armchair by the open window of her room; the *Daily Express* lay open across her knees. Her chin nodded against her chest and she made a gentle snoring sound. I glanced at my watch then put aside *Hatter's Castle* and took out my sketch pad and a pencil. I had fifteen minutes of drawing time before the rattle of the tea trolley coming out of the lift down at the far end of the corridor would wake her.

That drawing of my grandmother is one of my best. Yes, she does look old and in a way ugly but it is a strong ugliness. You know this sleeping woman is indomitable; a rugged cliff of a woman, a city wall.

As I laid down my pencil Gran's eyes opened and swivelled in my direction. 'I hate you drawing me at any time but particularly when I'm asleep. It's an invasion of my privacy.'

'Want to see it?'

'Not really. You'll have made me old and ugly well before my time.'

'I hope I've caught your years of wisdom.'

'No woman wants her years of wisdom caught.'

She looked at my drawing and sniffed. 'You could at least have tried for handsome. I don't know why people pay you to draw them.'

'Nobody pays me to draw them – I'm a knitwear designer not an artist.'

Gran put the drawing carefully on top of a pile of large print books on her bedside table before saying, as if following on from an earlier conversation, 'You and Susan never got on, did you? You were chalk and cheese. Such a pity.'

I took my time retrieving the drawing and slipping it into the back of my sketchbook before replying; I tried to keep my tone casual as if I was imparting some not very interesting information. 'You know, Gran, Susan was a terrible bully or she was where I was concerned.'

There, it was out in the open. I'm certain that my heart rate

72

accelerated. I'd waited years, decades, to tell my grandmother that, to put in front of her a fact about my childhood that she should have acknowledged. I sat back in the white plastic chair and waited. Like the child I'd momentarily become I yearned to hear her say, 'Bonnie, we had no idea. How you must have suffered.'

'Where the devil's the tea trolley?'

'It isn't three-thirty yet. Yes, she bullied me – in a way mentally as well as physically. If you remember she was quite a bit bigger than me, quite intimidating.'

'Stuff and nonsense.' Gran put on her spectacles and opened the newspaper.

'But don't you remember how she pushed me down the stairs? On my birthday as well.'

'Oh for Pete's sake – a tiny bruise on your bum. Horse play. If you'd had children you'd know what I'm talking about. Anyway, I heard the pair of you later on, laughing together up in your bedroom, so you couldn't have been that upset.'

'We didn't laugh for long.' Within a few moments my advantage, if I'd had one, was lost. 'Susan hated me.' My voice sounded shrill.

'Of course she didn't.'

'Gran, she did.'

'Can we change the conversation?'

'She was always your favourite. You always took her part.'

Gran angrily crackled her newspaper. For a second she disappeared behind the open pages then she folded them back, folded and folded again, till the newspaper was neatly quartered in size. She studied the crossword puzzle, her biro hovering next to 1 across. Without looking up at me she said, 'Susan had one proper parent, you had two. She was parcelled off to boarding school from eight years old to keep her out of Ed's way. Yes, I may have appeared to take her part but I loved you both equally. You chose to see anything concerning your cousin as competition, and what amazes me is that you still do.'

'I don't.' I reached for one of her tissues.

'You can pack in crying. What's the capital of Turkey?'

'I've no idea. Gran, if there was a fly on the wall watching us, it would think you were a hard and unreasonable woman.'

Automatically we both glanced up at the same expanse of magnolia coloured wall then looked at each other. I read in her eyes

73

that she was on the verge of laughter and suddenly so was I, both of us imagining a larger than life cognisant fly listening attentively to our argument and reaching a decision about Gran's behaviour. The humour in her eyes died, her lips tightened, and she said quietly, 'You were jealous.'

I stood up and began to put on my jacket. 'Of course I was jealous. Susan was always the centre of attention while I trailed behind moaning "It's not fair". But it wasn't fair.'

'Bonnie, if any child was bullied it was Susan or is your memory so convenient? Once a fortnight, you come waltzing in here decked out in your expensive clothes with your expensive baskets of fruit – I know what you're after. Me to make a comparison between the two of you. Well, all right then. For a start, at school you shone while your cousin was useless.'

'Excuse me; *I* was the useless one at school.'

'You see. You can't even allow her to have been more useless than you were at school. I rest my bloody case.' The newspaper slipped to the floor. Gran pulled herself up in the chair, her eyes blazing. *Oh my God*, I thought, *she's going to have a stroke and I'll be blamed for it!* 'Yes, you have done better than Susan. You always did do better than Susan. Satisfied?'

At that point the tea trolley arrived, Moira the attendant looking furious.

'My God, Mrs Benson, you and your granddaughter can be heard all over the building. Button it the pair of you.'

She took hold of Gran's wrist and measured her pulse. 'Surprisingly normal. Shall I check yours as well?'

I shook my head, gave her a watery smile. I rammed my sketchpad into my shoulder bag. 'I'm sorry. I won't stay for tea after all.' I didn't even pause to drop a kiss on Gran's cheek.

'Oh yes. You run off. The truth isn't comfortable, is it?'

74

TWELVE

Autumn 1964

Mum hopes I'll pass the Eleven Plus and go to grammar school.

'One day you could be a secretary.'

'I want to be an artist.'

'But that's not a proper job.'

'What about other artists, like Henry Moore?'

'I expect this Henry Moore has a proper job during the day just like everyone else.'

Dad doesn't help. He is pre-occupied. 'Not now Bonnie. Ask me about being an artist in six years' time.'

Only my gran quite likes the idea. 'If you show commitment – like I said about the knitting.'

'I have shown commitment to the knitting.'

'No. Commitment doesn't mean doing something for a fortnight or even a couple of months, it means sticking with a project for years and years.'

'But I don't necessarily want to knit forever and ever.'

'You don't have to – just have a sense of purpose, Bonnie. Make "to finish a project" your goal. Anyone can get started but they don't all see things through.'

'If I get the weaving loom for my birthday and find I like weaving better than knitting, am I allowed to swap?'

'Yes, but don't build your hopes up about the weaving loom. I think it's highly unlikely that anyone can afford to buy you that.'

The knitting and my search for more and more wool doesn't mean that I've forgotten about Joanna Bayliss. I watch her without appearing to watch her, taking in every detail of what she wears, what she says – I know which of Joanna's friends are in or out of

75

favour with her, while noting that Joanna is always in favour with her friends.

Joanna has started wearing a selection of scarves. In silk or chiffon. Sometimes just squares tucked into her raincoat or blazer collar, sometimes long embroidered scarves sent from her brother in New York.

'Originally from India,' she tells her friends, but loud enough for everyone to hear. 'Cathy McGowan wears them on *Ready, Steady, Go*. She looks fab.'

I've never paid much attention to scarves. I do have a cowboy neckerchief but that's not the same thing at all. Mum has several; ugly faded ones she wears over her hair while she does housework, also a couple of large shiny squares she's been bought for birthday or Christmas presents. When she goes shopping she wears an in-between scarf with a border of horses and horseshoes, which she says is not unlike those worn by female members of the Royal Family. Gran also wears a headscarf for shopping but she likes to wear hers in turban fashion to hide her hairnet. Sometimes I wonder why they don't just cut their hair short instead of hiding it under scarves, hats or hairnets.

A few weeks ago I was late for school. My mum had a cold and Gran a bad knee. Gran thought she'd be all right to take me but got as far as the gate before turning back, which meant I had to wait while Mum put on her powder and lipstick and comb her hair before squashing on a hat that resembled a brown bucket.

'Why can't I go to school on my own?'

'Because you're not old enough.'

'But lots of children, even in the year below, go to school on their own.'

'You're not "lots of children", you're my child. Hold hands crossing the road.'

Just supposing I ever have children I'll never expect them to 'hold hands crossing the road' once they reach the age of about six.

I walked through the empty playground. From the assembly hall came the sound of singing, 'We Plough the Fields and Scatter'. Unlike 'To Be a Pilgrim', this isn't one of my favourite hymns as it has: a) too many very low notes as in 'the good seed on the land', which seemed to require my voice to sink right down into my shoes,

76

and b) I don't like the thought of 'God's almighty hand'. I went into the cloakroom. I'd been told off before for loitering in an empty cloakroom. I liked the feeling that only a few minutes earlier it had been filled with other children and noise – and then it emptied out and fell silent, dark and quite secretive! Grey light filtered in through the dirty windows and fell like a blanket of dust over the many dark coats hanging from steel pegs.

I hung up my blazer and stood looking about for Joanna's coat. Even though it was a warm day she'd worn her rabbit fur. Nearly every girl in the class had been allowed to stroke it and murmur about how soft the fur was and such a beautiful tan colour. Only I'd kept my distance.

A pale blue scarf hung from her pocket. I moved closer. The blue was shot with a silver thread. Gently I pulled at the scarf till it was out of her pocket and in my hand. I crumpled it into a tiny ball then stuffed it into my skirt pocket. I wasn't sure what to do next. Suppose Joanna reported her scarf stolen and the teachers searched us? I grabbed my blazer and hurried back out of the school gates. As I reached my road I saw Mum coming towards me down our path. I set my face in an expression of extreme pain and managed to make myself cry.

'Whatever's the matter?'

'Mum, my head's hurting so much. Miss Wozencroft sent me home.'

'But you were all right when I left you.'

'I wasn't really. But you and Gran weren't well and I didn't want to worry you. I think I might have meningitis.' (Our neighbour Mrs Brown's son had died of meningitis the previous year.)

Mum looked horrified. 'Dear God,' she said, grabbed my arm and marched me indoors.

Gran was on her way downstairs. 'What the devil's she doing home? Is she swinging the lead?'

'Her head's hurting. Do you think it could be meningitis?'

'I'd be very surprised if it was.'

Mum manoeuvred me into the light.

'She looks pale.'

'She always looks pale.'

'I feel sick.'

'You said you had a headache.'

'A sick headache.'

'Get her the Jamaica Ginger, Eileen. That sorts the men from the boys.'

'No, Gran.'

'Yes, Gran.'

Jamaica Ginger is the most loathsome, horrible mixture in the world, far worse than Senacot which we take to keep our bowels healthy and even worse than Virol, a sticky brown liquid we take every day before dinner for no good reason. I gulped down the Ginger and Mum gave me a sherbet lemon to take the taste away. Then they settled me on the kitchen settee with cushions and a blanket. A perfect day.

Up in my bedroom that evening I smoothed out Joanna's scarf. It was very fine. Quite a small square. Just big enough to tie cowboy fashion around my neck. It smelt of perfume. The only other person I knew who wore perfume was Aunt Ed. In one corner of the scarf was a little white label – *Macy's*. With my Junior Miss manicure scissors I carefully cut the label out. Then I folded it in two and pressed it flat between the pages of the *Daily Mail Annual for Girls*.

The next day at school nobody mentioned Joanna's scarf. I apologised to Miss Wozencroft for my absence. I told her that we'd all had to go to Birmingham General to see my aunt who was dangerously ill.

'We think she'll pull through this time,' I said.

THIRTEEN

Gran and I both like going to jumble sales. Mum hates them. She says they are a breeding ground for fleas and bed bugs. She says she imagines all the Mallaby clothes come from jumble sales and 'I rest my case'.

Mum's rules are strict about what she'll allow into our house; no clothes, no books, no home-made jams or what she calls 'comestibles'.

Gran becomes much nicer at jumble sales. She knows most of the women organizers from the church and the WRVS. 'From the old days,' she says. I never ask her 'Which old days?' in case I get a lengthy answer, as my gran has a lot of 'old days' to look back on. In the past the helpers have asked her to man a stall, but she always refuses.

'You could bag all the best bargains, Mother,' Dad teases her.

'That's where you're wrong. Helpers have to be impartial. They're there to raise money for charity, not to snaffle the antiques.'

'Other folks' rubbish,' my mum says.

Gran uses me as Fagin used the Artful Dodger. Because I'm small and skinny, I'm useful for nipping between hips and elbows. Gran says, 'There's something about your sticky-out ears and spectacles that seems to charm the helpers.' I think she means this to be a compliment but I don't take it as one.

'How much for this?' I'll ask, holding up, say, a flowered water jug while trying to imagine myself as a motherless child.

'Why do you want to waste your pocket money on something like that, dear?'

'It's for my granny.'

'Go on then. A penny.' Turns to other helper, 'Bless her.'

All through the school's summer holidays I thought about possible

79

'woollens'. In my best daydream our kitchen was transformed into a magical cavern, skeins of brightly coloured washed wool hanging from the wooden clothes airer that is attached by pulleys to the scullery ceiling. I would look picturesque and interesting in patched velvet trousers with a knife tucked in my bejewelled belt. I'd be like the Robber Girl in Hans Andersen's *The Snow Queen*, 'as wild and as savage a little animal as you could wish to find', as I unravelled pullovers; winding my balls of pink, blue and yellow wool, although I realise unravelling pullovers doesn't sound so 'wild'.

But where was I going to find pullovers to unravel? No luck with Aunt Ed. She didn't like woollen clothes. Like Mum she had a fear of moths. She'd converted Susan and Uncle Brian to cardigans and jumpers made of Courtelle, which she said kept their shapes and colours much better. 'Machine washable,' she said proudly. I didn't waste my time asking Mum and Gran. I knew exactly what was in their cupboards; everything in black, navy, beige and brown.

'Nothing wrong with autumnal colours,' Mum said, but there was.

I was after reds, anything in pastels. I'd accept green providing it was lime or emerald green. Suddenly people were only as interesting as the woollen content of their clothes.

Over the school holiday I campaigned. Summertime is out of season for jumble sales. There are Spring Fayres and Summer Fetes outdoors – weather permitting. 'Fetes worse than death' Gran and I tell each other, which is an old joke but always makes us laugh. We avoid fetes and fayres. We are fish out of water amongst ladies in pretty summer dresses and straw hats all being polite to one another as they drink tea from matching cups and saucers. The two of us prefer the dust and smells of wintry church halls heated by a lone bar fire. We enjoy the regulars at the front of the queue rapping on the doors with their entrance pennies if the organisers are ten seconds late opening up. And the surge forward as if we are all running for our lives instead of in search of a broken bargain.

In my fervour to find wool I was helped by Mum having been impressed by my hot water bottle cover. As a surprise she bought me three ounces of rainbow wool and some purple plastic knitting needles. For two hours I knitted away and completed a rainbow coloured rectangle in stocking stitch. It looked very agreeable, but what next? If I had twenty more rectangles I could sew them together and have a useful, pretty blanket to liven up my attic bedroom. Gran said I was like a hungry cuckoo, beak open, 'Feed me wool. Feed me wool'.

By the time autumn came my mum had given in. Yes, I could buy woollens in the jumble sale but before they came through the front door she would check them 'rigorously' for moths, etc. They must look clean and be smell free.

The first jumble on our jumble calendar was held at a church some distance away. Gran wasn't keen.

'Supposing I find that little mahogany tallboy I've been after – I won't be able to get it home on the bus.'

'But if we don't go, we won't have the option of trying to get it home on the bus.'

Mum said, 'Well if you can't bring it home on the bus that's a blessed relief to me. We've got enough clutter in this house without a mahogany tallboy to add to the mayhem.'

'What about waiting a week or two and going to St Clements?' my gran asked.

'That's two weeks off the jumbling season, Gran; we'll be running into Christmas Fayres.'

She looked only half convinced. I continued, 'And we may get better bargains in a church where we're not well known.'

'We're not bank robbers, Bonnie.' But she gave in. The 'better bargains' had their effect.

It poured with rain. We were soaked, apart from our heads, because Gran had wisely brought plastic hats. I was glad we were out of our area as I'd have hated to bump into Joanna Bayliss and her mother.

Joanna's mother: 'Isn't that Bonnie Benson going into that jumble sale? You've only got to take one look at how she and that old lady she's with are dressed to know that they're not our kind of people. Joanna, you've had a lucky escape.'

Joanna: 'I have indeed, Mama.'

There wasn't much of a queue. Gran and I were near the front and because of the rain the organisers opened the doors early. In we went, a second to get our bearings, then heads down and rushing across the hall, me to the clothes stalls, Gran with nearly everyone

81

else to the White Elephant and Electrical Goods.

Left to myself I had plenty of time to sift through the piled clothes. Not much selection, the same drab colours that we had at home, but on the men's stall I found a scarlet cardigan, a pale blue cable knit pullover and a renegade, lady's multicoloured scarf and matching hat.

The woman serving said, 'That will keep you warm. There are gloves to match.'

'I don't want the gloves.'

'We can't split up the set.'

So I bought the gloves as well and went in search of Gran. She was haggling over a battered crocodile-skin handbag. I rummaged under the stall through boxes and boxes of odd china and glass and then something took my breath away as I stared into two insolent, beady eyes. It was a large stuffed seagull. I drew it towards me. It had a grey back, the rest of its feathers were mostly white. They felt crisp and hard under my fingers. He (in my head I was sure it was a 'he') had bright pink legs and a yellow bill with a red mark on the lower part of the beak. I leant my bag of woollens against the table leg and picked him up.

'It's a herring gull,' the woman serving said.

I felt as if I was actually carrying a live gull. Already he had a character; cheeky, naughty, with too much to squawk about. I imagined him in pride of place on my bedroom window sill looking out over the back gardens. What would the few blackbirds and starlings make of him? I'd call him Sinbad. I'd introduce Sinbad to Aunt Ed. 'What an amusing child Bonnie is. Susan would never come up with anything so original.'

'You're not buying that seagull are you?' Gran said, having bought the handbag. 'I'm not sure your mum will allow it through the door.'

'How much?' I asked.

'Sixpence,' the woman said.

'Sixpence for a tatty old seagull that nobody apart from this daft, addled-brained child would want – it's outrageous!' Gran roared.

'Threepence?'

'I wouldn't give you a farthing.'

'Threepence,' I said. 'Fair enough.'

'Oh, madam's got money to throw away, has she? Don't forget

82

your wool,' and Gran marched towards the church door.

Outside on the pavement I felt a bit ashamed of us. People stared as if we were a comic turn, my gran with a large roasting dish under one arm, the crocodile-skin handbag banging against her old black leather handbag and a grubby raffia basket full of china, me with my wool and a stuffed seagull.

'I'm calling him Sinbad, Gran.'

'Call him what you like, Eileen won't be pleased. Come on, there's the bus. Run!'

The bus driver saw us running and waited. We trundled up to the top deck in buoyant moods. I bagged the window seat and positioned Sinbad so he could look out. Gran put on her reading glasses to inspect her pieces of china, turning the pieces upside down to study at the maker's mark.

'Meakin. Not bad. Windsor, Coronet – cheap but definitely cheerful. My pièce de resistance is a little Wedgwood dish for my hairnets. The basket was free.'

We became quiet but happy. I'd got everything I'd wanted and still had tuppence left in my purse. We were travelling past *Cox's Bakery* on Coventry Road where, had we been on foot and unencumbered, we might have bought a bag of doughnuts, when Gran let out a loud, frightened squeal. It was a sound I'd never heard her make before which startled me and also, even more dramatically, made my blood truly run cold.

'Whatever's the matter, Gran?'

'His back,' she said, like a ventriloquist through lips tightly pressed together. 'Look at his back.'

I stared hard at the back of the man seated two seats in front of us.

'You fool,' she said. 'Your bloody seagull.'

Rearing up between the gull's grey feathers was a thin white worm. I insisted afterwards, and for once Gran didn't disagree, that it had a nasty pink nose. The worm raised itself at least two inches above the gull's back and twisted round to look at us. Dad later said that worms couldn't possibly look around and they definitely didn't have pink noses. (This one definitely could and did.) The worm looked from Gran to me. We pressed ourselves against the bus seat as if it were a cobra about to strike.

'What will I do with it, Gran?' I wailed.

'Don't give it to me.'

'Perhaps it's full of worms.'

Gran groaned as if she'd been shot. Other passengers turned to look at us. Gran stood up. 'Leave it on the seat and come on,' she ordered.

I edged out from under the seagull, put it down carefully on the seat and joined her in the aisle. We headed briskly for the stairs.

'Hey, you can't just leave that there,' a woman said as we hurried past.

Gran said, 'I'm afraid we must.'

Luckily the bus was just about to stop at a zebra crossing and off we jumped. We looked up. The woman who'd told us off was staring down at us mouthing, 'Disgraceful.'

I carried Gran's roasting dish for her. It was quite heavy. At home we had another six roasting dishes – at least five of them Gran had brought from jumble sales, her motto being 'You can't have too much of a good thing'.

I said, 'The gull's made me feel a bit sick. It reminded me of the caterpillars.'

'It reminded *me* of the caterpillars, only it didn't smell.'

'It might have started smelling.'

'Yes it might.'

Suddenly we were both laughing.

'Not far now,' she said.

Ahead of us were the tall iron gates of Small Heath Park. We waited at the Belisha beacon as several cars passed. Suddenly Gran stepped forward holding up her hand – the two handbags bumping back down her arm. The car she was waving at didn't stop, in fact it speeded up.

'Good grief. That's odd.'

'What is? Did you know the driver?'

'I thought I did. I could swear it was our Brian.'

'That wasn't Uncle Brian's car.'

'It's a new one. Not many navy blue Jags in this part of Birmingham. He never said he was coming over. I hope Ed's ok.'

Slowly we walked along next to the park railings. The leaves on the trees were already turning yellow, red and orange. I thought about my mum saying how she preferred autumnal colours and how proper autumnal colours were very different to what she meant.

'Well I'm blowed.'

I looked in the direction Gran was looking. Inside the park, twenty yards away from us, there was my dad and Aunt Ed walking hand in hand, heading down the avenue of tall trees that led to the boating lake. Dappled afternoon sunshine fell on them and around them. As I opened my mouth to call out Gran yanked my arm and turned me to face her. 'No Bonnie,' she said.

'But it's Dad and Aunt Ed.'

'No it isn't. I was mistaken.'

'It *was* them.'

She paused, thinking, then nodded. 'You could be right. They were probably discussing something private; could be Eileen's birthday. Could be yours – I think discretion would be the better part of valour.'

'What does that mean?'

'We keep our mouths shut. Don't mention this to your mum. We don't want to spoil a possible surprise, do we?'

'But they were holding hands.'

'Holding hands doesn't mean anything. Shut up now, Bonnie.'

FOURTEEN

'If Ed will be civil so will I,' Mum said, 'although what she's got to be uncivil about I haven't the faintest idea. *I'm* the wronged woman.'

'But it's not as if you're overly bothered in that department.'

'That's hardly the point.'

'Well in this instance can't we just let sleeping dogs lie?' Gran shut the kitchen door with me on the hall side of it wondering what 'department' they could be talking about.

It was about to be my eleventh birthday and a PARTY was being planned. Not a big grand party. Nothing like Joanna Bayliss might have with friends of her own age and party games and wonderful presents sent from her doctor brother in New York. Gran's friend Miss Venables was coming. Mrs Brown, our next door neighbour, and her daughter Celia and, if Mum agreed, Aunt Ed and Uncle Brian. Susan would be delivered from boarding school at some point in the afternoon. Six guests. Ten people. A crowd.

Mum had asked if there was anyone I'd like to invite from school. I said a firm 'no'. I couldn't for one minute imagine Joanna Bayliss's mother dropping Joanna off in our street, not with Mrs Mallaby a permanent fixture on her front wall.

Even Aunt Ed can't compete with Joanna Bayliss's mother, although my heart remains true. From my desk by the classroom window I watch her two-tone Vauxhall arrive at the school gates every afternoon at ten to four. Mrs Bayliss doesn't just get out of her car; she unwinds like a snake who wears pastel coloured Capri pants and figure hugging shirts with their collars turned up. Her hair is worn in a similar style to the film star Leslie Caron, pinned up and back-combed with a long straight fringe. Waiting for Joanna she slouches against the car bonnet with her cigarette. She blows smoke up into the sky and watches its trail as if something private is amusing her. Sometimes men in passing cars have wolf whistled but she never looks round. I'm glad Mum or Gran always turn up late to collect me. I'd hate them to bump into Mrs Bayliss and comparisons made.

I felt very pleased with the way I looked. My hair is now long enough to cover my ears and thick enough to take a bit at the back up into a pony tail and back-comb it a little, with hair left to cover my neck in a smooth curtain. Gran says I look like a chihuahua. I take that as a compliment.

I wore a dusty pink, corduroy skirt ordered from Gran's catalogue and leather sandals with a one-inch heel. I'd practised coming down the stairs several times while glancing sideways at my descending reflection in the hall mirror. I looked at least thirteen. Sophisticated.

My birthday present from Mum and Dad was a Minnie Mouse Watch which I was fairly pleased with.

Mum said, 'I wanted to get you the Cinderella watch with the pink strap but your dad vetoed that.'

I wish they had bought me both. The Cinderella watch strap would have matched my new skirt, which is the kind of detail Susan would have noted and been impressed by. I could have kept Minnie Mouse for everyday use.

'Bonnie,' my gran called from the kitchen, 'will you stop admiring yourself in that mirror and help butter some bread?'

'I can't butter bread. I've got my party clothes on.'

'Why?'

'Because it's a party.'

'It isn't a party till three pm.'

'But it's my birthday all day.'

I walked, not skipped as I wanted to do, into the kitchen. I posed with one hand on my hip. 'Don't I look nice?'

Gran looked at my mum, who turned her head anxiously towards the scullery door. 'Of course you look nice,' Mum said. 'Mrs Brown, are you all right now?'

I sighed in frustration. Here was Mrs Brown coming out of our scullery with a red nose and eyes. She'd been crying. She was always crying.

'Come and sit down.' Gran took Mrs Brown by the elbow and

steered her to a chair as if unaided she was likely to topple over. What I'd have liked to say was, 'Mrs Brown, I'm sorry about your son Gary dying but this is my birthday so cheer up. What do you think of my ensemble?'

'Bonnie, perhaps you'd better…'

'I can't butter the bread.'

'Amuse yourself somewhere else then.' Gran gave me one of her looks.

I marched out into the hall. Mrs Brown was saying, 'Forgive me Eileen. I don't think I'm quite up to a party. Celia said she'd stay and keep me company, bless her.'

Which suited me because I hadn't wanted Celia coming to my party anyway. I hardly knew her. She was in the year below me at St Benedict's and I'd heard her described as 'vivacious' by Miss Bryant the English teacher.

'I can do without vivacious,' I told my reflection as I passed by the mirror on my way back upstairs to check out the guest facilities of my bedroom.

Susan had never stayed the night at our house before. Although it was agreed (by me, with me) that I hated Susan, I was still excited at the prospect. Of course my bedroom was nothing like hers but I'd decided it was at least picturesque. It reminded me of illustrations in books of fairy tales when the heroine finally after many hardships reaches a cosy cottage with a bedroom in the eaves of a thatched roof. Of course my roof wasn't thatched but would a heroine be able to tell the difference once she was indoors?

Dad was going to sleep on the settee and his put-u-up bed now stood next to mine with a rag rug covering the floorboards in between. Across the foot of both beds lay a small blanket made up of brightly coloured knitted squares. I was proud of these blankets. Gran had sewn up the squares but I'd done all the knitting.

Along one wall were two white shelves crammed with books; purple velvet curtains (from my gran's old house) hanging at the small window and across the door to keep out any draughts and hide the view of the rickety staircase. Near the window was the paraffin stove and a white wicker armchair. I sat in the armchair and tried to see my bedroom as Susan might see it. Yes definitely picturesque.

At a quarter to three I ran downstairs just as Uncle Brian and Aunt Ed's car pulled up outside. I met them on the front step.

'Bonnie, you look a picture.'

What picture Aunt Ed? I was hugged, kissed, admired and promised my present after birthday tea. Dad came out into the hall and suggested sherry. They both said 'Yes' just as my mum said, 'It's far too early.'

'Far too early for you, Eileen,' Dad said and led them into the kitchen.

'Far too early for anybody,' she muttered under her breath but loud enough for me to hear, then she picked up the best tablecloth from where she'd left it on the telephone table and went into the front room.

'In or out?' she asked me over her shoulder. 'If it's in, shut the door please.'

I followed her in. Together we spread the cloth over the old chenille cloth that Gran says is to protect the table top. Mum crossed to the fireplace and looked at herself in the mirror, turning her head each way.

'How do you think I look compared to your aunt?'

Mum had kept up with the *Blonde Mink*. She wore a new white blouse with beige piping on the collar that matched the beige of her pleated skirt.

'You look great, Mum.'

'Do I?' She seemed doubtful.

Mum didn't look quite 'great'. Aunt Ed looked great. No way could my mum's skirt and blouse look better than Aunt Ed's sheath dress worn with a red patent belt and scarlet high-heeled, winkle-picker shoes. No, never mind great, Aunt Ed looked splendid.

'Well, I'll have to do. No one's bothered how I look anyway. Susan and Miss Venables should be here shortly. Go and tell everyone that tea will be ready around three-thirty.'

From the kitchen window I observed Uncle Brian. He stood very still next to the water butt which was full to the brim with dark stagnant water. The butt had only ever been used to drown Lindy Lou's kittens, but now Lindy Lou was buried under the bench all it did was gather water and attract clouds of midges to our back door on warm, damp evenings. Uncle Brian glanced at his watch, he looked up at the sky, then from his pocket he took out the familiar battered tin in which he kept his discarded cigarette stubs. Uncle Brian smoked *Capstan* cigarettes although Aunt Ed would have preferred him to smoke *Dunhill* or another brand with a filter tip. Aunt Ed liked to see good looking men with a cigarette in their mouths. She said it looked sexy, a word that made my mum shudder. Aunt Ed said cigarettes looked most sexy when first lit; stubs, particularly stubs with ash waiting to drop didn't look sexy at all, they looked working class. Mum and Aunt Ed both shuddered over the words 'working class'.

Methodically Uncle Brian unrolled the thin cigarette paper to reveal the remaining tobacco which he tossed into the water butt. I rapped on the window. He looked up and grinned.

'Tea at three-thirty,' I mouthed.

'Okey-dokey,' he mouthed back and returned to his stubs.

Normally the door of the scullery was hooked back against the kitchen wall. That afternoon the door was shut, the hook dangling loosely from its hasp. I could hear laughter, my dad and Aunt Ed, laughing as if something was very funny indeed. I rattled the hook before pulling the door open. Aunt Ed was perched on the stool we kept next to the sink. She'd taken off her red shoes and her stockinged feet rested on the bottom rung of the stool.

The scullery sink only has a cold tap which is hard to turn on and when you do the water gushes out with icy force. Aunt Ed's hands were stretched out under the stream while my dad lathered up the bar of carbolic soap.

'Tea's almost ready,' I said.

'Ken, that water's freezing,' Aunt Ed said.

He took both her hands in his and began to wash them.

'My hands are warm.'

'Tea's almost ready,' I said again.

'I heard you the first time – we'll be along shortly, Bonnie.'

Dad didn't look at me but Aunt Ed flashed me a ravishing smile. 'Your dad's a treasure.'

Dad ran the water even harder to wash off the soap and she squealed. Then he grabbed the tea towel warming next to the oven and began to gently pat her hands dry.

'That's the tea towel, Dad. Mum won't like you using that.'

'Don't tell her then.'

He took ages drying her hands. Aunt Ed said, 'You've missed my wrists, Ken.'

He dried her wrists.

'All done,' Aunt Ed said beaming.

'Not quite.' Dad turned Aunt Ed's hands palms downwards and kissed her knuckles. She stared at his bent head, not smiling anymore. Was she annoyed with him? I'd never seen my dad ever kiss my mum; a peck on the cheek for Gran, for me just a kiss on the nose or my forehead with a 'Night, night Bonnie-tops'.

'Ugh!' I said. 'That's disgusting, Dad. Aunt Ed, you'll have to wash your hands again now.'

'Go away Bonnie,' he said.

'But Dad.'

'You're beginning to get on my nerves.'

In all my life I've never, ever got on my dad's nerves. I am his pet, his favourite above all *and* it was my birthday.

'Any chance of getting to that sink?' Uncle Brian stood in the doorway. He grinned at us, a fresh cigarette stuck cheekily out of the side of his mouth.

Aunt Ed slipped off the stool. 'You're a mucky fellah,' she said, inspecting his fingers stained brown from the tobacco. 'Whatever have you been doing out there?'

'Putting my tobacco stubs in the rain water butt. Use it on your vegetables Ken and you'll never be troubled by aphids.'

'Brian, we're never troubled by aphids because we don't trouble ourselves with growing vegetables.'

Cheerfully he threw the tea towel at Uncle Brian who caught it and slung it over his shoulder. He turned on the tap but instead of washing his hands he put his whole head under the jet.

Aunt Ed laughed. 'Mind your jacket.'

Uncle Brian shook his head like a dog springing out of a river and water showered over them.

'You're a bloody idiot,' my dad said. 'Bonnie, tell your mum we're on our way.'

Uncle Brian looked at his watch again. 'I can't wait to see Susan.'

'I can,' Aunt Ed said and winked at me.

'Your mum's upstairs putting on her lips,' Gran said. She sat with her slippered feet up on the uncomfortable ottoman. It was still chilly in the front room. She'd draped the fox fur around her shoulders and it stared up at me with navy blue, malevolent eyes.

'It's cold in here, Gran. Aunt Ed won't like it.'

'Your dad was supposed to light the fire but that's men for you.'

The table was laid and ready. There was Gran's best china, tinned pink salmon and salad cream sandwiches (Mum says tinned pink salmon is classier than tinned red salmon), corned beef and chutney sandwiches, and *Dairylea* cheese spread and cucumber sandwiches. Crowding the three-tier cake stand were macaroons, sliced marble cake and lemon curd tartlets.

'I thought there'd be jellies and a birthday cake,' I said.

'There will be jellies and birthday cake.' She studied my face. 'What's the matter with you? You look like you've swallowed a dose of cod liver oil.'

'Nothing's the matter.'

'Something's the matter. Spit it out.'

'Dad kissed Aunt Ed's knuckles.'

Her mouth fell open then she started to laugh. 'As long as that's all he kissed. I'd better get this fire going.' Gran stood up. From behind the china lady she took a box of matches and with an 'ouf' squatted down in front of the grate. Yellow flames crinkled the paper spills peeping out from between lumps of coal. Above us came the sound of Mum's footsteps crossing the landing from the bathroom.

'He dried them on a tea towel,' I said to the back of Gran's head.

'Dried what?'

'Aunt Ed's hands.'

'It's not a hanging offence, Bonnie; although I'm surprised Ed let him. Our tea towels are none too clean.'

From out in the hall came the noisy joshing sounds of my dad, Uncle Brian and Aunt Ed. The doorbell rang and kept on ringing.

Gran smiled at me. 'That will be Susan. I've missed that girl.'

She made for the front door but Aunt Ed beat her to it.

'Stop ringing that bloody bell. We're not deaf.'

In bounced Susan in her grey school coat, grey school hat with a maroon and black striped band around the brim. She carried a small pink suitcase.

'Hello everyone! Aunt Eileen, is it okay to go up to your bedroom and change?'

'Of course dear.'

Without another word to anybody, Susan rushed up the stairs.

'She should have gone up to my room,' I said.

Mum patted my shoulder. 'It doesn't matter which room she uses. Ken, I will have that sherry now. Shall we all wait in the kitchen till Miss Venables arrives? Give the fire a chance to get started.'

In the kitchen Gran had put a bowl of peanuts in the centre of the table. Everyone stood, holding their glasses of sherry.

'Shouldn't I have a sherry too? After all it is my birthday.'

Dad came in with a bottle of lemonade and two glasses. 'I'm making you and Susan lemonade shandies.'

'Oh I think the girls could have a small sherry,' Aunt Ed said.

'Not in this house they can't, Ed.' Mum gave Aunt Ed a look.

'Peanut anybody?' Gran shook the peanut bowl. I took a handful. 'Bonnie, put at least half that handful back. Miss Venables is partial to peanuts.'

Dad and Uncle Brian started talking about cars; Uncle Brian saying that Martin Rossiter had bought a new car and was willing to let my dad have his old car for a song.

'Only eight hundred miles on the clock,' Uncle Brian said.

'How much would "a song" be?' Dad wanted to know.

'Fifty quid.'

Dad whistled.

'It's a brilliant price, Ken. The car's in mint condition. Not a scrap of rust. He could get ten times that much at a garage.'

'Why doesn't he then?' Gran asked.

'As a favour to me, that's why.'

Aunt Ed smiled affectionately at them both. 'Men. Eileen, I can't get over your hair colour. What did you say it was called again? It's taken years off you. Years and years.'

Aunt Ed was on best behaviour. She admired our new biscuit barrel: 'Isn't it amazing what you can pick up for next to nothing? Whatever it's made of it still looks perfectly charming.' She agreed that 'Yes, *Surf Washing Powder* probably was as good as her own *Lux Flakes*. It's certainly far cheaper!'

93

Behind the conversation I listened for Susan. Twenty minutes passed. Aunt Ed looked at the clock on the mantelpiece and frowned.

'We won't start tea till Miss Venables arrives,' Gran said.

I heard the click of heels on the stairs. Aunt Ed's frown changed to a small, pleased smile. Mum's eyes widened as Susan sauntered into the kitchen.

'Sorry I've taken so long.' She posed on the hearth rug. 'Fab dress, isn't it?'

It *was* a fab dress; a black and white Op-Art shift that ended just above her knees. In Gran's *Sunday Express* there had been a whole page devoted to shift dresses the previous week. I'd said, 'I think that style would suit me, Gran.' And she'd said, 'It would if you want to look like a stick of rock.'

Susan had accessorised (*Sunday Express* fashion pages) with white lace tights, black and white bootees. She wore make-up; plum coloured eye shadow and mascara, plum coloured lipstick. FALSE EYELASHES. Susan looked like a model out of a magazine or the *Sunday Express.*

'It's rather an adult ensemble for a child,' my mum said.

'Times have changed,' Aunt Ed laughed, 'and anyway she's not a child, Susan's almost a young woman. By Christmas she'll need a brassiere. Bonnie's going to need one soon as well.'

There was an awkward silence. Mum's face turned scarlet. The word 'brassiere' even made me feel a little warm. Mum picked up the tea pot and walked out of the room. Gran said, 'Bonnie, why not show Susan the weaving loom I bought you. I'll give you both a shout when Miss Venables arrives.'

'A weaving loom. Yeah. Wow,' Susan said and pulled a disgusted face.

Reluctantly she trailed back upstairs behind me.

'It's really dusty everywhere.' She ran a finger between the banisters.

I ignored her. I was racking my brains for something to say that would impress her before we reached my bedroom and she found my facilities equally disgusting.

'You need a stair carpet,' she said. 'These stairs are very steep. I'm going to snag my nylons.'

Suddenly out of my mouth came the words, 'Sometimes I fly

94

down these stairs just like Peter Pan.'

She said nothing till we got to the landing. As I drew back the curtain leading to the flight of steps leading up to the attic she caught hold of my arm. 'What did you say?'

'I said, sometimes – not always, I can fly like Peter Pan... Only not when people are watching,' I added hastily. 'Perhaps one day I'll show you.'

I pulled my arm away and continued upwards, threw open my door with a flourish. She walked over to the window and looked out.

'You can see the park,' I said.

'Big deal! Do you ever see courting couples?'

'No. I don't think so.'

'I bet there are loads of them in the bushes after dark. Tell me about the flying.'

We stood shoulder to shoulder looking out over the park. 'The first time was amazing,' I said. 'I could see my feet in my grey felt slippers, close together as if they were glued and I was flying an inch or two above our stairs. I landed on the hall rug.'

'Wow!' Susan said, this time really impressed. 'Like Superman. Weren't you frightened?'

'Oh no. It was exciting.'

'What if you'd broken your neck?'

'I didn't think of that.'

Susan walked across to my book shelves, stood with her head on one side reading the titles.

'Have you read all these?'

'Yes.'

I showed her my chemistry set instead of the weaving loom. I explained how to turn pink litmus paper blue. She admired the dinky test tube rack, tripod and mini Bunsen burner.

'Can we do an experiment?'

'Well no. Dad said, in the wrong hands it could be dangerous.'

'We could attach the Bunsen burner to the gas tap behind the cooker.'

'We'd better not.'

She flopped onto my bed and lay on her stomach. After a minute she said, 'What do you think of Richard Burton?'

'Who?'

95

'The film star. He's just got married to Elizabeth Taylor.'

'Has he?'

'I go for older men.'

'Do you?'

'He's Welsh.'

'Is he? Mum says as a rule the Welsh are a miserable race.'

'It was her fifth marriage.'

'Phew.'

'Who would you marry if you had the choice?'

'Davy Crockett.'

'That's silly. Davy Crockett isn't a real person.'

'He was.'

'He isn't now. What about Anthony Armstrong-Jones.'

'Isn't he married to Princess Margaret?'

'By the time I'm grown up they'll probably be divorced.'

I said stiffly, 'Dad doesn't approve of the Royal Family.'

Susan looked smug, 'Then I won't ask him to my wedding.'

'Dad says there's no earthly use for royalty although he thinks Princess Margaret is quite attractive.'

'Are you in love with your dad?'

'No, of course not.'

'Then shut up and sit.'

I squeezed into the small amount of space on my bed that Susan had left me. I felt a new feeling; happy and pleased with myself. This was our first ever proper conversation; my first ever proper conversation with somebody who wasn't my dad, mum or gran.

'I quite like the cowboys on television. I don't think I'd like to marry one though. I'd rather marry the ladies.'

'Bonnie, you're weird. Ladies don't marry each other.'

'Then I won't get married. I'll go to America and be a cowboy.'

'I bet cowboys are really smelly people. They never take their trousers off. I bet they have to wee in them while they're in the saddle...'

'No they don't. And sometimes they have baths with lots of soap suds. They do keep their hats on in the bath, and their gun-belts within reach. And there's always a romance, every single week.'

Downstairs the front door bell rang again. Susan rushed over to the window.

'Who's that old lady?'

96

'Probably Miss Venables. She's Gran's best friend.'

Mum came to the foot of the stairs and shouted, 'Come on you two – the party's starting. Wash your hands first.'

We clattered down to the bathroom on the next landing. I washed my hands while Susan sat on the edge of the bath and admired her reflection in the chrome door plate.

'Sorry,' I said. 'You're the guest. I should have said "after you".'

Susan waved her hands under the tap then flicked water at me in a friendly fashion. I wished I'd flicked water at her. Suddenly I felt I knew her well enough to do that sort of friendly flicking thing.

At the top of the stairs she said, 'After you, Bonnie.'

I grinned, 'No, after you.'

'Age before beauty,' she said and we both laughed. I stepped forward then felt a thump between my shoulder blades.

'Off you go. Fly!' She hooted as I fell forward.

I fell four steps, slithered painfully down the rest, coming to a stop on the bottom stair just as Aunt Ed came out into the hall carrying a plate of sandwiches.

'Bonnie, are you okay?'

From above Susan shouted, 'She slipped mum. They need to get their stairs carpeted like ours.'

'Did you fall, Bonnie, or did Susan push you?'

Aunt Ed looked up at Susan.

'She did slip. Tell my mum you slipped, Bonnie.'

I managed to grin. 'I did slip, Aunt Ed. I'm not quite used to these new sandals.'

Aunt Ed rested the plate of sandwiches next to the telephone and held out her hand. I grasped it and she pulled me to my feet. Susan came down the stairs, walking in an affected manner, pretending to be a model on a cat-walk.

'You've got dirt on the back of your new skirt,' she said. 'May I pass please, Bonnie, my audience awaits.'

I stepped aside and let Susan swan past, head high, nose in the air. I could see that Aunt Ed was trying not to smile, as if she actually found Susan amusing. I decided that I would never speak to Susan again. Ever. And if anyone noticed that I wasn't speaking to my cousin and asked 'Why?' I would say, 'Because she tried to kill me.'

FIFTEEN

I hadn't said a word to Susan for almost six hours. Annoyingly Susan had made no attempt to speak to me either. It wasn't very satisfying sending my cousin to Coventry if she didn't realise she'd been sent. Also I had the niggling worry that perhaps she might have sent *me* to Coventry. As we changed into our pyjamas in my bedroom, I was almost ready to say something just so she might be forced to say something back, and then I might get *my* chance to snub her.

'Does your bum ache?' Susan asked, which was so surprising that I immediately answered, 'Yes it does.'

She climbed into the put-u-up bed. 'Sorry, but you did say you could fly. You know Bonnie, your bedroom's much nicer than mine.'

This time I was surprised into saying, 'Do you think so?'

'Of course.' She settled herself against the pillows and studied my room. 'I just like it a lot.' Her voice wasn't quite her usual confident one; not envious either, more sad as if she was missing out on something. I removed Susan from Coventry and got into bed.

'What did you think of my birthday party?'

'Hmm. Well it wasn't what I'd call a proper party. Certainly not a proper birthday party – why weren't there any paper hats or birthday cake?'

'The iced sponge *was* my birthday cake.'

'Nobody even sang "Happy Birthday to you".'

'They forgot. Do you think your mum was very bored?'

'I expect so. Why does your mum always look so miserable?'

'I don't know. Gran's friend Miss Venables didn't say much but she gave me ten shillings...'

'Did she? I thought she looked like she'd got a stick stuck up her bottom.' We both giggled. 'I helped my mum choose your handbag.

98

Do you really like it?'

'I love it. I've never had a handbag before.'

'It's real leather. Pink's a mod colour.'

'Is it?'

I wriggled my toes under the light weight of my patchwork blanket. Suddenly I felt very happy – my room seemed as snug as I'd hoped it would.

'Bonnie, can you really fly?'

'Of course I can.'

'Then why didn't you when I pushed you on the stairs?'

'I couldn't be bothered.'

'You fibber.'

I ignored her. Suddenly her head and shoulders appeared over the side of my bed.

'You can't fly, can you?' and she started tickling my neck just under my ear.

The door opened. Mum said, 'Susan get back into bed.'

'I can't sleep Aunty Eileen. Bonnie keeps making me laugh.'

'Bonnie, pack it in. It's getting late.'

'Are my mum and dad still here?'

'They'll be off in half an hour and if you're not asleep by then they can take you with them.'

'That's not a bad idea,' Susan said.

'Don't be cheeky.'

Susan climbed back into the put-u-up bed and Mum closed the door. We listened to her retreating footsteps. Downstairs, as she went into the front room, there was a burst of conversation and laughter. For a few minutes we lay quietly. Had Susan fallen asleep? I didn't think so. I held my breath and waited. Then, out of the orange gloom came a low saucy voice more like Aunt Ed's than Susan's: 'What are you waiting for, Bonnie?'

'What do you mean?'

'Why don't you come into my bed?'

'That bed's uncomfortable.'

'Then shall I get in with you?'

Again silence stretched between us before I heard her quietly pushing back the covers and the sound of her body moving stealthily across the floorboards between us.

'What are you waiting for?' she said again, her breath warm

99

against my face.

'I don't understand,' I said.

She put her hand on the waistband of my pyjamas and stretched the elastic. Then she let go so that it snapped against my skin.

'That's what my mum says to my dad,' she whispered. 'They think I'm asleep. Mum opens his bedroom door and says "What are you waiting for?" Sometimes she calls him "big boy".'

'Well he is a big chap.'

'No. She's talking about his tinkie.'

'His what?' My voice came out as a squeak.

'His tinkie. Men have tinkies, we have minkies.'

'That's disgusting.' I squeezed my knees and thighs together to hold onto the spasm of excitement. 'What does he say when she says that?'

Susan laughed. 'Usually, "Ed go back to bed please".'

Susan walked her fingers over my pyjama jacket probing between the buttons.

'Susan suck titty,' she said.

I gasped. Excited but embarrassed as well. 'Titty' was a rude private word I'd heard my gran use a few times, always to be 'shushed' by Mum. 'Suck' a word never used at all except in connection with boiled sweets. Susan opened two buttons and stroked my chest. I undid the rest of my buttons. I was so hot. I felt like a bright red balloon stretching bigger and tighter. Susan licked my skin.

'Yum, yum,' she said. She giggled. I groaned. And then I froze. Over Susan's head I saw my bedroom door swing open. Frantically I pushed Susan's head away.

'I haven't finished. I want to see if there really is a bruise on your bottom.'

She tried to slide her fingers into my pyjama trousers. And then she felt my fear and she looked where I was looking – at Aunt Ed standing in the doorway. In her hand she held her red winkle-picker shoes.

'Mum,' Susan whispered.

Aunt Ed switched on the light. She smiled at us. In slow motion she put her shoes down on the floor and stepped into them. Aunt Ed's lips were slightly parted, her eyes huge; no colour in them except black. Her mouth hung open. Suddenly, as if somewhere in

100

the house a starting pistol had been fired, Aunt Ed sprinted the few feet between us. Susan clung to me. I tried to hold her but I was no match for a furious Aunt Ed. She grabbed hold of the neck of Susan's pyjama jacket and, as if Susan weighed no more than a rag doll, lifted her off the bed before dropping her. Susan sprawled face down on the floor.

'You – dirty – little – beast – ,' Aunt Ed screamed, her red shoes taking on a life of their own, the sharply pointed toes hammering into Susan's shoulder blades and back.

Then my dad was in the room. On the floor Susan was trying to crawl under my bed, one arm shielding her head.

'Don't, Mummy,' she whimpered.

Dad scooped Susan up, using his body as a shield from Aunt Ed. She pummelled his back yelling, 'Put her down. She's my daughter – ' Aunt Ed's spittle spraying the back of his shirt.

'Calm down Ed. Calm down,' he said. My dad sounded completely calm, as if he was absentmindedly quieting a wild animal. Then he was out of the door. For a second Dad and the bundle that was Susan were framed against the light from the stairwell. The light was blotted out as Aunt Ed rushed after them, her arms raised, her hands clenched into fists. I heard the noise they made racing down the stairs. Dad's slippered feet thumping, Aunt Ed's shoes pattering, but a furious chasing pattering.

I was left alone for several minutes before Gran came upstairs. Gently she fastened my pyjama buttons, straightened my sheet and blankets and tucked me in unnecessarily tightly. In a small voice I said, 'I'm sorry Gran.'

'Nothing to be sorry about.'

'What will happen to Susan?'

'I've no idea. Go to sleep now.'

She switched off the light but left the door open. She went downstairs, her footsteps slow and heavy. On the next landing, she stopped to use the bathroom and I heard the toilet flush, the cold water tap running. I tracked her as far as the front room. When she opened that door no party sounds rushed out.

A short time later, just as I was drifting off to sleep, I heard low voices in the hall. I couldn't make out what was being said. The front door opened and closed, there were footsteps on the path. The beam from Uncle Brian's headlamps shone through the curtains, illuminating the bedroom, and then the car pulled away. I listened to the engine and imagined I could still hear it long after the road outside had become silent again.

SIXTEEN

The next morning while I was eating my breakfast the telephone rang, which was unusual. We rarely got phone calls and only ever in the evenings. Gran answered it while Mum and I both strained unsuccessfully to hear what she was saying. Finally she put the phone down and came back into the kitchen.

'Brian's just gone with Ed to Birmingham General. She's had chest pains and trouble getting her breath. The doctor called an ambulance. He thought she might be having a – ,' she paused, 'an anxiety attack.'

'Is it serious?' Mum asked.

Gran gave her a meaningful look, meant for mum to interpret as 'not in front of Bonnie'. Sometimes I wonder why they do that, as if they think I'm blind or just not very bright.

'Is Aunt Ed having a heart attack, Gran?'

'Nobody said anything about a heart attack. It's just a matter of her learning to control that temper of hers. If she won't then the consequences will be chest pains and causing everyone a load of worry and disruption. I've now got to pack my case and hop on two buses to look after Brian and Susan. I'm not best pleased.'

Most evenings Uncle Brian drove over to our house to collect my dad and they'd go together to the hospital. Gran visited during the day while Uncle Brian or a neighbour came in to look after Susan. Mum said Susan would be better off returning to boarding school but nobody else seemed to think that was a good idea.

Mum didn't visit Aunt Ed. She bought fruit for my dad to take, and once a bunch of Sweet William from the market. Silently she left them on the table and silently he picked the bunch up on his way out to Uncle Brian's car. I wondered if mum secretly wished for Aunt Ed's death as I'd sometimes wished for Susan's.

Gran came home once to collect more clothes and sat talking to Mum in the kitchen with the door shut. Nobody included me in what was going on. Even my dad ignored me. I heard Mum telling Gran, 'He walks around as if he's in a dream.'

In bed at night I imagined Aunt Ed dying; no longer two bus rides away, or on the telephone, or the subject of our conversations. A world without Aunt Ed.

At my school there is a section of wall outside the assembly hall. Four times a year a different class makes a frieze to depict the season. Some of the frieze is painted, some of it made from felt or paper or card stuck on. Because it is autumn, Year Four collected fallen leaves and glued them into lovely patterns. It looked brilliant. Red and orange with yellow leaves like the sun was breaking through. Then the leaves began to wither and fade. Now the frieze looks horrible, almost frightening. The colours are dirty as if they've been trodden in mud and some of the leaves have curled and twisted to look like clutching hands. That is how a world without Aunt Ed might become. And then I think that is how Aunt Ed might become.

'But is she going to be all right, Mum?'

'How many more times – I don't know.'

'But doesn't anybody know anything?'

'Well it seems not.'

At school Miss Wozencroft stopped me in the corridor.

'Bonnie, you've seemed rather distracted of late. Is anything worrying you?'

I burst out with, 'My aunt's dangerously ill in Birmingham Hospital.'

Miss Wozencroft smiled down at me. 'Again? And do you think she'll pull through this time like she did before?' Her voice was teasing.

'I don't know Miss Wozencroft.'

'I'm sure your aunt will be as right as rain but I don't think you can use this excuse many more times.'

'It isn't an excuse.'

'Oh I think it is, Bonnie. Now enough of this silliness, you've got passing your Eleven Plus to concentrate on.'

Miss Wozencroft patted my shoulder and walked away.

That afternoon when my mum went to the corner shop for cigarettes I waited for the gate to click shut behind her before ringing Gran, praying that Susan wouldn't answer.

'Hello, Brian Benson's house,' Gran said.

'Gran, it's me, Bonnie.'

'What do you want? Does Eileen know you're using the phone?'

'She's gone out for cigarettes; I've only got a minute. I want to visit Aunt Ed.'

'You can't. They don't allow children in the adult ward. Only next of kin and that's in very special circumstances. Susan's only been allowed to visit once.'

'If I wait outside while you visit Aunt Ed could wave from a window.'

'Your aunt isn't up to waving from a window. It's not like the Queen at Buckingham Palace. Anyway your mother would be furious.'

'But if you asked her, Gran.'

'Then she'd be furious with me.'

'Please.' I sniffed.

'No tears, Bonnie.' Gran went quiet. I could imagine her in Aunt Ed's lounge-diner, sitting very straight in an armchair or the corner of the sofa, unwilling to let herself be comfortable.

'I miss everybody, Gran.'

A 'harumph'.

'If your mother says yes, I'll take you, but chances are that you won't be able to see Ed.'

'And will you ask Mum?'

'Yes. Now get off the phone. I'll ring her tonight but I won't mention this call – it wouldn't help.'

I fell asleep before Gran rang. The next morning Mum said nothing, but after tea, after she'd washed up, at the moment when I'd just decided that she wasn't going to mention Aunt Ed at all, Mum said, 'Your gran wants to take you to the hospital. She doesn't think you'll be able to see Ed but she knows – I know – how much you care about her, and that with everything at sixes and sevens you're anxious. I'm sorry I can't take you, Bonnie, but I just can't.'

'Because you don't like Aunt Ed?'

'It's not quite that straightforward.' Mum's eyes were narrowed.

105

She reached for a cigarette, lit it before saying, 'Ed's my enemy. I'm sure you're aware of that. I've perfectly valid reasons for considering her so but obviously that doesn't mean I want the woman to die.'

Her voice was clipped and hard and she looked at her cigarette as if it were Aunt Ed and hateful. I wanted to shout out, 'She's my aunty not a woman', but if I did Mum might change her mind.

'She's not going to die, is she, Mum?'

The skin on her face shivered and her head darted towards me like a snake's. 'Bonnie, if you ask me that question one more time I swear I'll slap you.'

The bus dropped us fifty yards from the hospital gates on a road running between fields full of tall, dry grass and straggling daisies.

'Very pleasant,' Gran said.

'What is?'

'The temperature. Not bad for the time of year.'

In silence we walked towards the hospital. When the fields stopped and the hospital car park began Gran put her hand on my arm.

'Now listen, I can't take you in with me. You're only just eleven and I'd have to leave you waiting in the corridor while I went up to the ward. Your mother felt it wasn't suitable.'

'But Susan visited.'

'That was when Ed was in a private room. She's in the general ward now. Anyway you're better off out here in the sunshine.'

'I wanted to see Aunt Ed.'

'I'll give her your love and when I come out in half-an-hour you'll get my blow-by-blow account of how she's faring.'

'What will I do for half-an-hour?'

'You've got your knitting.'

'I can't sit in a field knitting.'

'I don't see why not. It's perfectly dry. Just don't wander off. Keep an eye out for me coming through those doors.'

Gran kissed me on the top of my head, which was unexpected. I stood on the field side of the dividing brick wall and watched her walk briskly across the car park. In the raffia basket she'd bought at the jumble sale she carried fruit and changes of Aunt Ed's night clothes. At the swing doors she turned and waved. I waved back.

I considered the field. Above it the sky was a very bright blue, the field itself was cream coloured and pale green where everything had dried out after the hot summer. At the edges were trees and shrubs all with their leaves turned to gold and orange. I wished that instead of my knitting I'd brought my water colour set and some paper. I could have painted the scene but added poppies and forget-me-nots to give it some more colour. I imagined my gran taking the picture in to Aunt Ed on her next visit, Aunt Ed's eyes filling with grateful tears. 'The dear child.' My own eyes filled with tears at the thought.

I sat down on the grass with my back against the brick wall and took my knitting from my satchel. So far I'd knitted half of a very short scarf or a quarter of a very long scarf. The day grew warmer and it seemed like Gran had been gone for at least an hour. It was too hot to knit and the sun beat down on my head. What would happen if she never came back? I put the knitting away and headed across the field to a clump of gorse bushes. Patches of dull, dried blossom still clung to the branches. I found a twiggy alcove and crawled in, pulling my knees up to my chin. This was the sort of thing Susan would do with Lucy; make camp.

Suddenly, about six feet away from me a small brown rabbit popped up out of the ground. I'd only ever seen rabbits in books before and I was pleased and excited to see one in real life. I sat very still, held my breath. It hopped towards me. The little rabbit's eyes were runny. It sniffed the air before zigzagging to my left. Another bigger rabbit came up out of a different hole. It too sniffed the air then rushed at the first rabbit. It jumped on the first rabbit's back, pushing its lower half against the first rabbit's lower half. My rabbit made desperate unhappy squeaks. I clapped my hands. 'Shoo!' I shouted. The attacking rabbit shot away. My rabbit toppled over onto its side and lay panting. I crept towards it thinking how I'd slip it into the cool dark of my satchel and let it calm down. Its eyes were navy blue but encrusted in the corners and then they went milky. The panting stopped.

Its fur looked soft. I reached out and stroked it and then drew my hand sharply away. I'd felt nasty, nubbly lumps. I looked at my fingertips. There was dark brown pus on them. I could smell it. I scraped my hands across the grass. My rabbit was dead. A bus was stopping on the road and I began to run towards it. Two nurses wearing short capes got off. They paused to light cigarettes.

'Help!' I shouted and then my foot caught and I fell over.

I stood on a flight of stairs inside the hospital. One of the nurses held my hand. 'Is this your granny?' She pointed upwards to the top of the staircase.

'Yes.'

'Bonnie? What the devil? I thought I told you to wait outside.'

'A rabbit frightened her,' the nurse said.

'It was horrible, Gran.'

'The child's frightened of her own shadow.'

'Actually nearly all the rabbits around here have got myxomatosis. They're not a pretty sight. Your granddaughter had got some mess on her hands but we cleaned her up.'

'Bonnie,' a pleased, familiar voice called out from behind Gran.

Gran stepped aside so I could get to Aunt Ed. She wore a flowered cotton dressing-gown and turquoise velvet mules. I hugged her carefully. With a shock I realised we were almost the same height now. It felt like I was holding a fragile bird whose bones could easily be broken. Aunt Ed took me by the shoulders and stepped back so she could look into my face. Yes, she was still my Aunt Ed, still glamorous, eyes mischievous.

'What a devil you are, darling. Your gran nearly had a heart attack. We watched you pelting across that field screaming blue murder.'

'You saw me?'

'I had my eye on you every single moment.'

'And did you see the rabbit? It just died.'

'Yes well – never trust a rabbit.' She burst out laughing.

Two days later Aunt Ed left hospital.

SEVENTEEN

Winter

Today Gran is sitting at a table in the communal conservatory with another elderly woman. As I arrive the woman heaves herself out of the chair, puts her hand on my gran's shoulder and says, 'Don't let the so-and-so's grind you down, Shirley.' Which isn't reassuring. Am I one of the so-and-so's? I bet I am.

'Hello Gran. Is that a friend of yours?'

'It's Hilda. Her husband died at the weekend and we're planning a small celebration.'

'Didn't she like her husband?'

'She likes him better now.'

I kiss her on the cheek. She looks grimly gratified.

'That's a nice dress you're wearing,' I tell her.

She pulls at the bodice of the dress and makes a face. 'It isn't one of mine. They mix up our clothes in the laundry. Whoever's dress this was, the owner's either too polite or too batty to claim it back.'

It's a pretty dress; shirt-waister style patterned with white daisies on a cream background in a silky material. I can't remember ever having seen my grandmother wearing a light colour. As ever she picks up my thoughts.

'Yes, I expect it does look odd to you. I've always gone for navy or black — nothing flamboyant. I left that to your Aunt Ed and Susan.'

I'm slightly annoyed that I'm not counted as being flamboyant even though I'm wearing a scarlet wool trouser suit plus an embroidered felt hat, however privately acknowledge that if anyone had said 'Bonnie, you are a rather flamboyant woman' I'd probably have been offended.

Gran continued. 'Nowadays I find I'm wearing all sorts of odds

109

and sods I wouldn't ever have considered putting on before. I find it surprisingly exciting. I don't have to conform to my idea of myself. Do you know what I mean?'

I nod although I'm not sure I do know exactly what she means. I unpack the sweets I've brought her; *Turkish Delight* and a tin of *Quality Street*.

'If there's anything else you'd like,' I say tentatively.

Gran looks first at the chocolates, then at me. She clasps her hands on her stomach and puffs out her cheeks. 'Last time you visited, I wasn't really fair to you, Bonnie.'

Oh God, I'm thinking, *if she apologises I'm going to cry, which will make her regret apologising. Please, if anyone is watching over me, don't let me cry.*

'I perhaps didn't realise how little you understood about that time.'

I don't cry. I pull up my white plastic chair and prepare to listen. Just for a moment I think, *I wonder if Susan sits in this chair when she visits.*

'Of course you do remember the picnic?'

'When Aunt Ed bought you the electric blanket?'

'Yes, that's the one. I want to tell you what happened afterwards.'

Moira comes in with a tray of two cups of tea and some chocolate bourbon biscuits. These are a variety of biscuit I'd never dream of buying but when visiting Gran I find them rather tasty and comforting.

'Thank you, Moira,' Gran says.

'I hope there's not going to be any unpleasantness this afternoon.'

Gran and I look at each other. After my last visit I feel as if there's no fight left in me, and in my gran's face I read regret for her own part in the argument.

'Mind your own business, Moira. We're family. We're perfectly capable of falling out and then falling back in again without you to referee.'

Moira smiles. 'That's all I need to know.'

Gran:

You remember I went back with them in the car that afternoon? Ed wasn't at all well. She shouldn't have let herself get so angry with Susan. Brian should have stopped it but he always seemed helpless when faced with Ed's temper.

110

She went straight to bed when we got home. I spent a quiet evening with just Susan and Brian. Susan seemed pre-occupied and a bit miserable, which I put down to having upset her mother in front of all of us.

The next day, Sunday, Brian went off early to his office in Solihull – some spreadsheets he had to go over with Martin, he said.

He kissed me on the cheek and ruffled Susan's hair.

'Will you be okay?' he asked her.

'Of course, Dad.'

Ed came down briefly, late morning, to say 'goodbye' to me, then Susan walked me to the bus stop. It was a bright, sunny day but not quite as warm as the Saturday. As I hopped on the bus I almost repeated Brian's words, 'You will be okay, won't you Susan?' You see I was worried about her.

'I'll be fine, Gran.'

I waved from the bus window. She held up her hand and then closed her fingers. She looked very sad.

Susan went straight home. In the pocket of her summer skirt she had a florin I'd given her and I like to think she held on to it, turned it over between her fingers. I like to think it gave her comfort.

She went round the back of the house and came in by the kitchen door. From the kitchen she could see her mother. Ed hadn't gone to bed, she'd gone into the lounge and was resting on the sofa. She had her back to Susan, her head bent slightly forward as she flipped through a magazine. Without looking round she said, 'Susan, go upstairs to your bedroom and wait for me.'

Susan knew the drill. In her bedroom she waited. An hour went by. She sat on the chair by the window and looked out across the fields. Finally she heard Ed's footsteps on the stairs. Susan tracked her mother as she passed the bedroom door and went into her own room, a drawer opened and closed, then a moment later she heard Ed's footsteps coming back. Susan's door opened and there was Ed. In her hand she held a thin, metal ruler.

'Stand up.' Ed's voice was perfectly calm and friendly. Once upon a time that calm, friendly voice had fooled Susan into thinking that everything was back to normal. But no, just as she'd come to learn how and where her mother expected each cushion to be positioned, the correct way to hang up a towel and how the towel should never look as if it had been used by someone with dirt on their hands, Susan had learnt that her mother preferred to punish in cold blood. Yes, Ed might lash out at her or at Brian in a fit of temper but 'punishment' was to be administered when her anger had cooled. In Ed's mind she was unemotionally administering deserved chastisement. Spare the rod and spoil the child.

111

Susan took down her knickers so that they hung around her ankles then she bent forward gripping the seat of the chair. Efficiently Ed raised Susan's skirt and tucked the material into the waistband. Then she hit Susan as hard as she could.

Now Bonnie, you might say, 'Well just how hard could a pint-sized woman with a severe heart condition have hit Susan?' Hard enough. Three times across each buttock. The first blow was always the worst. Susan knew what it meant to see stars. She did not cry. Susan heard her mother's ragged breathing as she put all her strength behind the impact of ruler upon flesh. Twice Ed fluffed her stroke and the sharp corner of the ruler cut into Susan. Each time this happened Ed tutted as if only mildly annoyed.

When she'd finished she said, 'Stay where you are. I'm just going to dab some calamine on those two cuts.'

Susan stayed exactly where she was. The cold of the calamine lotion stung. Susan did not flinch.

'Let it dry,' Ed said and left her.

It was over. Whatever Susan had done was wiped away. After she'd heard her mother's footsteps go lightly down the stairs, she quietly closed her bedroom door. Then she cried but she made no sound.

Gran sits forward in her chair. She reaches for the bar of *Turkish Delight*.

'Did Susan tell you that?' I ask her.

'She did. Susan has children of her own now – I don't know if you knew.'

I shook my head. How could I know? We hadn't spoken in years. Gran rarely mentioned my cousin and I've never asked for information about her.

'They're in their teens. You have a niece and a nephew. They adore her, and I believe Susan when she tells me she has never laid a finger on either of them. Years ago Brian spilt the beans about Ed punishing Susan. One evening when he'd had too much to drink. There'd been no real need for him to go to his office that Sunday. He said he couldn't face being in the house whenever Susan was punished. He loved his daughter, but frankly my son was a coward.'

Gran unwraps the chocolate and takes a small bite. She chews thoughtfully, avoids looking at me.

'Ed was never the motherly type. She was always jealous of Susan, behaving as if her daughter was a grown woman instead of a child. Ed never could bear competition of any kind. I expect you're thinking "worse happens".'

'No Gran, I wasn't thinking that at all.'

I'm seeing my cousin from a distance of nearly forty years. The ten-year-old Susan in that house that was always really Aunt Ed's house, nothing much to do with Uncle Brian; no room at all for a boisterous, opinionated child – a quiet, pristine, unshifting place where my beloved Aunt Ed exerted total control. A perfect place, a perfect house, but never a proper home. Worse still; now, today, in the present – I'm acknowledging my own jealousy!

As if at a signal from Gran (which I certainly didn't spot) her friend Hilda re-joins us carrying a family photograph album. Gran amazes me by appearing interested in every single photo. She asks numerous questions, following up Hilda's answers with 'Well I'll be blowed' and 'Isn't it a small world?' This last directed at me. I agree that yes, it is indeed a small world but I don't actually know what I'm talking about.

EIGHTEEN

Winter 1964

Joanna, Estelle and Lesley call themselves 'The Triumvirate'. Every lunch time they take over the playground bench – the same bench where Joanna first spoke to me. They talk in low voices with their heads close together. If anyone comes near they stop talking and wait till the person moves away. Then Joanna tosses her head and says 'Thank *you*' and, to Estelle and Lesley, 'Really! Some people!'

At the end of break they walk with their arms linked behind each other's backs around the gym block to the main entrance, talking loudly and shrieking with laughter whenever they pass a group of boys. What can be that funny? Their conversation is all about boys. How can they find Bryn Preston 'cute' when he's at least three inches shorter than all of them? And his voice often comes out as a high pitched squeak. He reminds me of a mouse and, although I like mice (I've never seen a real mouse), I wouldn't want to go out with one, even if it was the same size as me.

Joanna says she's in love with Eric Burdon from The Animals, even though he has pimples and is short. For months 'The House of the Rising Sun' has been her favourite song. She sings it with Estelle and Lesley all the time. They look into each other's eyes as if they're in love.

I told Gran about them.

'Do these girls have boyfriends?' she wanted to know.

'No, but I think they want to have boyfriends.'

'They're only children.'

'They're eleven, same as me.'

'I hope you don't want a boyfriend. That can wait till you're at least sixteen.'

114

'And will I have to have one then?'

'You'll probably want one.'

'I don't think I will.'

'Wait and see. I'd steer clear of these girls if I were you.'

But I can't steer clear of them. Like a safety pin to a magnet I'm attracted to Joanna. She is the princess and Estelle and Lesley are her two less lovely attendants. I'm always hovering nearby while trying to make myself invisible. Sometimes they notice me and tell me to go away, sometimes they know I'm there but choose to just ignore me. Gran would say that I am putting myself in an 'invidious' position but I can't seem to help myself.

Last week Estelle called out from their indoor perch on the corridor radiator, 'So Bonnie, who's your favourite singer?'

'Marianne Faithfull.'

They looked at each other and said, 'Eugh!'

'But she's a girl.'

'Yes.'

'Who's your favourite boy singer?'

'Elvis.'

'He's not a boy, he's nearly thirty,' Estelle said. 'You're weird, as in *really weird.*'

Joanna laughed and shook her head as if there was no hope of me ever becoming a normal person.

Miss Wozencroft stood on the dais, her hands clasped on her stomach. She was smiling.

'Boys and girls, this term a great honour has been bestowed on the class.'

I thought, *how exciting if the great honour is to do with me.* With Gran's help I'd recently entered the *Fry's Chocolate* Painting Competition, sending in a picture of three pirates finding a treasure chest full of chocolate. I imagined Fry's contacting our Head Mistress: 'Is Bonnie Benson a pupil at St Benedict's? She is? Then your school is very fortunate to have a pupil who is such a talented artist.'

Miss Wozencroft continued, 'As you know each Christmas term one class is chosen to put on a play in front of the entire school.'

I nodded.

'This year 4B have been chosen. Quiet children.'

Because everyone had started talking excitedly except me. I rarely

115

said anything to anybody. However, I was silently excited.

Miss Wozencroft picked up a cardboard folder from the table behind her and waved it at us. 'I've chosen the story of Hansel and Gretel.'

'Can't we do Cinderella?' Estelle shouted out.

'Or Dick Whittington?' from Malcolm.

She ignored them but held up her free hand for quiet.

'Now, in the original story there weren't that many parts so I've added a few extras; fauns, nymphs and a flock of sparrows. For those of you who really don't like the limelight there's scenery and costume. I will direct the play and Mr Stevens from Music will advise.'

Gretel. I could play her really well. I was thin. I could easily look like an abandoned child.

'Hands up those wanting to play Gretel.'

My hand shot up. 'Miss, miss. Me miss.'

I looked round. The only girl in our whole class who hadn't put up her hand was Joanna. She was looking out of the window, a bored smile on her face. Straight away I knew that her bored smile was a tactic! Now Miss Wozencroft was turning towards her.

'Joanna, if we can tear you away from what is obviously far more interesting than being in the school play; I wonder how you feel about playing Gretel?'

Miss Wozencroft had fallen for it.

'Don't mind miss.' Joanna shrugged.

'Yes or no?'

'Okay.'

'Is that a yes or a no?'

Joanna shrugged again. 'Yes… I suppose.'

'Excellent.'

I stared hard at Joanna. Willed my hatred to travel across the desks and hit her right between the eyes. She met my gaze. 'Jealous?' she mouthed.

'Bonnie, face the front.'

And now I'd been almost reprimanded by Miss Wozencroft! I was furious. Nobody else seemed furious. I heard Estelle whisper, 'Well done Joanna. You're the natural choice.'

The natural choice! Joanna didn't look anything like someone who'd been neglected by a wicked step-mother or left in a forest by

116

her wood-cutter father. Couldn't Miss Wozencroft see that? She made me think of... strawberry ice cream. Joanna, not Miss Wozencroft. *She* made me think of fudge – which I don't like at all.

Miss Wozencroft handed out the other parts. John Seton (tallest boy in our year) was Hansel and Gretel's father, Bryn Preston was Hansel. Everyone was pleased about that, even me. Estelle was the wicked step-mother.

'But can I still be beautiful Miss Wozencroft?'

You've got to be beautiful in the first place, Estelle, to 'still be beautiful'!

Miss Wozencroft was smiling again. What was so funny?

'Wickedly beautiful, Estelle?'

Estelle looked bewildered, as if she had no idea what 'wickedly beautiful' meant. I knew what 'wickedly beautiful' meant. I had a 'wickedly beautiful' aunty.

'So, just the witch left to cast.'

Philip Stevens put his hand up for the witch, grinning and looking around at all of us as if he'd made a brilliant joke.

'Put your hand down, Philip.'

'But I want a part in the play.'

'You can be a faun or a sparrow.'

A very fat sparrow. (Philip Stevens is the fattest boy in our year.)

Miss Wozencroft stepped off the dais and advanced to the first row of desks.

'Now come on girls. Surely one of you wants to play the witch. It's the best part – a real chance to shine.'

None of us wanted a chance to shine at being old and ugly. We clamped our lips shut in case some tiny squeak might slip out and catch Miss Wozencroft's attention.

'Well, if nobody volunteers, I'll have to choose one of you.'

My heart sank.

'Bonnie – you'd make a terrific witch.'

Everyone roared with laughter – and relief.

'I'd rather paint scenery miss.'

Miss Wozencroft beamed at me. 'Of course you can paint scenery as well as being our witch.'

Gran laid down her newspaper and actually smiled. 'You lucky devil. I'd have loved to play a witch.'

'But I wanted to be Gretel.'

117

I turned to my dad sitting warming his stockinged feet on the brass fender in just the way a woodcutter father might. 'Dad, it's not fair. Joanna Bayliss gets all the star parts. She was Alice last year in our class production and she's been the Virgin Mary twice now.'

'Bonnie, you've never wanted to play the ladylike parts in your cowboy games, you've always wanted to be the man in the white Stetson who – '

'Yes Dad, but the man in the white Stetson doesn't have a wart on his nose.'

'Then don't have one.'

Gran said, 'Oh, she should have a wart.'

'You'd like to get laughs, wouldn't you Bonnie?'

'I would Dad but can't I get laughs and look pretty as well?'

'Well no, I don't think you can.'

A few days later I brought home Miss Wozencroft's script. At least the witch had the most dialogue.

I threw myself into the role. (That's how film stars describe taking on a part.) Gran belted a cushion across my shoulders to give me a hump and made me a grey wool wig. She said I was a 'natural'.

'What's a natural, Gran?'

'That's for me to know and you to find out.'

I did sort of know, dressed up in my costume and hobbling around our kitchen shouting out as I passed the stove, 'Light the oven, I'm going to have a tasty, toasted boy for supper.' I not only made my gran and dad laugh, but for a few seconds almost convinced them that this wasn't their Bonnie at all; I really was a very old woman with magical skills and a liking for roast children.

I haven't mentioned Mum, because my mum had very little to say about me being the witch. Now Aunt Ed was on the mend Dad was back to being his usual self, making jokes, teasing Gran, remembering to buy my comics on his way home from work. Mum seemed annoyed or upset, I couldn't decide which. She sort of removed herself from us and was hardly ever in the kitchen when we all sat down to tea, or afterwards when I rehearsed my lines.

'Eileen, are you joining us?'

'In a minute, Mother, just doing a bit of washing up.' 'Just rinsing my stockings.' 'Just peeling some spuds for tomorrow.'

'Ken, tell her to come in.'

But he never would tell her. So we got used to Mum being out in the scullery or upstairs in her bedroom and when she did sometimes join us even Gran seemed a little uncomfortable.

I was no longer upset about not being picked to play Gretel. Now I daydreamed about being the witch, how I would be a success like Judy Garland in *A Star is Born*.

Gran coached me.

'I used to tread the boards before I met your grandfather. At an amateur level of course but I learnt a few tricks.'

For instance the witch's house was made of thick cardboard; its walls painted to look as if they were fruit cake and the roof, marzipan. When I opened or closed the front door, the whole house wobbled and unless I ducked down the point of my witch's hat popped up above the pink marzipan roof tiles. Getting the cardboard door open wasn't easy either. Once I'd even walked around the stage wearing my little house.

'Use that for effect,' Gran said, 'like you use your wand.'

She bought me three green and three yellow bean bags that represented frogs and newts to toss into my cauldron for my supper while waiting for Hansel to fatten up.

Mum did come in there: 'Bonnie doesn't want to turn the school play into a farce.'

Gran didn't agree. 'It should be funny. The number of times I've sat through amateur productions and been bored to tears.'

'But it's not anywhere near as grand as an amateur production, it's a school play acted by ten and eleven-year-olds.'

At rehearsals Joanna and her friends watched me with a sort of horrified amusement. Sometimes Estelle and Lesley couldn't help but laugh but they'd stop quickly and look at Joanna to check her reaction.

One afternoon when I was in one of the toilet cubicles I heard Estelle say, 'The weed is funny.'

'Is she?' That was Joanna's voice. Then she yawned.

'Well funny for a weed.' Estelle again.

'Which isn't very funny at all. Can I borrow your comb?'

That was all. I heard them shuffle out.

119

The evening of the play I felt sick with fear but also excited. I found an empty classroom to change in and do my makeup. I sat at a desk and took everything out of my shopping bag; wand, wig, cushion for hump, theatrical make-up (thank you Gran), eyebrows, glue, bean bags and Gran's hand mirror. I repeated her instructions, 'Keep taking deep breaths. Don't hurry. Follow the procedure I've shown you.'

I took my first deep breath and began. First my face: I rubbed in a white base but not too thickly. I didn't want to look like a clown. Then I drew dark shadows around my eyes, under my cheekbones and lower lip. Ideally I wanted to look like a witch-zombie. I pulled on my grey wool wig and then I glued my black mono-brow and false nose in place. Dad had already stuck the chewing gum wart on the tip. 'Like a big, brown dew drop,' he'd said. It was easy to fit the cushion to my shoulders because Gran had attached a strap to it that buckled across my ribs. Over this went one of her old black dresses, and I'd borrowed the cracked leather shoes she wears in winter to bring in the coal from the coal shed. I studied myself in the mirror; sank my head down between my shoulders, pushed the lower half of my face forward – I wished we'd thought of a false chin but too late – I was ready. I put on my witch's hat.

As I slipped in backstage I heard Joanna's voice. 'Miss, I can do it myself. I wear make-up all the time at home.'

Then Miss Wozencroft. 'I'm not interested in what you do at home – you're supposed to look like a lost child not a little madam.'

Joanna spotted me as I came out from behind the curtain. She screamed. Miss Wozencroft glanced up and started laughing.

'Good God. Is that you, Bonnie?'

'Yes, Miss Wozencroft.'

'You look terrific.'

'Thank you.'

'If Bonnie can do her make-up, why can't I?' Joanna pouted.

'That's quite enough, Joanna. Now where is everybody?' She looked at her watch, 'Ten minutes – if either of you want to go to the toilet, go now.'

Joanna went to the toilet but I stayed behind and peered with one eye through the gap in the front curtains. The assembly hall was filling up. Three rows from the front Aunt Ed was already seated between Uncle Brian and my dad. There were Mum and Gran moving along a row into the middle. Aunt Ed turned and waved a white gloved hand. Gran waved back but Mum kept her head lowered.

'Bonnie, backstage now.' It was Mr Stevens, stage manager and musical director. 'We're almost ready. I must say, you look... extraordinary.'

And then we were off. The play rushed by and it was every bit as wonderful as I'd day-dreamed it would be, apart from me not getting spotted by a Hollywood talent scout. With the stage lighting I think I looked truly frightening as I emerged out of the gloom of the enchanted forest to take Hansel and Gretel by the hand. I forgot that they were really Joanna Bayliss and Bryn Preston and they forgot that I was Bonnie Benson. When they screamed they sounded and looked terrified. The audience boo-ed at me – I boo-ed back at them. I led the abandoned children into my little fruit cake house. The house trembled, my witch's hat bobbed above the roof. 'Whoops-a-daisy!' I said which wasn't scripted. Laughter swept around the hall. I lifted the house three inches above the floor. More laughter. Above everyone else's laughter I know I heard Aunt Ed's.

At the end of the play we ran back on stage to take our bows. I got the biggest cheer. I had never felt so happy. Then we took a final curtain call. Miss Wozencroft had instructed us; girls curtsey, boys bow. Well, blow Miss Wozencroft, I bowed! There was Gran beaming and trying to catch anybody's eye. 'That's my granddaughter up there!' Aunt Ed waved her handkerchief at me and blew a kiss. I stood in the middle of the line as the curtains slowly began to close in front of us. The audience disappeared.

'Well done, Bonnie,' Miss Wozencroft said. 'Well done all of you.'

I whipped off my witch's hat and made Miss Wozencroft a low sweeping bow. At that moment Joanna pushed between us, stepping hard on my foot. 'Show-off,' she hissed in my ear.

NINETEEN

My bedroom is lit by the flower-shaped pattern thrown onto the ceiling by the flame inside the paraffin heater. I've found the hot water bottle – at least my mum remembered that. I can just make out the roses on my wallpaper; dark splodges that in daylight I know to be different shades of red. I am too excited to sleep. So what if Joanna thinks I am a show-off – her mother, everybody else likes me. I don't care – much – about Joanna.

With my stage-make up and mono-brow still in place, but no false nose, I'd raced round to the corridor on the other side of the assembly hall. It was jammed with audience all talking loudly to each other. Dad and Uncle Brian towered above the other dads and uncles. As I pushed my way towards them I was clapped twice on the shoulder. 'Well done, young lady,' someone shouted. People looked at me with interest – I hoped they were thinking 'A star in the making!'

I recognised Aunt Ed's gloved hand waving frantically above heads. 'Over here Bonnie.'

I broke through. She grabbed my wrist. 'Bonnie, you were marvellous.'

I was laughing with happiness. 'Was I?'

'You know you were.' This from an unsmiling Gran. I looked into her eyes; warm – good – not cool or cold.

'But marvellous, Gran? Did you really think I was marvellous as well?'

Her features closed in as if she was sucking something sour. 'That's not a word I'd generally use but you were very good. We are all proud of you.'

'By heavens,' Uncle Brian grinned at me, 'that's one to treasure – a compliment from your gran.'

'Where's Mum?'

122

Gran began to button up her coat. 'Don't worry about your mum. She's popped on ahead of us to put the kettle on. She said to say "well done".'

'Excuse me.' Someone touched my shoulder. I turned. It was Joanna Bayliss's mother. All our eyes widened. It was like being approached by Leslie Caron or Audrey Hepburn. She was so astonishingly beautiful. Gran stopped buttoning.

'It is Bonnie, isn't it?'

I nodded.

'I thought you were excellent.'

'This is Mrs Bayliss. Her daughter, Joanna, was Gretel,' I explained.

Dad said, 'Your daughter was excellent too, Mrs Bayliss.'

'But not in Bonnie's league. I think your daughter has real talent. You were in a league of your own this evening.'

She smiled briefly and then very elegantly walked away from us.

'Crumbs. What a cracker!' Dad said. Uncle Brian whistled. Aunt Ed reached out for my dad's arm, stumbling a little.

'Damn it, I'm a bit shaky with all the excitement. Hang on to me, boys.'

They hung on to her, slipping her hands through both their arms.

'Can I hang on to you?' Gran asked, but with humour, and we followed them slowly towards the exit.

At home, no sign of Mum. No kettle on the stove, or cups and saucers arranged on the tray.

'You can talk to her in the morning,' Gran said. 'Just wash that muck off your face and get to bed. Tea, Ken?'

'I'm having a beer. Night-night, Bonnie. Well done.'

Dad kissed the top of my head.

Although I want to keep going over the evening, before I realise it I'm thinking about a batch of unravelled wool soaking overnight in the scullery. I wonder if Mum will rinse it out and hang it on the line tomorrow for me. I have plans for knitted snoods for winter. My snoods will be embellished with pom-poms. They'll be the envy of all the girls in my class. Perhaps Joanna's mother will stop me again and enquire in an admiring voice just where my collection of snoods comes from.

123

'I made them myself, Mrs Bayliss.'

'What an extraordinary girl you are, Bonnie.'

What had Mrs Bayliss said about me? I was in a league of my own? Which meant what exactly? Was she being complimentary or sarcastic?

Gradually, into my thoughts like a trickle of icy water, comes Mum's voice but as if from a distance. I turn over to face the wall and pull my knitted blanket up over my ears. They are always arguing now. The grown-ups. Their rows are like little bonfires that they take turns in starting up, then along comes Gran with a bucket of water. Some hissing, some crackling, and usually the bonfire goes out. I concentrate on a picture I've seen in mum's magazine of a model's head and shoulders. She is wearing the very knitted snood I plan to use as my prototype, while clasping mittened hands beneath her chin. In the background is a snow covered Alpine scene.

Downstairs both voices are growing louder. One low, one high, almost a harmony. My snood picture has gone. I am thinking of Joanna Bayliss and how she is in the school choir and I am not. My voice is much better than hers. I love singing, although at school we only sing the School Song and hymns. I go over the words of 'To Be A Pilgrim' in my head.

He who would valiant be 'gainst all disaster,
Let him in constancy follow the Master.

I start whispering the hymn to drown out their voices –

There's no discouragement shall make him once relent
His first avowed intent to be a pilgrim.

'As far as you're concerned I'm invisible.' That is my mum's voice.

'You've chosen to make yourself invisible. When was the last time – ' That is my dad's voice.

'What?' Mum almost screaming. 'What? After all you've put me through. I've no intention of ever…'

'Good. Thank God. Don't kid yourself! I was about to say, when was the last time you even took any notice of our daughter? The thought of having to go through the motions with you, ever again, makes my stomach heave.'

'You bastard! That's rich coming from you. Ed whistles and you start running.'

Her voice is awful; angry, as if she's trying not to cry.

Who so beset him round with dismal stories
Do but themselves confound – his strength the more is.
'The pair of you pack it in now. This minute!' The cavalry.
'Keep your nose out of this, Mother.'
'You'll wake, Bonnie.'
'It's high time she knew what a bloody swine her father is.'
No foes shall stay his might; though he with giants fight –
The wallpaper roses begin to shiver. The harder I will them to stay still the more they seem to spread out and slide away. Petals become legs, petals become bodies, fat swollen spiders' bodies, forming groups, *mumble, mumble, Bonnie, mumble*, then scattering, searching for a way to scuttle off the walls and crawl all over me.

Like in a bad dream I cry out but make no sound. I try to shout out the words. It's just a whisper against the scratching and squealing noise of the spiders and behind that sound comes the *boom, boom, boom* of anger reaching up through the floor boards. I imagine it as smoke and then as skeletal hands.

My voice breaks through. A horrible sound not like my voice at all. I shut my eyes tightly and scream: *HE WILL MAKE GOOD HIS RIGHT TO BE A PILGRIM.*

Dad reaches me first. He wraps his arms around me. 'Hush up, Bonnie. That's enough now.' His voice is gentle.

'The wallpaper came alive. Spiders, Dad, not roses.'

Gran switches on the overhead light. 'Is that all? I thought at the very least you were being murdered.'

'Where's Mum?'

'Washing up.'

'But there wasn't any washing up.'

'Well she found some. Ken, bring up a glass of warm milk and a couple of aspirins, then go to bed.'

I'm asleep before he comes back.

The next day I don't see Mum till the afternoon when she meets me from school. It's usually my gran who meets me and I feel awkward. I can see that she feels awkward as well. We set off for home, at first in silence before she asks, 'Any more compliments today about your performance?'

'Not really.'

'Any stars?'

I rarely get stars except in art but sometimes I have lied when she asks me that and say, 'Yes, I got a green star for English.'

Green is my house colour. On my tie I wear a small green enamel brooch in the shape of a shield with 'Turner House' written across it in gold letters. I have no idea who Turner is. If I feel like really cheering my mum up, which I don't today, I tell her I've been awarded a gold or silver star but I can't do this very often in case she boasts about it to someone and I'm found out.

'You went down very well yesterday,' she finally says. This is hardly a compliment of the 'league of your own' variety.

'Aunt Ed said I was marvellous.'

'Did she?'

'Coming home in the car she said I could go on the stage.'

'I thought you were going to be an artist.'

'I could be a film star too.'

'I'd rather you weren't.'

'Aunt Ed was in show biz.'

Mum begins to walk faster. 'Ed was never in "show biz". She was a night club hostess, there for the gratification of men with more money than sense. Men who should have been at home with their wives and children.'

'Slow down, Mum.'

'No, *you* walk faster. Your aunt was a waitress in a night club.'

I'm impressed. I imagine a dark smoky room, lamps with orange shades on every table, men seated at the tables, their shirt fronts and cuffs gleaming whitely, every face turned towards Aunt Ed as she crosses a dance floor carrying a tray of glittering drinks.

As we near our house Mum finally slows her pace, because there as usual sits Mrs Mallaby.

'Afternoon the two of you. Bonnie, you're growing more like your lovely mother every day.'

'Thank you, Mrs Mallaby.' I lift my chin and flare my nostrils so that Mrs Mallaby knows exactly what I really think of her remark. Mum puts her hand on my shoulder and steers me up our path. Indoors she says, 'I can't stand that woman.'

'I can't either.'

'But we do look a bit alike, don't we?' She pats her hair as she looks at her reflection in the hall mirror. I don't want to look at me and Mum together.

'I look like my dad as well.'

'Yes of course you look like your damn father. The pair of you are a perfect match.'

I take off my blazer and hang it with my satchel over the banisters. I follow her into the kitchen. Mum clatters plates. Cups and saucers are banged down, the kettle rattles against the cold tap. She is making such a noise and I know she wants me to say something nice about her and me, or she has something more to say about Aunt Ed.

She says, 'I've never mentioned this before but Ed and I have known each other since we were girls.'

I am astonished. 'What? Like me and Susan?'

'No. We worked in the same office.'

'I thought you said Aunt Ed was a waitress.'

'She was. In the evenings. We met when we were both sixteen. Once upon a time I thought we were really good friends. For a few years we were inseparable.'

'Were you?' I can't imagine my mum and Aunt Ed ever being good friends, sitting in the cinema, sharing a bag of sweets, gossiping over a cigarette.

'Then I met Brian.'

'Brian who?'

'Your Uncle Brian, who else? We went out together for several months.'

'*You* went out with Uncle Brian.'

Mum lights the gas under the kettle. When she turns round she's smiling but it is not a true happy smile. 'Yes, that's right, and then Ed got her hooks into him.'

'But what about Dad?'

'Ken was just a photograph on your gran's sideboard. He was away in the army and rarely came home on leave. If he had a leave he went down to London. I met him at their wedding. He was Brian's best man while I moved from being Brian's girlfriend to finding myself relegated to bridesmaid in two blinks of an eye.' Mum is looking into the distance at a memory. 'So I took up with Ken. I liked him very much. I still do when he remembers I'm alive. And then of course madam, not being satisfied with her own husband, took a shine to mine.'

'But if Dad was in love with you?'

127

'Get this into your head Bonnie; nobody was ever in love with me. Not Brian, not Ken, not anyone.'

She switches off the gas, pours boiling water into the tea pot. I think she's finished talking but she hasn't. 'It's a lesson in patience, Bonnie. If Ed had waited, left Brian alone, she would have met Ken at *my* wedding. They were and are made for each other. I can't argue with that. They would have no doubt been – what is that ridiculous term? Deliriously happy.'

I think for a moment. 'But why do you get so angry with Dad when he wants to see Aunt Ed, if you didn't love him.'

Her face hardens. She carries the tea pot out of the scullery and sets it down on the kitchen table. I follow her.

'He owes me some loyalty. I've played second fiddle to the three of them for years and now I've had enough.'

TWENTY

Yesterday was the last day of the Christmas term. Last week, a few days before the play, Miss Wozencroft brought in a post box she'd made out of cardboard and red crepe paper. Although I don't like Miss Wozencroft very much she is clever at making things. When I told Gran about the post box she said, 'The woman's a genius.' I think Gran meant it.

All week cards had been posted into the box till it was so full up you could see cards sticking out of the posting slot. I didn't post any cards. I'd mentioned cards to Gran but she'd said, 'We're not made of money.' She'd meant that too.

I didn't expect to receive any cards either, although immediately after my success in *Hansel and Gretel* I'd day-dreamed that I'd receive dozens, that Miss Wozencroft would come into class dragging a large sack of cards. *These are all for Bonnie Benson*, she'd announce. *Never in the history of St Benedict's has any pupil received such a bumper bundle of Christmas cards.*

Once the post was sorted and Miss Wozencroft, in a white beard and Father Christmas hat, had delivered them all, two cards lay on my desk. For a second I wondered if Miss Wozencroft had sent them, to save me the embarrassment of being the only girl in the class *not* to receive a Christmas card. But no, one was from John Seton (who may one day be classified as a giant) – the other card was from – Joanna! I recognised the green ink she'd used to write 'Bonnie Benson', I'd seen it on the cards she'd given to Estelle and Lesley in the canteen the previous lunchtime.

It was an expensive looking card. A wintry scene of reindeers pulling sledges; snow made of silver glitter dotted the night sky and also showered into my lap. She hadn't signed it but underneath the printed 'Happy Christmas' she'd written 'Dear Bonnie, it *was* the best day's play ever.'

I was very near to crying, but by now Gran had instilled into me not to show weakness in the face of the enemy, or a possible enemy. Once I'd sorted my eyes out I looked across to Joanna's desk by the window. She'd had at least twenty cards. She'd arranged them in three packed rows on her desk. Probably a card from every single person in the class – except me. Our eyes met. She hunched up her shoulders and stuck out the tip of her tongue which made me think of the aggressive behaviour of an armadillo, although I know nothing about armadillos except that they're poor swimmers and I don't know how I know that!

TWENTY-ONE

Spring

These were the peaceful few hours after lunch when those residents capable of sleep took their naps. Outside my grandmother's bedroom window the sky was iron grey but at least it had stopped raining. The red and purple tulips lay beaten down amongst clouds of pale blue forget-me-nots.

I helped myself to a soft centre from a new box of *Quality Street* while studying Gran's face for signs of life. She was asleep in her armchair. At least I hoped she was only asleep. For at least twenty minutes she'd hardly moved or made a single sound. Years earlier, when I was a child and Aunt Ed was having one of her increasingly frequent spells in hospital, Gran had told me (quite cheerfully) that a noise to listen out for when visiting the elderly or critically ill was a dry cough followed by the staccato rat-tat-tat sound coming from the back of the patient's throat.

'A sound very much like a machine gun being fired,' she'd said. This combined with the dry cough indicated that death was on the cards in a matter of minutes. 'Seconds in your grandpa's case.'

I moved away from the window and stood looking down at her.

'Gran, are you awake?'

Immediately her eyes flicked wide open. She looked up at me, not with any pleased surprise or affection; with annoyance.

'I am now, you little blighter.'

I sat down on the white plastic chair which has become a permanent fixture in her room.

'You were so quiet it unnerved me. I thought you were a gonner, Gran.'

'Pah!' The annoyance left her eyes. I'd known that word 'gonner' would win her round. Something we'd had in common; a remembered liking for the cowboy series on television. Gran had championed Rowdy Yates (a very young Clint Eastwood) in *Rawhide*, while my favourite and Gran's least favourite had been Matt Dillon, the marshal in *Gunsmoke*, played by James Arness. You didn't get much more quiet and no-nonsense than Matt.

As happened so often, she read my thoughts. 'Matt Dillon gave me the creeps. His chin was out of all proportion with the rest of his face, and why didn't he make an honest woman of Miss Kitty?' (Miss Kitty ran the saloon and it was accepted among the viewers that she and Matt were promised to each other.)

'There'd have been no backstory if he'd married her, Gran.'

'Backstory, my eye. Do you intend to eat all those sweets? If you bring me in sweets, then let me eat them. You can afford to buy your own box.'

'We can't both sit eating our way through separate boxes of sweets.'

'Why can't we?'

'The nurses will think we're greedy.'

'We are. Anyway I couldn't care less what anyone thinks of me. You mind, don't you? You haven't changed.'

'Let's not start on how awful I was as a child.'

'Why not? You were.'

'I wasn't. My teacher Miss Wozencroft said I was exceptionally clever.'

'Oh you *were* clever. Cleverer than a barrel of monkeys. No point smiling smugly. Being clever didn't make you more lovable.'

'Thank you.'

She helped herself to a strawberry cream. The colour had come back into her cheeks and her eyes twinkled.

'You've left it a bit too late to have children,' she observed.

I shrugged. 'I'm not the maternal type.'

'Doesn't your Jay have any say in the matter?'

'Not really.'

'I loved having boys. Ed would have been happier with a boy. She couldn't stand her own sex.'

'She liked me.'

'Only because she wanted what wasn't hers. But Ed was Ed and I wanted at least one of my sons to have his heart's desire.'

'But which son do you mean, Gran?'

132

She ignored my question. 'What a time to start talking about "heart's desires". How about you, Bonnie?'

'I'd say Aunt Ed represented my idea of a "heart's desire". I've never met anyone since who dazzled me like she did.'

'She intended to dazzle you; to dazzle everyone with the exception of your mother. What about your Jay.'

'I love Jay, but with a steadier emotion.'

'A "steadier emotion". That must be fun for him, Bonnie.'

I shrugged as if to say, 'That's not my problem', which of course I don't mean. But my relationship, my life, are areas I'm not ready to share with my grandmother. I've thought about this. How Gran has always been able to talk to Susan. I've progressed to bringing chocolates, sweets and magazines; stuff she actually wants, rather than fruit and flowers in tasteful wrappings, but each time I visit I recognise little touches in Gran's room that I know have come from my cousin. Postcards and newspaper cuttings, a blue felt elephant and a rabbit in a velvet waistcoat. Next to the small television is a radio and cd player and, next to that, a cheap plastic cd rack – every space filled with Frank Sinatra, Dean Martin, Bing Crosby and singers I've never even heard of. They're personal. They represent a different level of intimacy between Gran and Susan that I'm excluded from. I have no experience of the successes or the tragedies, the private jokes – the backstory.

When we were children, I remember Gran repeatedly saying, 'Your cousin's choc full of beans'. Mum would agree with her. It hurt me at the time but I'm beginning to realise that it wasn't meant to. It was a statement of fact.

'You don't have any photographs, Gran.'

'I do. I just don't put them out. You should see some of the residents' rooms, not an inch of space anywhere; dozens of family photographs in odd frames. One of these days I'd like one of you and Jay, if it's not too much to ask.'

'Have you got a picture of Susan?'

'Of course.'

'Can I see it? Them.'

Gran heaved herself out of the chair and crossed to her chest of drawers. Pulled open the top drawer and began to rummage about. I could see that the drawer was full of loose photographs. Finally she made a choice; she handed me one quite large photograph.

'It's taken in Small Heath Park,' I said.

'Yes.' She stood next to me, looking over my shoulder.

'Susan's put on weight.'

'A little.'

I swallowed. My eyes filled with tears which luckily Gran couldn't see. My cousin Susan, my flesh and blood; more like Uncle Brian but still something of Aunt Ed in the way she posed, one hand on her hip. Susan, older, plumper but still 'choc full of beans'.

'She looks absolutely lovely, Gran,' I said and I meant it with all my heart. I felt Gran's spasm of surprise as she took a step away from my chair.

'I hope you're not being sarcastic.'

'No. She does look lovely – and happier.'

'I think she's happy now. Considering. I don't suppose you'd like to have that photograph – I've got others.'

'Are you sure?'

'Quite sure.'

'I'd be very glad to have it then. Thank you.'

She picked up *The Lady* magazine. 'Tuck it in there so it doesn't get creased.'

TWENTY-TWO

Spring 1965

Dad has finally bought the car from Uncle Brian's office manager Martin. It's a Ford Poplar, beige coloured with beige leather upholstery.

We have all tried out the car seats and agree that they are more comfortable than our armchairs indoors. The driver's seat has several cigarette burns but Dad says, there will be several more by the time *he's* finished. Next to the front side windows are two neat little exterior indicators that flip outwards like twin tortoise-shell combs. At night they glow orange and make a regular ticking noise when in use.

Mr Mallaby said our car is 'a credit to the street'.

Dad has taken us out on short runs to the Black Country, Dudley Castle and Stourbridge. He was going to offer Mr Mallaby 'a spin' but Gran reminded him about Mrs Mallaby being fat, and that if she insisted on accompanying Mr Mallaby she might ruin the suspension. I wouldn't have imagined my gran would know a word like 'suspension' but it must have been the right word because Dad nodded. 'Point taken, Ma,' he'd said.

Yesterday after tea but before we switched on the television to watch *Emergency Ward 10* my dad announced from behind his newspaper, 'Brian and I thought we'd take the girls a bit further afield.'

Dad hadn't spoken for some time. He'd left the table and taken his newspaper to sit in the armchair next to the fireplace as he does every evening, even if a fire hasn't been lit. Sometimes we forget he's even in the room. Gran and Mum are very interested in Mrs Brown's 'predicament' at the moment. They have always preferred

135

Mrs Brown to Mrs Mallaby, because Mrs Brown is ladylike and it is 'a crying shame' that her husband and son are dead. She still has her daughter, Celia (vivacious), but now Mrs Brown wants to send Celia to a private school because she will almost certainly fail her Eleven Plus due to never being in class, due to Mrs Brown always needing her at home, due to Mrs Brown's nerves being in a terrible state, due to Mrs Brown's husband and son having died within a few months of each other. However, in their opinion, Mrs Brown has got above herself with her talk of 'private school'.

'Damn,' my mum said as she missed her tea cup with the sugar spoon and sugar dropped in her saucer and all over the table.

Gran started to get up. 'I'll get a cloth.'

'Sit, Mother.' Mum held up her hand. She looked across at my dad who was still hidden behind the paper. 'And who exactly would be classified as "the girls" you want to take further afield?'

Dad's face appeared above the paper. He was grinning. 'We were thinking – '

'We?'

'Brian and I were thinking – '

'Are the two of you joined at the hip? Do either of you ever have a thought to call your own?'

Dad's grin was beginning to look as if it was quite painful to keep in place.

'Eileen, if you'd just let me finish. Brian and I were thinking that it might be educational to take Susan and Bonnie to see – '

'The Queen?'

'No, the Spring Solstice at Stonehenge.'

If Dad had said he was taking us on a visit to the Taj Mahal we couldn't have been more astonished. Gran snorted with amusement. A flush ran up my mum's neck and into the lower half of her face, which meant she was *really* angry. Just beneath her eye a vein began to twitch. I'd never noticed that before.

'You want to take the girls *where*?'

'Stonehenge.'

Dad was grinning again but now as if he really wanted to laugh.

'You want to take two children on a cross-country jaunt in winter.'

'Spring. I've seen daffodils in the park.'

'And what do you know about the Spring Solstice?'

'Nothing, apart from it being celebrated at Stonehenge towards the end of March, which is another reason to go. Broaden Bonnie's horizons… and mine.'

Gran stood up and put a shovel of coal on the fire. The flames spat at her but she didn't seem to mind. She stood warming the back of her legs. 'Why not wait till summer, Ken? We could take two cars and all go. Surely there's more than one solstice?'

'But he doesn't want all of us to go. Do you Ken? And he's only taking Bonnie and Susan to use as an alibi. Ed is included in this trip, isn't she? I wouldn't be surprised if it wasn't her hare-brained scheme'

The silence that followed was finally broken by Gran. 'Don't mind me, but Bonnie's eyes and ears are out on stalks.'

At 1am on the twenty-first of March our car pulled up outside Aunt Ed and Uncle Brian's house. Gran had seen us off with a flask of tea and corned beef and mustard sandwiches. She'd tied my scarf so tightly round my neck I'd protested. 'You're choking me, Gran.'

'Don't tempt me. Ken, look after your daughter. I expect there'll be crowds at this time of year.'

'Don't worry, Mother. I'll keep an eye on her.'

He wore old corduroy trousers, two pullovers and his Crombie overcoat. Leather gloves that he kept slapping against his thigh. He wanted to be on his way.

'You look like a burglar, Dad.'

'Good. Are you fit?'

'Aren't you going to shout cheerio to Eileen?'

'No, Mother, I don't think I'll bother. Even if she isn't asleep she'll pretend to be. I'll only get the cold shoulder.'

All the lights were on in Uncle Brian's house. We stood on the doorstep waiting to be let in. Cilla Black's 'Anyone Who Had a Heart' drifted out through the letter box.

'That's one of my favourite songs, Dad.'

'Is it?'

'Is what?' Aunt Ed said, opening the door.

'Bonnie's favourite song is whatever it is you're playing.'

'Do you like Cilla Black, Aunt Ed?'

'I can take her or leave her. I think it belongs to Susan. Brian's

137

always playing her records. He's like a big kid.'

Aunt Ed stepped back to let us in. She posed on the circular hall rug.

'Will I do?'

She wore a tight fitting polo neck and a mohair skirt in different shades of lilac. Over her shoulders she'd thrown her fur coat.

'You'll break your ankle in those,' my dad said nodding at Aunt Ed's high heeled shoes.

'I've told her that already.' Uncle Brian came into the hall carrying a cocktail shaker. 'I thought we'd have one for the road. Nothing for you and Susan, Bonnie – Ed's not making hot drinks at this time of night.'

'Where is Susan?'

'In her bedroom. Nip up and tell her to get a move on.'

I nipped. Susan's bedroom door was shut.

'Susan.'

'Yeah?'

'Your dad says to get a move on.'

She opened the door. I'd never seen a girl of my own age in trousers before. Pale blue cord.

'I've been ready for ages. It's the two of them who are never ready.'

'Are your trousers new?'

'Yes.' She walked over to her bed and threw herself down on it. For a second the memory of Susan in my bedroom flashed into my head but I blotted it out.

'Isn't it exciting?' I said.

'Is it?'

'It is for me. Your mum looks excited.'

Susan sat up. 'Well she's not excited. She doesn't want to go. She's dreading it. All afternoon she's been trying to think of an excuse to stay at home.'

'Mum said it was her idea.'

'She's always having ideas, that doesn't mean she wants to carry them out. Can you really imagine her enjoying stumbling about in the dark just to watch the sun come up behind some mouldy old rocks?'

'She likes nature.'

Susan raised her eyes to the ceiling. 'You're so dense, Bonnie.

Mum likes the garden, sparrows and thrushes. She wouldn't like an eagle or a – a mongoose. She likes what's safe. Saying she'd like to visit Stonehenge is just her showing off. So she looks more interesting than your mother. You know my mum's in love with your dad, don't you?'

'Yes, I do know.'

'So you do have something up top?' Susan tapped the side of her head.

She jumped off the bed and walked towards me. I stepped back. 'I think we better go downstairs.'

'After you,' she said, grinning.

'No, definitely after you.' I grinned back at her.

'Cowardy custard. Come on then.' She barged past me and out of the door.

We piled into the back of Dad's car. It was thrilling leaving the lamp lit streets behind. Knowing that inside each house people were already asleep or getting ready to go to sleep. But not us. We were setting off on a real adventure. I was determined to stay awake. Uncle Brian sat in the front with my dad, Aunt Ed squeezed in between us, a blanket spread over our knees.

I peeped across Aunt Ed to Susan. She was drawing a face with a downward curving mouth in the condensation on the inside of the window.

'Sit back Bonnie,' Aunt Ed said quietly. I sat back. She took my hand in hers. 'My hands are cold. I forgot my gloves.'

'You can borrow mine,' Uncle Brian called out.

'No thank you. They'd look ridiculous. Bonnie's hands are nice and warm – she'll look after me.'

I chafed Aunt Ed's hands. They refused to stay warmed up. In the darkness, I knew she was smiling from the tone of her voice. 'It's okay Bonnie. I'm fine now. Thank you.'

Twice we stopped at transport cafes to stretch our legs and use the toilets. Susan and I stared at men with motorbikes wearing black leather jackets and they stared back at Susan. On the second stop Aunt Ed stayed in the car. Uncle Brian bought her a bacon sandwich but she said the very smell of it made her feel nauseous.

At one point it began to rain. Dad switched on the windscreen wipers. They made a sound like an old gate creaking in the wind.

'Steady Ken.' Uncle Brian reached over and touched the steering wheel with his leather gloved hand as the car skidded on a corner.

'Can't see a bloody thing,' Dad muttered.

'I'm cold.'

'Ed, I've got a bottle of *Bells* in my jacket if that would warm you up.'

'She'd better not,' Uncle Brian said. 'She's taken tablets.'

Aunt Ed didn't argue. She shrank down under the blanket. She had most of the blanket now. Susan and I tucked our hands into the sleeves of our coats for extra warmth. It was cold in the car even with the heater on.

I stared out of the window, watching for stray pin points of light in the darkened countryside. Aunt Ed sighed loudly, 'Oh God.'

'Nearly there.' Even Uncle Brian sounded tired. 'We've cut it a bit fine.'

It was quarter to six. The sky was fading from navy to a pale green. More lights showed now, like the glowing tips of cigarettes. Then a stretch of nothing much, but on the grassy verges cars, motorbikes, motor scooters, even a horse and cart, were randomly parked. Dad rolled down the window and cold air blew in.

'Dad!'

'It's fresh. Not like Brummie air.'

'Please Ken.'

'Sorry Ed.' He shut the window.

We got out of the car and Aunt Ed moved over into my space. She peered out of the car window at us almost as if she was frightened.

'It doesn't seem to have rained here, Mum,' Susan said. 'The ground's quite dry.'

'Not dry enough for me, thanks all the same. If you're going, go – you're letting the cold air in.'

It was cold – but exciting. Dad and Uncle Brian seemed to somehow come to life, inflate – not fatter but fill more space. They stood next to the car stamping their feet and blowing on their hands, although they could easily have put on their gloves. They smiled hugely at each other as if being in the midst of something different suited them. Aunt Ed rolled the window down an inch.

'You're not going to be ages are you?'

Dad looked irritated. 'Come on Ed, we didn't drive all this way

140

for you to sit in the car. It was your idea after all.'

'Yes it was my idea Ken, but I didn't realise we'd be marooned in the back of the back of beyond. I thought there might be a nice cafeteria.'

Dad put his hand on Uncle Brian's shoulder, 'Brian, let's get moving – we don't want to miss the bloody dawn. Okay Ed, you sit and guard Mother's sandwiches and the flask.' He started laughing. Aunt Ed wound up the window and pulled the blanket around her so that only her nose, eyes and the top of her head showed.

'Ready girls? Susan, you hold your dad's hand – Bonnie, take mine.'

'Dad, we're eleven years old.'

'And you're in the middle of a crowd of strangers. I don't intend to lose you.'

'Shouldn't one of us stay with Mum?'

'No Sue. Ed's made her choice. Come on.'

Dad grabbed my hand and tugged me along. I looked back; Uncle Brian and Susan were moving more slowly. Susan looked unhappy, continuously glancing over her shoulder towards our car.

It was like a huge party but everyone was quite quiet; groups of what mum would have called 'beatnik types' wearing donkey jackets and jeans, then men *and* women in dresses. 'Hippies,' Susan said later. 'I want to be a hippy.' And people like us; families. Lots of children and music, guitars – a tambourine, someone singing, but nothing loud, nothing that would frighten anybody, certainly not Aunt Ed.

I saw the wavering flame of candles and the light from torches shining weakly in the green light before the dawn. I looked at Susan. She pulled a face at me but not an unfriendly one.

'Everyone's weird,' she whispered.

We joined the edge of the crowd. I felt proud to be standing with my dad and Uncle Brian. Uncle Brian was handsome. When he was with my dad he wore a particular lopsided smile and squared his shoulders. And Dad in his Crombie coat with the collar turned up so his pale yellow hair showed like a beacon. People nearby glanced at them because, although they weren't twins, together they looked striking.

We pushed forward a bit to get a better view. Dad made me

141

stand in front of him, his hands on my shoulders. The stones were huge. Behind them the sky glowed a greenish blue.

'They look like a family,' I said.

'What's that, Bonnie?'

'The stones. They look like a family. A really big family. Grown-ups with flat heads looking after the smaller ones.'

'Grown-ups with flat heads, eh?' Dad chuckled.

I itched to draw them but I hadn't brought my sketch book. In my coat pocket my right middle finger outlined their shapes on the palm of my hand. The taller stones seemed to be looking outwards, proudly; their shoulders held back, scanning the distance for a possible enemy.

We waited. The whole crowd was waiting, their voices kept low. Only Dad and Uncle Brian talked in their normal voices, making jokes, laughing. Inside I was a bit embarrassed that they wouldn't keep their voices down. If my gran had been with us, she'd have known that they were talking too loudly. She'd have called them a pair of yobbos. 'Keep the noise down you pair of yobbos. Don't you know how to behave?'

'Oh-oh, here comes the sun,' Uncle Brian called out.

My dad turned to Susan. He put his hand under her chin and tilted her face upwards. 'Susan, run back to the car and tell your mother to get her arse over here pronto. Tell her I said. Take Bonnie with you.'

We raced back to the car. In the half-light Aunt Ed was trying to read a copy of *Woman's Journal* she'd brought with her. Susan rapped on the window. Aunt Ed must have only been pretending to read because she didn't seem at all startled. She closed the magazine and rolled the window down. Through the inch of open space Susan panted, 'Mum, Uncle Ken says to say, get your arse over there right now!'

It was like a lamp going on inside Aunt Ed's face. 'Did he? Oh bugger it, why not? If I go base over apex, no doubt someone will scoop me up.'

She beamed at us both. Threw down her magazine and got out of the car. 'It's perishing.' But she didn't sound complaining anymore. She wrapped her coat around her, threw back her head as if she was a woman who welcomed a wild breeze in her hair, and teetered across the rough ground. I held her arm while Susan marched on ahead of us.

'Excuse me,' Susan said. 'Can we get through please. My mother isn't well but she wants to see the sun come up.'

I was amazed at how in command Susan was and that people took notice of her. I mean, Susan's younger than I am – only just eleven – but she cut through the crowd, knowing exactly where she was heading. Dad and Uncle Brian stepped apart and let Aunt Ed slip in between them. Each took one of her arms and hugged it against their sides.

From all around us came a low sound, like the beginning of a wail or a moan and then a gasp.

'I can't see,' Susan said.

'I'll pick you up.'

'Then you can't see.'

'Never mind.'

I put my arms around her waist and lifted her. She was heavy but not too heavy. For a moment I imagined I was lifting up Joanna Bayliss.

'Can you see now?' I gasped.

'Yes. The top of the sun looks like a gold coin.'

I turned my head sideways. Aunt Ed was looking up at my dad who was concentrating on Stonehenge and the dawn. But suddenly, as if it was just a thought, way behind a dozen other thoughts, he opened his overcoat and pulled Aunt Ed inside it.

'I'm coming down,' Susan called out. She landed on my feet. 'Sorry. Shall I ask my dad to lift you up?'

'No.'

'Shall we go back to the car and eat our sandwiches?'

'Yes.'

Susan tugged Uncle Brian's sleeve. 'Dad we're going back to the car.'

Uncle Brian looked down at us. I thought his face looked sad; his shoulders had gone back to drooping again.

'Don't talk to strangers. I'll be along in a minute.'

I followed Susan. I wanted to ask her what she thought about her mum being in my dad's overcoat. In the car she said, 'Pity you missed the sun coming up – it was great.' And the moment to say something was lost.

TWENTY-THREE

Mum had been 'invited' to St Benedict's for an 'informal chat' with Miss Wozencroft. I half-hoped Miss Wozencroft was going to suggest that a pupil with my artistic and dramatic flair should immediately be enrolled at a stage school in London, as had happened to Pauline, Petrova and Posy in Noel Streatfield's *Ballet Shoes*. But no, Miss Wozencroft wanted to discuss 'The Eleven Plus' and 'What Was Going Wrong?'

Mum is often quietly annoyed, but when she came home from St Benedict's she was furiously annoyed – with Miss Wozencroft and also with me. I watched her from the bay window coming up our front path, through the front door, the hall and into the kitchen as if she were on roller skates.

'I want a word with you,' she said, taking off her raincoat and throwing it over the banisters on her way through.

'I'm just going to the toilet.'

'Well hurry up.'

I took as long as I could, washing my hands and admiring my new hairstyle in the mirror door of the bathroom cupboard. My hair is now long enough to wear in a ponytail like Joanna's friend Estelle wears hers, although my hair isn't as thick as Estelle's.

Gran said, 'It is not your crowning glory, Bonnie.'

'What is my crowning glory then, Gran?'

Gran thought for a moment then said, 'You don't have one – yet.'

'I told her,' my mum was saying to Gran, 'that *I* had no idea what was going wrong – I'm not the one taking the exam. Why not ask Bonnie, I said. She said she had asked Bonnie and Bonnie had told her she couldn't concentrate due to her aunty being seriously ill.' Mum turned her attention to me. 'How many times must I tell you, grey school skirt, white knee socks and black lace-up shoes. I ignored my school blouse and tie – instead I wore my favourite turtleneck jumper. This had been a birthday present from Aunt Ed and was not made of wool but Courtelle. I am beginning to quite like Courtelle because, as Aunt Ed says, the garment does keep its shape and colour. I knotted the blue chiffon scarf I'd stolen months earlier from Joanna cowboy fashion around my neck.

Mum came into my bedroom with a cup of tea. 'You're up early. Why aren't you wearing your school blouse and tie?'

'Not everyone wears school uniform, Mum.'

'Not everyone can afford to. Fortunately we're not quite in that situation. Where did that scarf come from?'

'Jumble sale, ages ago.'

'I hope you washed it.'

'Of course I did. Joanna Bayliss will be wearing a party frock.'

'If Joanna Bayliss jumped off a cliff would you jump after her?'

'Yes I would.'

'Don't be silly. Well, if you get told off, don't blame me.'

She walked over to the window and looked down into our street. 'So, I expect your friend Joanna will be going on to Grammar?'

'She's usually top in everything apart from music and art. I'm always top in art.'

'If you work hard you could get transferred when you're fourteen.'

'It doesn't matter, Mum.'

'It does to me. I don't want you picking up the Birmingham whine. That won't further your career.'

'I'm going to be an artist. I can talk any way I want then.'

Briskly she turned away from the window. 'You will get a good job in an office. You will speak like a young lady. You will not end up as a housewife or an unmarried mother.'

After she'd gone downstairs I positioned my hand mirror on the bookshelf so I could at least see my middle section if I stood against the facing wall. Something was missing. Perhaps a brooch. I tried the enamel Scottie brooch I'd dug up in the garden, but that wasn't the effect I wanted. I remembered the cowboy outfit my dad had bought me years earlier after he'd taken me to see John Wayne as Davy Crockett in *The Alamo* at the cinema in Lime Street Railway Station. I'd loved the leatherette waistcoat and chaps, the plastic gun

146

we don't wash our dirty linen in public?'

'It was the truth, Mum. I can't concentrate.'

'You can concentrate quick enough if there's a pullover to be unravelled.'

'That's different.'

'You do not tell perfect strangers our business.'

'Miss Wozencroft isn't a perfect stranger.'

Gran said, 'Can't you pull your socks up?'

'I don't want to pull my socks up.'

'But surely you can try harder? You've got an answer for everything when you're at home.'

'That's not the same at all, Gran. It's not like you're asking me questions on nature study or geography or how many pints of water it takes to fill up the bath tub.'

'You see,' Mum appealed to Gran, then the ceiling light, 'There's no point reasoning with her. Her mind's full up with drawing or weaving or… some other time wasting project that will get her nowhere.'

Gran said, 'Can we all calm down? The bottom line, as I see it, is that unless there's a miracle Bonnie will be going to the secondary modern in September?'

Mum nodded. 'Yes, that is the bottom line and I don't appreciate having it spelt out to me by some dried up, patronising school ma'am. I wouldn't be at all surprised if it isn't Miss Wozencroft who has filled her head with this nonsense. She actually said, 'I do hope Bonnie will be able to keep up her art at her new school.' Her art! She said Bonnie has 'potential and could make quite a fine artist'. Well I told her straight; my daughter will not be scraping out a living as an artist. She'll do her time at Secondary and then take a secretarial course. Bonnie is going to be financially independent and not end up being everybody's bloody doormat.'

I slipped out of the room and upstairs to my bedroom. I thought about my 'potential'. That was quite an exciting thought. I imagined a skein of dark brown wool and then spotting two brightly coloured strands. How to stop them getting lost or fading?

I didn't care too much about going to secondary modern but I'd really miss seeing Joanna Bayliss.

On the morning before half-term I dressed carefully. I put on my

145

grey school skirt, white knee socks and black lace-up shoes. I ignored my school blouse and tie – instead I wore my favourite turtleneck jumper. This had been a birthday present from Aunt Ed and was not made of wool but Courtelle. I am beginning to quite like Courtelle because, as Aunt Ed says, the garment does keep its shape and colour. I knotted the blue chiffon scarf I'd stolen months earlier from Joanna cowboy fashion around my neck.

Mum came into my bedroom with a cup of tea. 'You're up early. Why aren't you wearing your school blouse and tie?'

'Not everyone wears school uniform, Mum.'

'Not everyone can afford to. Fortunately we're not quite in that situation. Where did that scarf come from?'

'Jumble sale, ages ago.'

'I hope you washed it.'

'Of course I did. Joanna Bayliss will be wearing a party frock.'

'If Joanna Bayliss jumped off a cliff would you jump after her?'

'Yes I would.'

'Don't be silly. Well, if you get told off, don't blame me.'

She walked over to the window and looked down into our street. 'So, I expect your friend Joanna will be going on to Grammar?'

'She's usually top in everything apart from music and art. I'm always top in art.'

'If you work hard you could get transferred when you're fourteen.'

'It doesn't matter, Mum.'

'It does to me. I don't want you picking up the Birmingham whine. That won't further your career.'

'I'm going to be an artist. I can talk any way I want then.'

Briskly she turned away from the window. 'You will get a good job in an office. You will speak like a young lady. You will not end up as a housewife or an unmarried mother.'

After she'd gone downstairs I positioned my hand mirror on the bookshelf so I could at least see my middle section if I stood against the facing wall. Something was missing. Perhaps a brooch. I tried the enamel Scottie brooch I'd dug up in the garden, but that wasn't the effect I wanted. I remembered the cowboy outfit my dad had bought me years earlier after he'd taken me to see John Wayne as Davy Crockett in *The Alamo* at the cinema in Lime Street Railway Station. I'd loved the leatherette waistcoat and chaps, the plastic gun we don't wash our dirty linen in public?'

'It was the truth, Mum. I can't concentrate.'

'You can concentrate quick enough if there's a pullover to be unravelled.'

'That's different.'

'You do not tell perfect strangers our business.'

'Miss Wozencroft isn't a perfect stranger.'

Gran said, 'Can't you pull your socks up?'

'I don't want to pull my socks up.'

'But surely you can try harder? You've got an answer for everything when you're at home.'

'That's not the same at all, Gran. It's not like you're asking me questions on nature study or geography or how many pints of water it takes to fill up the bath tub.'

'You see,' Mum appealed to Gran, then the ceiling light, 'There's no point reasoning with her. Her mind's full up with drawing or weaving or... some other time wasting project that will get her nowhere.'

Gran said, 'Can we all calm down? The bottom line, as I see it, is that unless there's a miracle Bonnie will be going to the secondary modern in September?'

Mum nodded. 'Yes, that is the bottom line and I don't appreciate having it spelt out to me by some dried up, patronising school ma'am. I wouldn't be at all surprised if it isn't Miss Wozencroft who has filled her head with this nonsense. She actually said, 'I do hope Bonnie will be able to keep up her art at her new school.' Her art! She said Bonnie has 'potential and could make quite a fine artist'. Well I told her straight; my daughter will not be scraping out a living as an artist. She'll do her time at Secondary and then take a secretarial course. Bonnie is going to be financially independent and not end up being everybody's bloody doormat.'

I slipped out of the room and upstairs to my bedroom. I thought about my 'potential'. That was quite an exciting thought. I imagined a skein of dark brown wool and then spotting two brightly coloured strands. How to stop them getting lost or fading?

I didn't care too much about going to secondary modern but I'd really miss seeing Joanna Bayliss.

On the morning before half-term I dressed carefully. I put on my

145

belt and holster. I rummaged amongst the boxes and bags at the bottom of my wardrobe till I found the waistcoat. Too small. The silver sheriff's badge in the shape of a five-pointed star winked at me. I pinned that to my jumper. On my way out Mum called after me, 'Oh Bonnie, not the sheriff's badge.'

'But I like it.'

'At least hide it under your blazer.'

I walked to school on my own now. Most of us did. Not Joanna. Her mother still dropped her off in their car, always early as her mother worked in an office.

'She's not just a secretary,' I'd overheard Joanna telling Estelle. 'There are people under her.'

I wondered what sort of office Joanna's mother might work in. I knew when my mum talked about her dream to have me work in an office, she imagined I'd be wearing a sombre suit in grey or navy, perhaps a string of pearls at my neck; never in Capri pants and tight sweaters, with brightly coloured clip-on earrings.

As I neared the school gate I could see Joanna. As always she was the centre of an admiring group. Today she looked like Cinderella on her way to the ball. No ringlets, her hair falling in shining gold waves to her waist. She wore a white ballerina length dress with a blue sash and matching blue satin ballet pumps.

I told myself, Bonnie, imagine you are Steve McQueen in *The Magnificent Seven.*

I tried a laconic grin as I sauntered across the playground. I wished I'd worn my gun belt because that would have given me something to do with the hand that wasn't holding the strap of my satchel. Joanna's group turned and stared at me then they turned back and stared at her. Not once did Joanna glance my way.

'Anyway,' she said, 'my brother bought this dress in *Macy's* in New York. New York, America, you know. It's a proper ballet dress. I'm starting lessons in the summer holidays.'

She raised her arms above her head and pirouetted. Her skirt filled up with air and looked like a flower, its petals unfolding.

'Howdy, Joanna,' I said tucking my spare thumb into my skirt waistband.

Her pirouette subsided.

'What?'

147

'Just saying howdy. That's a mighty purty frock you're wearing.'

'Are you making fun of me?'

'No sirree.'

'Yes you are. Push off.'

I tipped my invisible Stetson at her.

'Stop that.' Her cheeks were scarlet.

'Leave her alone, Bonnie Benson,' Estelle shouted. 'They should lock you up in the loony bin.'

Joanna's eyes widened as she spotted her scarf. She grabbed my arm.

'You little thief.'

We faced each other. The other girls stepped back, just like in the cowboy films when there's a shoot-out in town. I stared hard at Joanna's pretty nose and lips.

'Who you calling a thief?' I drawled.

Frowning she let go of my arm. 'You're creepy.'

I swallowed. This wasn't turning out anything like I'd imagined. Joanna wasn't amused or acting flirtatious like the western ladies did while sashaying around the men folk in *Bonanza*.

'Why am I creepy?'

'Pretending to be a cowboy.'

'Underneath I am a cowboy.'

'No you're not. You're a stupid girl who's stolen my scarf. I want it back.' She held out her hand.

'You can't have it back.'

'But it's mine.'

Estelle stepped forward. Estelle has got fat this term, fat and tall. 'Give it back to her.'

I took a deep breath. 'I'm keeping it to remember you by.'

Joanna's bottom lip trembled, her eyes filled with tears, her nose went bright pink – with a sob she ran into the school.

'Joanna, wait,' Estelle shouted and ran after her.

The whistle blew. Mrs Skeffington marched into the playground. We all rushed to line up in our forms, shuffling into position, resting our fingertips on the shoulder in front of us. I stood at the end of my form line. Mrs Skeffington inspected us. She stopped in front of me.

'Take off that ridiculous star before I confiscate it Bonnie. And the scarf.'

'Yes miss.'

'Forward.' Mrs Skeffington took her place at the front of the line and marched, arms swinging towards the Girls entrance. Inside I made straight for the toilets and locked myself in a cubicle. I put the scarf back on. I stayed there till I heard the first bars of *All Things Bright and Beautiful*, the signal that assembly had started, before setting off in the direction of home.

The rest of the day I spent by the lake in Small Heath Park. Some of the other schools had already broken up for half-term so nobody took any notice of me sitting on the grass on my own with my sketch pad and packed lunch.

It was only the end of April but quite warm and there was a green haze over all the trees where the leaves were just beginning to arrive. I sat staring at the lake with its island in the middle. There were no rowing boats out that afternoon. They were moored neatly by the small concrete jetty waiting for the weekend.

I drew a picture of my dad and Aunt Ed, their rowing boat rocking gently, half concealed behind the overhanging branches of a willow. Each time my thoughts strayed back to Joanna I shied away from the pain like a hot nugget of coal lodged in my chest. At 3.30 I unpinned my sheriff's star and walked down to the water's edge. I pressed the star into the mud and put a large stone over it.

As I came out of the park I saw Mum walking ahead of me. She wore her faded red raincoat with the belt dangling. I wasn't pleased to see her – I didn't run to catch up – my spirits sank even lower. Mum, from the back looked no happier than I felt. She walked very slowly, her head bent, but suddenly she glanced over her shoulder, saw me and her face broke into a smile.

'Hello darling, you're early.'

I took one of her shopping bags.

'Heavy,' I said.

'You've got the bag with the potatoes. How was your day?'

'Okay.'

'Only okay?'

'Yes.'

'You're not wearing your star.'

'I gave it to Joanna.'

149

'That was generous of you. She's the girl you said you'd follow over a cliff, isn't she?'

'Yes.'

I scuffed into the house after her. She picked up the post scattered on the mat and went through into the kitchen. As she dropped the bags and letters on the table there was a knock at our front door. Gran was away looking after Susan, Dad at work – Mum put her head on one side in surprise. 'Whoever can that be?'

'Mrs Mallaby?'

'She wouldn't knock, she'd bang. Or stick her nose through the letterbox and shout something. Put the kettle on.'

'I'll get the door.'

'No, you put the kettle on.'

She went out into the hall. Kettle in my hand I followed her. Through our half glazed door I saw two blurred images. I saw gold colour – lots of it. The gold of Joanna Bayliss's hair. Mum opened the door.

'Yes?' she said.

'Are you Mrs Benson?' Joanna's mother drawled.

'Yes.'

'It's about your daughter, Bonnie. Can we come in?'

Mum looked back at me standing in the kitchen doorway hugging the kettle. Joanna's arm shot out, pointing at me. 'She pinched my scarf.'

'She did what?'

'I didn't, Mum.'

'Yes you did, Bonnie Benson.'

'Come in.' Mum led the way. 'Bonnie – kettle on. Now.'

Joanna and her mum filled our drab kitchen with colour. Mrs Bayliss in a bright pink v-necked jumper with elbow length sleeves and her favoured Capri pants; Joanna still wore her white frock. They stood close to each other as if afraid they might get a smudge of dirt on their nice clean clothes. I wished Mum would take off her mac, then she did and I wished she'd kept it on. She was wearing her oldest, drabbest, brown and orange patterned dress with odd buttons on the bodice.

'Would you like to sit down?' she asked.

Mrs Bayliss smiled thinly. 'No thank you. This isn't a social call. That scarf your daughter's wearing belongs to Joanna. It

150

disappeared from her coat pocket in the school cloakroom some time ago. When Joanna challenged Bonnie this morning about it, your daughter behaved in an extremely odd and threatening fashion. In fact she reduced my child to tears.'

I said, 'I told you, Mum, I got the scarf in the jumble sale. Gran will bear me out.'

'That scarf is mine.' Joanna said.

'I expect there are thousands of similar scarves.'

'I think you'll find a *Macy's* store label on it.' Mrs Bayliss was looking at me very unpleasantly as if I'd at the very least stolen her car.

Mum sighed, 'Bonnie, give me the scarf.'

I untied the scarf and handed it to her. She spread it out on the table. There was no label, only a thin white uneven edge where a label had once been.

'There you are,' Mum said.

'It's obvious. She's cut it off.'

'Bonnie, did you cut the label off?'

I shook my head vigorously, 'No I didn't.'

'Thank you. Now Mrs Bayliss, my daughter isn't in the habit of telling lies.'

'Nor is Joanna.'

'She may have been mistaken.'

'Bonnie said she wanted my scarf to remind her of me,' Joanna said.

'I didn't, Mum.'

Mum ignored me and concentrated on Joanna. 'Why would Bonnie steal your scarf so she'd be reminded of you? Are you going away?'

Joanna stiffened. 'I'll be going to grammar school in September.'

'I wasn't aware that the exam had been taken yet.'

Well done, Mum.

Mrs Bayliss's turn. 'Oh we're pretty certain that Joanna will pass her Eleven Plus.' Another of her thin smiles which made her look much less like Leslie Caron.

'Even so.' Mum had adopted a bewildered frown and something of Perry Mason's manner of questioning – interrogation. 'I say again, if Joanna is continuing at St Benedict's till the end of the summer term why ever would Bonnie want her scarf now to remind

151

herself of your daughter and why would she be so silly as to wear it into school?'

And if I couldn't answer that question, nor could they.

'What about the strange behaviour?' Mrs Bayliss's voice sounded less confident.

For once I felt proud of my mum. She wasn't intimidated, if anything she looked annoyed. 'Bonnie is an unusually imaginative child. Darling, you didn't intend to frighten Joanna, did you?'

'No Mum.'

Mum went eye to eye with Mrs Bayliss. 'I'm sure Bonnie would never upset your daughter. After all she did give Joanna her sheriff's badge and I know how much she treasured that.'

Mrs Bayliss looked bewildered.

'Did she give you a sheriff's badge?'

Joanna stared down at her ballet pumps, then pointed one toe and began tracing the pattern on the carpet.

'Well did she?'

Joanna said, 'I was so annoyed with Bonnie over the scarf, I threw the badge away.'

'But that's dreadful,' Mrs Bayliss said. 'Then perhaps you were mistaken over the scarf.'

Joanna shrugged and stared at her pumps as if she was bored.

I said, 'Can I show Joanna my weaving loom?'

Mum hesitated. 'Actually I don't think Mrs Bayliss – ' she frowned, staring down at one of the letters on the table. It was unstamped. Her name 'Eileen' was written on the front in black ink and underlined. I recognised my dad's handwriting.

Mrs Bayliss said, 'We'd better go. I'm really sorry about this misunderstanding. It's not like Joanna at all.'

We trooped through the hall, my mum and Mrs Bayliss out in front. I tweaked one end of Joanna's blue satin sash. She'd stopped crying. She whispered, 'Is it really not my scarf?'

'Of course it's your scarf,' I whispered back.

'You're mad, Bonnie Benson.'

'Why did you agree that I'd given you my sheriff's badge?'

'Because I'm mad, Bonnie Benson.' She pulled a face at me.

I remembered a phrase Aunt Ed had used once, that I'd found very sophisticated, when she'd burnt the cauliflower cheese.

'C'est la vie,' I said.

I expected ructions from Mum, but no, she hurried back into the kitchen and opened her letter. One small sheet of note paper. She sank onto a chair and put her face in her hands.

'Mum?'

Without looking up or moving her hands away from her face she shook her head.

'What's the matter?'

'Your dad's gone away with Ed.'

I picked up the letter. More a note really.

Dear Eileen, I'm sorry. A week is all Ed and I ask for. Brian has agreed. Please try to understand. Ken.

'It's only for a week, Mum, not forever.'

Mum looked up at me. Her face was drained of all colour, no blood left in her lips. She said, 'Bonnie, it feels as if it's been forever.'

'I don't understand.'

'Would you open the scullery door – I need some air. And that cup of tea please.'

TWENTY-FOUR

Mum and I spent the week of my half-term alone together. Usually she took me on outings with Gran. Not far; to the park, the cinema, window-shopping in the newly opened Bull Ring, but Susan was home for her half-term so Gran remained at Uncle Brian's house to look after them both.

The first morning without Dad, my mum was still in her dressing gown when she brought up my cup of tea. She sat down on the edge of the bed. I watched her and waited. Our house seemed unnaturally quiet.

'Bonnie, you mustn't expect too much of me at the moment. You must make your own amusements.'

'But Dad will be back by the weekend, won't he?'

Her voice hardened. 'He said he would be. Who knows?'

'But where's he gone?'

'He and Ed are in Bournemouth. I spoke to Brian after you'd gone to bed. They're at the Majestic Hotel. Very salubrious. Of course Brian's footing the bill – your father couldn't afford it.' Mum seemed more angry than upset. 'I can't believe that he could just swan off with that woman and expect me to grin and bear it.'

'But if Dad thinks Aunt Ed's going to die – '

'Don't *you* give me that nonsense. I've been listening to it from your father day in, day out for over two years. That doesn't make it okay. I want a specific year, month, day and hour in that day – then I might believe it.'

'You don't want to share him, do you?'

'Married people don't share.'

'But Uncle Brian doesn't seem to mind sharing Aunt Ed.'

Mum looked at me. She was biting on her lower lip. She took a deep breath, 'Brian doesn't care enough to mind.'

'But of course he does. He loves Aunt Ed.'

154

'Yes, he does love her – but not in the same way. Brian has resources to fall back on that I don't have.' She stood up. 'I shouldn't be talking to you about these things.'

'Yes you should. What resources has Uncle Brian got?'

'That's enough Bonnie.'

'Dad hasn't gone away forever, has he?'

'You'd be sorry if he had, wouldn't you? Stuck with me?'

That week Dad was away, my mum altered. I'd expected her to be crying all the time, banging doors and saying things like 'your bloody father', but instead she was serious and thoughtful as if she was watching a particularly interesting documentary on the television. If I mentioned Dad and Aunt Ed, she said very firmly, 'Bonnie, I don't want to talk about them. If you've any questions you better save them for your dad, when and if he comes home.'

Several times she popped next door to speak to Mrs Brown, which I understood as Mrs Brown has also experienced tragedy, and on three evenings, after I was in bed, Uncle Brian came to our house. I'd hear the murmur of their voices down in the kitchen, and once as Uncle Brian was leaving he said, 'Time and patience, Eileen', and she answered, 'Easier for you, Brian.'

Gran rang every day but she never asked to speak to me. Once I yelled over the banisters, 'Give Gran my love.' Mum didn't give Gran my love; she finished her telephone call with, 'Well Mother, what choice do I have?'

The weather was quite warm. I sat in the garden on the bench beneath the laburnum tree, which was heavy with pale yellow blossom. I had my book and my sketch pad but I never read or drew anything. Once, just for something to do, I stood on the bench. The morning was misty and I could almost imagine I saw Mount Everest. Mum was at her bedroom window staring out. As I raised my hand to wave at her she turned back into the room. Most of the day she'd stay upstairs, only coming down at lunchtime to make sandwiches for us both.

'Bonnie, your sandwiches are ready,' she'd call out, but by the time I reached the kitchen there was no sign of her, just my sandwiches on a plate on the kitchen table and the plod of slow footsteps going back upstairs.

Dad stayed away for eight days. On Sunday morning he

telephoned to say he'd be home by six that evening. She let me sit on the stairs and listen to her side of the conversation. Mum kept her voice very pleasant, the voice she used with the insurance man or in shops. 'Will you be wanting tea or will you have it there?'

Pause.

'Well, there's ham and pickle in the larder.'

At exactly six o'clock that evening my dad's car pulled in outside our house. He'd brought Gran with him.

I heard Mrs Mallaby call out, 'Where have you been Ken? Anywhere nice?'

'The whole bloody street knows our business – no doubt Mrs Brown and her big mouth,' my mum said.

Something held me back from just running out exuberantly like I usually did when Dad came home from work. I stood with my mum on the door step as he took their suitcases from the car boot. Next to me I felt Mum shiver. Dad was tanned like a film star as if he and Aunt Ed had been sitting out in the sun all week. It didn't seem right for Dad to have to come inside our dark, gloomy house in shabby Waverley Road.

Mum looked down at me and said in a low voice, 'What would you have me say, Bonnie, "You look marvellous, Ken"?'

As he reached us my mum suddenly said in a high, brittle voice, 'Ken, you look marvellous. Good holiday was it?'

Then she turned and walked back indoors.

Dad's tan faded quickly. Gran remained Gran but not so cross or argumentative. Mum held herself aloof. She wouldn't gossip with Gran any more. Aunt Ed's house, clothes, behaviour were no longer a favourite topic of conversation. Even Gran seemed awkward if she let any mention of Aunt Ed slip out. Dad hid behind his newspaper until it was time for him to move to the settee and switch the television on. I didn't always join him even if it was one of our favourite programmes like *Bonanza*.

I couldn't get out of my head what Susan had told me, Aunt Ed's 'What are you waiting for, big boy?' I knew what my dad had done with Aunt Ed in their week away and I didn't want to think about whether my dad was 'a big boy' or not. I didn't blame Aunt Ed, I blamed my dad. He was my good guy, my cowboy in a white Stetson, now the word 'mucky' kept flashing through my head. I'd see his hands spread out on his knees and wonder where they'd been. Inside Aunt Ed perhaps? In moments of high drama or high romance on television I'd always cuddled up to him or he'd put his arm around my shoulders and hug me, now I didn't want him to. I'd sit ramrod straight with space in between us and if he touched me, I'd freeze or pull away.

'Whatever's the matter with you, Bonnie?' he asked at first but that soon changed to a shrugged, 'Please yourself.'

I spoilt watching television together for both of us.

One afternoon Mum brought home a puppy. Not for me as I immediately assumed, for herself. She'd seen it in a pet shop window.

'He was the only one in the litter who wasn't running round. He sat at the back of the pen and looked miserable,' she told Gran. 'I felt sorry for him. It was like looking at myself.'

Gran ignored the bit about 'looking at myself' and said, 'He's probably sickening for something. I hope he's not going to die.'

'No. He's not going to die,' Mum answered firmly. 'What shall we call him? Any ideas Bonnie?'

'Sinbad?'

'No, I think I'll call him Bill.'

'Why Bill? That's a boring name.'

'I used to have a boyfriend called Bill years ago. He was a decent chap.'

Bill had a very sad, ancient looking face for an eight-week-old puppy. He was black and brown with watery eyes. Not as easy to love as I'd always imagined a puppy would be. Mum insisted there was a hint of King Charles spaniel about his ears and the curl of his coat but really there wasn't. Mum said that anyway it was a well-known fact that mongrels were far more intelligent than pedigree dogs. Gran said she had heard that well known fact but feared Bill might be the exception to the rule.

I don't know if it was because Bill was ugly or whether it was that Mum had made this momentous decision to buy a puppy without consulting anyone else, but without any prior discussion we found ourselves unanimously disliking Bill.

I was jealous. Before Bill, my mum had always asked *me* to go with her to the shops or park or just to keep her company. I could

157

say yes or no, which suited me. Now there was no choice. She stopped including me. Inside I was often angry with my whole family. What was I supposed to do with myself? I slammed doors, huffed and puffed, tried Susan's heavy sarcasm, 'Oh wow! Park again! Big deal!' Nobody noticed.

Now Bill went everywhere with her, even to the lavatory. If she went out and left Bill behind he whimpered... and whimpered... and whimpered. I'd try to distract him, tickling him under his droopy chin. In return he'd award me a quick quite pleased look with a hint of apology as if he knew I expected more, and then he'd start whimpering *again*. Until she came back Bill could not be cheered up. He'd lie with his head on his paws on the fireside mat, in the best position for everyone coming through the kitchen to trip over him, watching us dolefully as if we'd played a rotten trick on him by kidnapping her.

'That dog depresses me,' Gran said.

'He depresses me too, Gran. I wish he'd take a running jump.'

'Slang Bonnie. He's a puppy, for heaven's sake. But why doesn't he play? I wouldn't even mind if he chewed my slipper. If he was a person and not a dog, Eileen wouldn't have him in the house.'

Bill chewed no slippers, chased no rubber ball unless mum threw one for him, he looked heart-breakingly sad which we determinedly ignored. However the more we ignored Bill the more my mum loved him.

'What's to love?' Dad wanted to know. 'If he widdles against my chair leg one more time, he's out.'

'It's a sign of affection,' my mum said stiffly.

'Well don't you ever try that on me,' and he started laughing.

Mum wasn't in the least amused. 'You're the last person I'd waste affection on.'

Dad stopped laughing and looked annoyed. Mum picked up her cigarettes and went out into the garden. Bill peeled himself off the mat and trotted after her.

Mum had always preferred to be indoors whatever the weather; suddenly with Bill she found she liked being outside. She'd sit on the bench beneath the laburnum tree with Bill lying across her sandaled feet. Sometimes she read a magazine; sometimes she put her feet up on the bench and just blew her cigarette smoke thoughtfully up into the tree's branches.

From the odd cigarette with a cup of tea in the afternoon she now smoked twenty-five a day. She owned two summer cardigans, a beige one and a navy one, both with pockets. In the right hand pocket she kept her *Kensitas,* in the left a small box of *Ship* matches.

If I joined them she and Bill seemed quite pleased to see me but Mum wouldn't immediately take her feet off the bench or move up so I could sit down next to her. I had to fend for myself. That was the phrase she used all the time: 'Bonnie, you'll have to fend for yourself.'

Up until then I'd always thought I could read her face. She was easily offended, often irritated, rarely what could be called 'happy'. Suddenly I couldn't read her at all. She appeared to be concentrating on a knotty problem that didn't necessarily include us or more importantly - me.

Right in the middle of the serial about a young woman who dresses up as a gondolier to protect the man she loves, my mum cancelled her subscription for her weekly magazine *Woman's Own*. It caused consternation for both me and Gran. We'd always insisted that we only glanced at the magazine because it happened to be lying about. Secretly we both read it from cover to cover; the stories, *Matron's Page*, the horoscopes. And the serial – all week I looked forward to the next episode.

'Are you sure you don't want the magazine?' Gran asked her. 'I would have liked to know what happened to Ventura – ' (Gondolier heroine.)

'You know what happens – they fall in love and live happily ever after – I don't think.'

Mum behaving differently and often indifferently in and around the house was bad enough but then gradually she and Bill were never at home. Without telling anyone she took Bill to the vet for his hard pad injection and while she was out she bought him a smart red leather collar and lead from Woolworth's. Now every day they were off across the road and into the park. And beaming at people who stopped to pat Bill. And talking to them! And patting other dogs and talking to *their* owners! However, at home she'd virtually stopped talking and beaming at us.

'Where the devil has she found the cash for the vet and the collar and lead?' Gran asked my dad. 'Has she come into money, Ken?'

159

'She says she's saved it from her housekeeping. I said, "In that case any surplus should go back in the kitty." She then says, she'll get a part time job if I'm going to adopt that attitude. I said, "Eileen, I'm not adopting an attitude, I'm talking common sense." Then she blows a stream of smoke from her cigarette in my face and comes up with, she's redressing the balance and I'm the last person to stand between her and the only bit of enjoyment she can find.'

'That's quite a conversation,' Gran said.

'It was a conversation to end all conversations because she's said bloody nothing much since.'

Dad was rattled (although still going over to see Aunt Ed twice a week). Gran was rattled. I was rattled. For the first time ever we found ourselves taking notice of Mum, we began to see her as a person in her own right; she wasn't just my mum or dad's wife.

The change interested me. Why was it that although she wore the same clothes, the same orange lipstick, made the same indifferent meals, she was more – a woman to be noticed, like say Joanna's mother?

We didn't intend to but eventually we all fell in love with Bill. It was like my year-long dislike of *Heinz Spaghetti* and then one day thinking it was a long time since I'd been given *Heinz Spaghetti* and feeling that spaghetti on toast was the only thing I wanted for my tea.

One Saturday Mum took Bill for a long walk. They went all the way to the Botanical Gardens. She took sardine sandwiches and coffee in a flask. She was gone all day. Dad came in from work at one o'clock and said the house felt like a morgue with no dog whining. It was too early to turn on the television. Gran had gone up the road to see Miss Venables, leaving me with my drawing and Dad with the newspaper. At four o'clock he folded the paper, looked at me and misquoted a *My Fair Lady* song title: 'I've grown accustomed to Bill's face, Bonnie. Go and see if there's any sign of them.'

I went into the front room and lifted the net curtain. Bill rounded the corner of our road first. Then Mum appeared, her arm stretched out as Bill pulled on the lead. She didn't look quite like my mum. I thought this lady could be walking on a cliff path, or across a field, somewhere remote, she'd be happy then. She saw me at the window. I held up my hand and waved. She held up her hand then

160

let it drop. A dull pain in my chest, the fear that she might not love me any more, made me race outside to meet her.

'We've missed you, Mum,' I said.

'I find that highly unlikely,' she said, but affectionately.

'Dad's definitely missed Bill. He says he's grown accustomed to his face.'

TWENTY-FIVE

Dear Bonnie,

Hilda has been staying with her son and his wife for a fortnight and it's been mighty quiet here. I thought I'd try my hand at writing down a bit about Ed for you. I'd wanted to remember some nice things, but wherever Ed went she caused trouble and pain. Now I didn't mean to write that but I've started this letter three times now and don't intend to begin again.

About two months after the holiday with your dad (if you can call it that) Ed became really ill. She was told that if her condition deteriorated further she would have to go into hospital. Complete bed rest and complete peace – no more visits from Ken, no tantrums. The next morning while you were at school your mum helped me pack and Brian drove over to collect me. Ken went off to work the same as usual but there was a dreadful atmosphere in the house – not anger anymore, a heavy sadness. By then I think all of us knew we were entering some final stage with Ed.

    As soon as I arrived I went straight up to see her. Physically Ed looked awful, really ill, but she was at her best; the kind, playful woman who could charm the birds from the trees. I couldn't help thinking, 'You are a courageous little body'.

    'Treat the kitchen as if it's your own, Mother,' she said. 'I appreciate you coming over. I really do.' She gave me a smile, very much like Susan's and just for a moment I doubted all that I'd seen and heard of her tempers, her machinations.

    The next few days the sun shone so Susan, who'd remained at home, could go out on her bike or over to Lucy's. Other people, myself for a start, would have wanted the comfort of having friends and family around them but not Ed – she looked for a silent, empty house, no disturbance. Temperamentally she was like a cat, any unwelcome noise and she jumped, then she'd spit and next she'd start attacking the furniture – so to speak. So for most of the time Susan stayed

162

outside, Ed stayed upstairs and I was able to settle into feeling as if I was running an orderly ship.

You know I couldn't help liking that house whatever I might have said about it being overly fancy. It was comfortable, it was welcoming. My bedroom was very nice too. The blue room – Ed said you'd liked it when you'd stayed with them. At the time I remember thinking rather sourly, 'Well yes, all this fuss and frippery would be right up Bonnie's street.' However I've thought since that you didn't have much comfort at home, stuck in that draughty attic full of paraffin fumes – you deserved a little luxury.

In the mornings before I got up to make a pot of tea for Brian and wake Susan, I'd lie in bed and just look around and admire everything;, the fitted carpet, matching curtains, lace nets, pastel coloured bed clothes, even that shelf of twinkling glass ornaments that at first I'd dismissed as 'dust collectors'. I grew to appreciate Ed's house, her knick-knacks, the cushions, her need for order

The third day in charge started well. I decided to cook a cottage pie for tea and felt almost like a young woman again, making myself at home in Ed's labour saving kitchen. I stood in front of the window rolling pastry and looking out at the garden. No sweet peas planted but Brian's beans were already flourishing. I was remembering years earlier when your grandpa and I grew runners. How satisfying it was to go out each evening and pick a bunch for our dinner, and just when we'd thought we'd picked the last ripe bean we'd spot a cluster of them hiding in amongst the leaves. So there you are; I've remembered a happy time with your grandpa – they were few and far between but already the chore of writing this letter has proved worthwhile.

Suddenly drops of rain splashed against the window. Susan was down at the bottom of the garden fiddling with her bicycle. I rapped on the glass as the rain came down harder. With floury hands I opened the back door. 'Come on in, Susan, it's pouring.'

'It's not too bad.'

'Come in right now.'

She wheeled her bike into the shed then ran down the path towards the house.

'You're soaked.'

'Keep your hair on, Gran.'

'You are a cheeky devil,' I told her. 'Wipe your feet. Get rid of those wet clothes then come downstairs. Do not wake your mother. Do not whistle or hum.'

'Can't I watch television?'

'Not till your dad comes in or Ed wakes up.'

163

Susan did as she was told. She changed out of her wet clothes and didn't whistle or hum. Nor did she bang her cupboard door. I found myself looking up at the ceiling and saying 'praise be to Allah' and I have no idea where a phrase like that came from.

Do you remember Ed's bedroom? That cream and gold furniture. The suite cost Brian a small fortune. It wasn't to my taste but it was impressive. The double bed with a carved headboard, cream satin quilts, embroidered pillows, satin cushions – pure Ed or pure film star. I could imagine Rita Heyworth or Ava Gardner having a bedroom like that in the nineteen-forties.

In amongst all those pillows and cushions and quilts Ed lay sleeping. For some reason that I've never quite fathomed Susan was fascinated by the alteration in her mother's looks. Ed knew this. She dreaded seeing Susan unless she was wearing her full war paint. It was the first time in Ed's life that she found herself at a real disadvantage to her daughter. Without make-up, and probably due to the medication, she'd put on weight, her skin was dry and puffy and her pink and white complexion mottled as if her blood ran much nearer to the surface. She'd not been well enough to have her hair dyed and now the roots showed very black against the gold. The change in her looks was really shocking but if she was in a good or even a vulnerable mood, once she became engaged in a conversation, I'd find myself forgetting about how she'd altered and all I saw was Ed at her most appealing.

It was easy to be quiet in that house if you chose to be, with those thick fitted carpets, so I didn't hear Susan making her way across the landing, listening at Ed's door before going in. Susan stepped closer to the bed. Somehow, even in her sleep Ed knew she was being studied; she groaned and rolled onto her side.

Susan moved away from the bed and sat down on the dressing table stool. In the mirror she looked like a curious puppy, clumsy and grubby handed (this is Susan's recollection).

The dressing table had always been a denied delight to her. I remember the ornate perfume sprays; a crystal unicorn, a silver galleon, a ruby red flagon with crystal stopper. Ed's precious bottle of Chanel Number 5 hidden inside cardboard packaging to resemble a gentleman's top hat, a circular box of pale pink face powder, the lid always askew – pushed up by the impressive swansdown powder puff. Day cream, night cream, hand and foot cream. A Chinese lacquer bowl for Ed's dress rings and good paste brooches. I could itemise every darn thing because at one time or another, I've had to dust it all.

At the back of the dressing table were narrow drawers for Ed's silk underwear – a velvet lined cubby-hole for her very best jewellery – all presents

164

from Brian; the two strand necklace of cultured pearls with matching earrings, a marcasite broach embellished with seed pearls, an amethyst bracelet (amethyst was Ed's birth stone), and her engagement ring.

Ed's dressing table was like a treasure chest to a young girl like Susan. She opened every single box, tumbling their contents onto the glass top. On her scabby finger she slipped Ed's engagement ring, around her wrist she wrapped the amethyst bracelet. She opened other drawers. Susan told me later that she was searching for something like a diary, although I don't think I'd ever seen Ed with either a book or a pen in her hand! She never even wrote a shopping list. But Susan thought somewhere there might be clues to the affair with your dad. And she did find a book; the book of poetry with the shabby green cover left to Ken. She shook it by the spine just in case it held a love letter or a photograph. As she shook, the book fell to pieces, the inside pages still held together by thread and glue falling with a soft thud onto the carpet.

Ed stirred. Susan froze. Quietly she placed what remained of the book down on the dressing table. She slipped off ring and bracelet trying as quickly and quietly as possible to put everything back in their correct boxes and drawers.

In the mirror she saw Ed's body turned away from her, reflected lying so still Susan was sure Ed was either dead or wide awake. As Susan got to her feet the stool tipped back and she reached for it. Susan saw the reflections of her own face looming towards her in the three-way mirror. For a second she was trapped between stool and dressing table, the stool hit the carpet; Susan fell forward and pressed her hand against the central mirror as she turned towards the door.

Ed was now fully awake. She knew someone was in her room and tried to push back her quilt. Finally she forced her eyes open and pulled herself up into a sitting position. She heard the click of her bedroom door closing. The stool lay on its side, drawers were half open and jewellery lay piled in a heap. There was the handprint on her pristine mirror, pages from the book scattered on the floor.

'Susan, you fucking little bitch, come back here now!'

Downstairs in the kitchen I heard Ed's shout. By then Susan had gone, letting herself out through the front door and away down the street towards Lucy's house.

I don't know why but I took my time. Before I went upstairs I untied my apron and folded it neatly over the back of a chair. Possibly I hoped the worst of her tantrum would be over but when I reached her room I saw straight away that Ed was just revving up. She had pulled herself into a sitting position by holding onto the bed post and managed to swing her legs off the bed. I thought if Ken could see her now he wouldn't be quite so besotted.

'When I get my hands on her I'll flay her alive. Look at the mess. My book,'

165

she yelled.

'You'll do nothing of the sort. Come on now, I'll tidy everything away and Brian can buy you another book.'

She stared at me as if I was talking Double Dutch.

'Brian can't buy me another book. It's irreplaceable. She is a vicious little bitch. Vile. Vicious. Bitch.'

'That is enough, Ed.' I had to shout to be heard over her shrieks.

'Don't you tell me what's "enough" in my own house. Fuck off. Piss off. Get out.'

But she was fading. I caught hold of her elbows as she slipped down onto the rug and managed to manhandle her back onto the bed.

'Calm down Ed. You're your own worst enemy. I've never heard such language in my life.'

Downstairs we heard the front door opening and we both tensed into silence.

'Mother? Ed?' It was Brian.

I looked at Ed. 'You're not a pretty sight.'

I couldn't help saying it – I'd had just about enough of Ed's behaviour and anyway it was true. Together we turned towards the dressing-table mirror. I wasn't reflected at all, it was just Ed's face transformed into three gargoyles. She began a dreadful wail of despair that rose and rose till it became an ear-splitting scream. At which point Brian burst into the room.

'What the devil's going on? Ed, stop it.'

Of course she didn't stop, if anything she got louder. I couldn't bear the noise. I let go of her, quite roughly letting her fall back onto the pillows. That didn't stop her either. She lay there on her back, this banshee screaming coming out of her mouth.

I said, 'Brian, she's hysterical. What she wants is a glass of ice-cold water chucked in her face.'

He ignored me. He took Ed by the shoulders and began to rock her gently – 'There now, hush, hush' – as if he was soothing a baby.

I backed away, righted the dressing table stool and sat down. Ed wasn't comforted in the least by Brian. She twisted and turned her head, snapping wildly with her teeth at his forearms, flailing her arms, her fingers knotted into claws.

'Watch your eyes.'

Brian jerked his head back just in time. The excruciating noise continued. I covered my ears but didn't dare leave in case she did him any real damage. I'd never seen her in such a state.

'I have had enough. Do you understand me? I have had enough. Do you

understand me, Brian? I have had enough. Do you understand me?'

The repetition and sheer volume of desperation was more unnerving than her screaming at the top of her voice. 'DO YOU FUCKING UNDERSTAND ME?' again and again. Brian risked her nails and gnashing teeth to put one big hand over her mouth.

'Careful, Brian,' I said, getting to my feet.

'Don't interfere – I know what I'm doing.'

I didn't interfere. The screaming died away; her arms fell to her sides. Under his hand her head ceased to struggle. At first I thought it was a trick – he'd take his hand away and she'd go for him again. It wasn't a trick. We both watched as the fury left her eyes. For a second I saw the frightened child she really was and then she became our Ed again. It was like watching someone take the step back into sanity. Her eyes closed. Brian removed his hand.

'You haven't killed her, have you?'

'I don't think so.'

Ed had suffered a small stroke. In the hospital waiting room Brian started crying which upset me – as you know I'm not good with tears. He said, 'It was so odd, Mother. I felt as if that angry Ed had left the room and closed the door behind her.'

I wasn't so easily convinced. 'I'll believe that when I see it.'

Susan went missing for three days. The police finally found her hiding out in Lucy's parents' garden shed.

Some weeks ago I told you that I wanted at least one of my sons to have their 'heart's desire'. Of course that son was Ken. He never saw Ed at her worst apart from that one night in your bedroom when she attacked Susan. With Brian, Ed had the care she needed and from your father, the love she wanted – two things she'd never had during childhood. That's the best I can say for your Aunt Ed. I will never forgive her for the way she treated her own daughter.

TWENTY-SIX

Spring 1965

Aunt Ed is finally out of hospital. She's been taken in an ambulance to a nursing home near Bognor Regis for two weeks. Uncle Brian and Susan are staying in a nearby hotel on the seafront and visiting her every day. Gran is back living with us 'To let them have time for themselves as a family' she said.

She and my mum talk. Sometimes they even walk Bill together. Everyone has something or someone for themselves; Mum has Bill, Gran has Susan and Uncle Brian to worry about, my dad is lost in his own thoughts. What do I have? I don't want my aunt, uncle and cousin 'having time for themselves as a family'. I see them in Bognor Regis; Aunt Ed restored to health, sitting in a deck-chair, her bare feet scrunching in the sand. Uncle Brian has gone to buy ice creams while Aunt Ed is talking to Susan, who is leaning her head against her mother's knee. Aunt Ed has realised that after all she really loves Susan. Nobody, least of all Aunt Ed, is thinking about me.

They arrived home on Saturday. In the afternoon Uncle Brian telephoned and spoke to Mum.

'I've asked them to Sunday tea and Brian said "yes". Ed's coming as well,' she announced as she came into the kitchen. 'Ken, Brian wants a quick word with you. Bonnie, better tidy up your room.'

'It is tidy.'

'Then tidy it again.'

I sat in my bedroom for five minutes then went back downstairs. No one was on the telephone; Dad stood at the end of the garden smoking a cigarette while Mum and Gran were galvanised into action as if Royalty were visiting. Gran had tied a scarf round her head, turban fashion, which meant she was about to start serious cleaning, and my mum wore her raincoat and was scribbling a shopping list on the back of a used envelope.

'Fruit flan, do you think?'

Gran nodded. 'A tin of double cream and look out for a good Dundee cake. Ed likes that. I wish we'd had more notice. How long has it been since they all came here?'

'My birthday,' I said. 'But Aunt Ed was fine when we went to Stonehenge.'

Both of them looked at me. 'Well, we mustn't expect any miracles,' Mum said.

'No don't.' Dad stood at the back door. 'Ed is extremely ill.'

'But Dad, didn't she recuperate in Bognor Regis?'

Sometimes he looks at me now as if he almost dislikes me.

'Bonnie, are you trying to be clever?'

'No.'

'She's worried as well, Ken.'

'Worried as well? As well as who else? Surely you're not worried, Eileen? At long last Ed will be out of your hair. That's what you've wanted, isn't it?'

'This isn't a time for the two of you to be arguing.' Gran picked up the poker and pushed it under the coals. 'What's wrong with this fire?'

'Ken, I *am* sorry.'

'Oh I bet you are.' Not looking at her, Dad took his cigarettes from the top pocket of his shirt. 'Anyway the doctor says it won't be long now.'

Gran straightened up. 'Not in front of Bonnie.'

'What won't be long?'

Dad ignored me. He took a spill from the jug on the mantelpiece and lit it in the embers of the fire.

Gran asked, 'Bonnie – I won't tell you again, will you please find something to do somewhere else, I need to talk to your father.'

'He's not my father, he's my dad and I haven't got anything else to do anywhere.'

'Bonnie, go before I lose my temper,' Dad said, his tone really nasty.

I sat on the stairs and listened. They didn't even notice the kitchen door was still open.

169

Gran: 'Is Ed okay to do the drive over here?'

Dad: 'No, but she wants to.' Dad's footsteps going out into the garden.

Mum to Gran: 'I keep wondering why I've made such a fuss all these years. Ken will make this a rod for my back for the rest of our lives. I could never compete with Ed; I certainly won't be able to compete with a dead woman.'

I got to my feet and went silently up to my bedroom.

The next day there were new towels in the bathroom and unheard of bars of *Cusson's Damask Rose* soap in the soap dishes. Unheard of soap dishes. Mum had bought them in *Woolworth's*. I caught her peeking through our half-open bathroom door. She looked embarrassed. 'Just trying to see the room freshly as Ed might see it. You know your aunt's taste better that I do; will she think our bathroom looks acceptable?'

I swallowed my first answer. I couldn't imagine Aunt Ed ever setting foot in Woolworth's, but Mum's expression was so hopeful that I replied, 'She'll really like it, Mum. The dishes are very pretty. And the towels.'

'Only cheap.' She smoothed down her skirt self-consciously. I could tell she was pleased.

I hadn't seen Aunt Ed since our trip to Stonehenge. Coming back in the car she'd seemed really happy, cheeking my dad and Uncle Brian. We'd ended up singing a song Dad and Uncle Brian remembered from their time in the Scouts,

You'll never get to Heaven in an old Ford car,
Cos an old Ford car won't get that far
I ain't gonna grieve my Lord no more.

Whatever Uncle Brian had said to my dad on the phone, whatever my mum said about 'a dead woman', I expected Aunt Ed to be *my* Aunt Ed; the glamorous, saucy, loving, sing-a-long Aunt Ed sashaying in, bosoms thrusting proudly, eyes sparkling ready as ever to do battle. Aunt Ed would not, could not die. She was nothing like Grandpa, the old, smelly labrador who hadn't lived up to Gran's expectations, Aunt Ed was ALIVE – she exceeded all expectations – always and forever.

The four of us crowded into the front bay window watching for

170

their car. We saw it turn into our road very slowly. Dad called out, 'Here it is now', as if he'd been the only one to spot it. He was the first out of the room. Gran's fox fur swayed wildly on the back of the door as if it was trying to follow him. We followed him. Mum took my hand and we stood at Dad's side at our open garden gate. Gran pushed between us to wait on the pavement. If someone had taken a photograph of us we would have looked like a real family; a mum, a dad, a daughter and a granny – united and loving each other. But we weren't, we were disconnected; all we were linked by was this other family.

We waited. Gran had said, 'Don't overwhelm them. Give Ed time to get out of the car in good order.' Giving 'Ed time' had seemed like a silly instruction. My Aunt Ed didn't need time to get out of any car.

Uncle Brian sat alone in the front. Aunt Ed was in the back seat obscured by Susan. Uncle Brian got out, Susan got out. Nobody was smiling. Susan walked round to the far side of the car and held the door open while Uncle Brian helped Aunt Ed. Susan was crying. Two lines of tears glinting in the sunlight. I could see she was trying to control her lower lip. Mum let go of my hand and hurried forward.

'How was the traffic? Not too bad I hope? We're so glad you could come.'

Then my gran following her, waving a tea-towel: 'Come on in, you galoots – there's quite a spread.'

Only Dad left behind, with me standing next to him, the two of us as frozen as a couple of stone statues.

Supported on each side by Susan and Uncle Brian, Aunt Ed moved slowly towards us. No more reason for my mum to be jealous. Aunt Ed puffed up, wearing slippers, her feet dragging. My Aunt Ed turned into Mrs Mallaby. Gran retraced her steps. She gripped my hand fiercely and gave me a look that said, 'Don't you dare let me down.' It broke the spell. I pulled my hand away and ran past her to Aunt Ed. I put my arms around Aunt Ed's waist and hugged her gently. Then Dad was pushing me aside, pushing Susan aside. 'Come on Brian; let's get our best girl indoors.'

Mum slipped her hand under Susan's arm and said, 'I want to hear all about your holiday.'

Aunt Ed never got to admire my mum's soap dishes and towels. We sat around the table decked out in the Sunday best white cloth. Dad shifted the rocking chair up between his chair and mine and piled it with cushions. Aunt Ed didn't move from the chair for the entire visit. It was a splendid tea. There were ham sandwiches and tinned salmon sandwiches, the fruit flan and cream, the Dundee cake. Aunt Ed nibbled a salmon sandwich.

'Dundee, Ed?' Gran tried to tempt her.

'I don't think I can.'

Susan hardly said a word. All her noisy nature had disappeared. She stared down at the tablecloth, and when I tried to talk to her she hardly answered.

'Was the sea warm, Susan?'

'Not really.'

'Was it a sandy beach?'

'Sort of.'

'Tell Bonnie about the knickerbocker glories,' Uncle Brian said.

'Every day I had a knickerbocker glory at a café on the sea front.'

'What's a knickerbocker glory?' I asked.

'An ice-cream.'

'Something more than just an ice-cream.' Aunt Ed's words were slightly slurred. 'At the bottom of a tall glass like a flower vase they put strawberries and fruit salad, then strawberry ice-cream, then more fruit salad, then more ice-cream, then whipped cream.' She paused for breath, smiling at us. 'Then hundreds and thousands and then a little paper parasol to finish it off.'

'Do you eat the paper parasol as well?'

Everyone laughed except Susan. 'No Bonnie, it's just for decoration.'

Aunt Ed didn't say much more. Describing the knickerbocker glory had tired her. Afterwards I thought that her longest bit of conversation she'd reserved for me; that the connection we'd always had was back in place. I wasn't jealous any more. Aunt Ed hadn't scrunched her feet in the sand and forgotten me, she would have been too ill.

Gran got up to make a fresh pot of tea. She opened the sitting room door and Bill burst in. Mum had shut him in her bedroom but somehow he'd managed to get the door open. He rushed to Mum, squealing with happiness, as if he'd thought he'd never see her again.

'Naughty Bill,' she said, but laughing.

Susan looked up. 'You've got a dog. Oh he's great. Can I pat him Aunty Eileen?'

'Of course. He won't bite. Bill's as soft as... clarts.' Everybody, including dad, laughed. It was so unlike my mum to use a word like 'clarts'. Susan left the table and knelt next to Bill and Bill seemed to quite like her. Uncle Brian turned his chair so he too could admire the dog.

'How long have you had him, Eileen? He's a nice looking chap. We always intended to get a dog for Sue.'

Under the folds of the table cloth Aunt Ed's swollen hand pressed mine. Our fingers linked. I felt a small square of paper pressed into my palm. She closed my fingers around it. Her head bent towards me. In a low voice she said, 'Pass it on.'

I put the square into the pocket of my skirt. At six o'clock my dad helped Aunt Ed out to the car and carefully settled her into the back seat. He leant in and kissed her on the mouth. 'Goodbye darling.'

Aunt Ed said, 'Goodbye Ken.'

Dad straightened up, shut the car door. He didn't look at Aunt Ed again or at any of us. The car pulled away and I watched with Gran till it turned out of our road.

That night we didn't bother with television.

'Wagon Train will manage without us for one week,' my gran said.

I am sitting on my bed which is strictly not allowed. Gran says that unnecessary sitting on beds ruins the bed springs and results in poor posture. I accept the bit about poor posture because I am slumped rather than sitting, but what about lying in bed? Doesn't that ruin the bed springs? This is the type of question that my gran considers not worthy of an answer.

Below I hear her come out of the kitchen and into the hall where she pauses. There is no mistaking my gran's footsteps because even over the short distances within our house she still marches as if in time to a military band. From the bottom of the stairs she yells, 'Bonnie, are you up there?'

'Yes, Gran.'

'I'm coming up.'

'I'll come down, Gran.'

'No. Stay where you are. I want a word.'

Hurriedly I slide Aunt Ed's piece of paper under my pillow, pick up a book and move to the wicker chair by the window.

By the time she reaches my flight of stairs her steps are slower. I can hear her panting. She stops dramatically in the doorway, one hand on the door knob, the other on her bosom. 'Those stairs will be the death of me.'

'I would have come down.'

She crosses the room and sits very straight backed on the edge of my bed and looks around as if she's never seen my bedroom before. Then she turns her attention to me.

'So, what are you reading at the moment?'

I turn my book over. '*Scarlet Wanton*, Gran.'

'What?'

'It was in the book case.'

'Give it here.'

I hand her the book. She studies the cover; a glamorous woman with long black hair wearing a scarlet sheath is pointing a revolver at a man in a belted raincoat and trilby hat.

'No wonder you have nightmares. I'm confiscating this.'

'But Gran – '

'You can't just help yourself to books from the book case. They're grown-up books.'

'I'm nearly twelve.'

'You're eleven and a bit.'

I know better than to argue. She will most likely return *Scarlet Wanton* to the book case and in a few days I'll retrieve it. I try to look not bothered but then I remember Aunt Ed and change my expression to sombre. I wait. It isn't like my gran to have something on her mind without coming straight to the point but no, she emits one of her loud sighs as if emptying her body of all oxygen. I wonder if she has come up to sympathise with me over Aunt Ed. 'How are you coping?' People ask on the television or in radio plays. 'Bearing up', would be my reply or 'not too good'. I don't know how I'm coping. I can't believe that Aunt Ed is about to die. The memory of how she was at the weekend is fading. I don't want that

174

memory in my head. The Aunt Ed I want stands on her front door step. She is looking along the road to see if she can spot me. She wears a pink gingham dress, the sleeveless, flouncy style of dresses that Brigitte Bardot wears. Maybe under her breath she is singing a silly song that has just popped into her head: *Oh where, tell me where has my Bonnie Benson gone?*

'What did Ed give you?' Gran cuts across my thoughts.

'Pardon?'

'What did she give you at the tea table when everyone was distracted by Bill's antics?'

'Nothing, Gran.'

'Yes she did.' Gran's tone isn't unpleasant.

'I promise you; Aunt Ed didn't give me anything.'

She slaps her hands palms down on her lap as if just a bit impatient. 'Bonnie, I may be getting on in years but my hearing and sight remain perfect. Ed handed you something under the table and said, "Pass it on".'

I can't help thinking that my gran is remarkable and should have been in the Secret Service. 'It was nothing much. Just a note saying she'd missed me.'

'Show me.'

'I haven't got it anymore.'

Slowly and distinctly she says, 'Bonnie, if I have to take this room apart with my bare hands I will.'

Which sounds so unlike her and so much more like Cheyenne Bodie one of her cowboy heroes that I start laughing. Gran also laughs which is a good sign.

'Were you being Cheyenne Bodie, Gran?'

'Yes, I believe I was.' She wipes her eyes with one of Grandpa's checked handkerchiefs and begins again. 'Bonnie, when Ed said "Pass it on", she didn't intend you to keep whatever it was she gave you.'

I don't answer her.

'Did she?'

In a small voice I say, 'She gave it to me.'

'Not really. Now we both know who she wanted you to pass the note on to, don't we?'

'Why did she give it to me then? Dad was sitting on her other side.'

Gran thinks for a moment. 'I don't suppose she dared hand it to your dad, not under Eileen's nose.'

We both sit very still. Gran is waiting. I try to think of an excuse or a lie but come up with nothing.

'Should I pass it on to Dad then?'

'It might be better if I gave it to him. Your mother would be very hurt if she ever found out that Ed had used you as a messenger.'

'I'd never tell Mum.'

'Are you sure?'

I'm not sure. That folded square of paper has given me a feeling of power. I could hang on to it forever, in fact I'd almost decided to do just that. I'd wanted to think that the note was meant for me.

'It's under my pillow.'

Gran reaches under my pillow and unfolds the piece of paper. In a low voice she reads out, 'Oh! Death will find me, long before I tire of watching you.' *

She scratches her head. Her hand is gnarled and old. Gran sniffs.

'Well I'm blowed,' she says. 'It's from that poetry book your grandpa left Ken. Who'd have thought Ed would take the time to read poetry and pick one out. She couldn't have picked better.'

Mum has taken Bill into the park for his evening walk. From my attic window I watch my dad leaning against the tree smoking a cigarette. Gran comes out of the kitchen. He watches her as she approaches. As she hands him the scrap of paper, for a second his face lights up. Before he starts to read he looks up and sees me at the window. He nods and I hold my hand up. Gran turns and looks up at me as well. She smiles a grim smile and waits while Dad reads Aunt Ed's few words.

Dad faces the tree. He presses his forehead against its trunk. Gran raises her hand to touch his shoulder. Her hand shrinks back. She tries again and this time she is successful.

* Rupert Brooke

TWENTY-SEVEN

It is Sunday afternoon and our house is quiet. Mum and Bill have gone off with one of her new dog-walking friends, Sandra; my dad is washing his car while Mr Mallaby makes admiring comments from the tattered armchair he's recently put in his front garden. Mrs Mallaby is having a 'lie down' which Gran says is a euphemism for 'sleeping it off'.

I like being at home, indoors with my gran. I wondered if she likes being with me. While washing up after Sunday dinner we've listened to *The Navy Lark* and then discussed how we imagine Chief Petty Officer Pertwee looks in real life. I thought tall and handsome in a cheeky way, she thought short and handsome in a cheeky way. Chief Petty Officer Pertwee is one of the stars. In my head I have very clear images of all the cast. My favourites, apart from CPO Pertwee, are Commander Povey (in command of HMS Troutbridge) and his bossy wife Ramona – always telling the Commander to eat up his eggy and toasted soldiers.

Now, while I knit and Gran unravels a sleeveless pullover in grey fleck she's bought for me at a WRVS coffee morning, we aren't listening to the afternoon play because after the first ten minutes she said 'It's a bit near the mark' and turned the sound down so the actors were reduced to mumblings. Gran switches on the standard lamp that is behind her armchair.

'Biscuit, Bonnie?'

'Yes please.'

She gets the biscuit barrel from the cupboard, opens it and places it on the fold-up table between us.

'Help yourself but don't spoil your tea.'

She falls back into the armchair with an 'Ouf' and returns to her unravelling.

'Not long now,' she says.

'Not long now until what?'

'The end of your school year. Finish, kaput – in the autumn you'll be somewhere else.'

'The secondary school.'

'You're not too bothered are you?'

'I'll miss Joanna.'

'Would that be the Joanna you stole the scarf from?'

'I didn't steal her scarf.'

'Oh I daresay you did.'

I wish I were at least the same age as say my mum (only much lovelier looking) and then I would be able to reply 'Well you daresay wrong' without being told off for answering back.

I change the subject a little. 'Nowadays I'm the fourth most popular girl in our year, possibly in the whole school.'

Gran doesn't say, 'Congratulations Bonnie, I'm not surprised.'

'Since when?'

'Since Joanna and I became friends.'

Gran worries at a knot in the wool before replying thoughtfully, 'Just remember, reflected glory is no glory at all. You've told me before that this Joanna is very popular, well for the moment she's taken a shine to you. In my experience those kinds of friendships don't last. She won't be with you at secondary; you're going to have to start from scratch in the popularity stakes.'

I carry on knitting. Gran glances sideways at me and adds, 'Not that there's any reason why you shouldn't be popular... '

I would like to talk to her about being popular because I have been very unpopular for the whole of my school life so far, and to suddenly find myself popular is very exciting. Often now in the playground I'm included in conversations. Sometimes I don't answer because I don't realise that a comment or question has been directed at me. I am the girl that other girls want to sit next to, the girl who is picked for a netball team even though I'm not very good at netball.

Not that I'm picked first, I'm usually third or fourth, but before Joanna and I became best friends I wasn't picked at all. Miss Skeffington, who took us for games, would say, 'Well I'm sorry but Bonnie will have to go in one of your teams.' And the team she chose to have me would groan and exchange despairing looks with each other and then walk off in pairs and threes to the netball pitch leaving me to follow on behind.

All this and more I'd like to share but I can see that Gran is not the best person to have the conversation on 'the popularity of Bonnie Benson' with. I think Aunt Ed would have listened. I realise that I'm now thinking of Aunt Ed in the past tense.

'Gran, Aunt Ed is going to die, isn't she?'

'We're all going to die.'

'But Aunt Ed is going to die soon? She won't get better.'

'No, I'm afraid not.'

I really like Joanna. She is not as stuck-up as I'd imagined her to be. In fact I am so comfortable with Joanna now that I was able to tell her this.

'You know Joanna, for some reason I thought you were quite stuck-up.'

She wasn't at all annoyed. She'd laughed – a nice, really amused laugh as if I'd said something cleverly original.

'I think I am a bit stuck-up, Bonnie – it's my mother's fault, she spoils me. I'm all she's got.'

'What about your brother in New York?'

'He's only my half-brother. We just share the same father. My father was married to someone else before he married my mother.'

'Isn't that bigamy?'

'They divorced. Then he married my mother then he divorced *her*.'

'Is he married now?'

'He's thinking about it.'

'Gosh.'

I've noticed how Joanna calls her mum 'my mother' and thought about calling Mum 'my mother' as well. I can't quite get the words out confidently so that they sound as if I'd always called her that. Even more impossible to call my gran 'my grandmother'. I wish they'd both wear higher heeled shoes.

Every day at break and lunchtime we 'monopolise' that one special bench. Often Joanna puts her feet up on the bench and stretches out with her head in my lap which means there is no room for anybody else to sit next to us, which suits me, but sometimes she doesn't want to put her feet up and stretch out and I can't very well insist that she does. Nor do I want to put my feet up because

179

this will draw attention to my shoes, which are scuffed and old fashioned. Then Estelle and Lesley, who are always hovering as I used to hover, join us. Lesley sits one side of Joanna and sometimes Estelle pushes her big bottom between me and Joanna, forcing me to move along the bench.

I have to pretend that I don't mind at all. They go on and on about The Beatles. Joanna joins in although she never mentions The Beatles when we are on our own. Joanna says she's in love with George Harrison. Estelle and Lesley are both in love with Paul. They swap pictures they've cut out of newspapers and magazines. I have to pretend that I like John Lennon. I can't bring myself to say 'I love John Lennon', however I like his round spectacles and think that of all The Beatles he would be the one to sit next to on a long train journey.

Cilla Black is my favourite singer at the moment. I think because she is ordinary looking. Joanna, Estelle and Lesley also like Cilla but with reservations. They like her hair, her clothes and her hits, but they would rather look like Sandie Shaw. Joanna says she goes barefoot all the time indoors.

Sometimes Estelle sings Cilla Black's 'You're my world'. Her voice is quite good and she gets so caught up in the song that tears appear in her eyes, which Joanna says her doctor brother in New York says 'is the mark of a true star'.

It is Friday. We are sitting on the bench at lunchtime but everyone else is in the canteen having their lunches because today is fish and chips, which is delicious apart from the fish bones. Joanna and I have foregone our fish and chips so we can be alone together. We kept back our sandwiches from break and she has given me a section of her *Bounty* bar.

It is ten past one and any moment now, girls will start streaming out into the playground. Estelle and Lesley are usually the first, followed by Linda Portman, because they eat really quickly as they think they're missing something happening outside.

Joanna's hair is tickling my nose. I'd like to rub my nose hard but then she'd move her head away from where it's almost touching my shoulder. We haven't spoken a word in several minutes. The last thing Joanna said was, 'I don't know why I like you so much, Bonnie.' I think she meant to say it in a jokey way: 'I don't know

180

why I like you so much, Bonnie – you're as daft as a brush.' But she stopped speaking after she'd said my name so the way she said it was more as if she was asking herself why she liked me.

In my head are the lines from one of Dean Martin's songs – 'I Don't Know Why I Love You Like I Do'. If my life were a film I would sing it to her right now, although I know for a fact that Joanna thinks singers like Dean Martin and Frank Sinatra are old fashioned. Joanna doesn't like Elvis Presley or Cliff Richard either, although I remember she did like them last year. Once I asked her what she thought of The Shadows, my dad's favourite group. Dad says that, given his time again, he'd have liked to have been a guitarist like Hank Marvin. Joanna said, 'I don't think anything at all about The Shadows, Bonnie.' Which was quite a rude reply but I wish I could come out with replies like that to my gran.

Gran: What's your opinion of Alma Cogan? (one of *her* favourite singers).

Me: Sorry, Gran, I don't have an opinion where Alma Cogan's concerned.

I watch an elderly woman walking briskly through the school gates. She wears a dark overcoat which is far too heavy for such a warm and sunny day. The woman carries a battered crocodile handbag just like the handbag my gran bought in the seagull jumble sale, and flat sensible lace-up shoes just like she wears as well.

'Isn't that your grandmother?' Joanna asks.

Gran sees me and waves urgently. I don't want to leave Joanna to be claimed by Estelle and Lesley but slowly I get to my feet. Gran shouts, 'You've got to come home now.'

I shout back, 'But why?'

Although I am annoyed at my gran coming into the playground dressed so shabbily and yelling at me in front of Joanna, I am already walking towards her.

'See you,' I call back to Joanna and wave my hand lazily behind me as if I'm not bothered at all about leaving her.

Miss Wozencroft comes out of the main building. She and I reach Gran at exactly the same time. Gran straightens up. 'How do you do,' she says to Miss Wozencroft. 'I'm Bonnie's grandmother. She's needed at home.'

'Nothing serious I hope.'

Gran gives me a quick glance. 'I'm afraid it is.'

181

Estelle walks past carrying a grease stained brown paper bag, staring at us as if amazed that someone looking like my gran is allowed in the school playground, then she sees that Joanna is sitting on her own and she starts to run.

'Brought you some chips, Joanna,' she shouts.

TWENTY-EIGHT

'Susan isn't in a fit state to go anywhere,' Gran says when I ask what Susan will be wearing for Aunt Ed's funeral. 'She will stay at her friend Lucy's house till we get back.'

Gran says I'm an unnatural child because all I'm interested in is what people are wearing. I don't think I'm unnatural – if my gran was a disembodied spirit entity mingling with Joanna and her friends in the playground she would find that they're all interested in what people are wearing. I'd like to know what Aunt Ed is wearing in her coffin because I know Aunt Ed would have worried about what they'd dressed her in. For instance I don't think she'd have liked to be buried in her dressing gown no matter how pretty it is, or wearing any shoes that didn't have a heel, and she'd have wanted her hair to look its best. I'd like answers to my questions but I know everyone will come down on me 'like a ton of bricks' and think I'm insensitive. I am not insensitive. Quite the opposite.

Also it seems extraordinary that nobody worries about me even half as much as they worry over Susan. Every night since Aunt Ed died I've cried myself to sleep. Nobody climbs up my stairs carrying a warm drink to ask what's wrong. Nobody sits talking in hushed voices about *me*.

Mum has written to Miss Wozencroft telling her that I won't be back this term. I almost wish I was back at school but in spirit form or as a disembodied entity (Mrs Brown has recently been trying to contact her dead son through a medium in Golden Hillock Road and has explained 'entities', disembodied etc, to Mum who says she'd rather not be called back from beyond the grave, thank you very much). I would have liked to be in the classroom, hovering just below the ceiling, when Miss Wozencroft announced that due to a tragic death in the family, Bonnie Benson 'wasn't in a fit state to go anywhere'.

Gran has told me to 'count myself lucky that I still have a mother', and that this (Aunt Ed's death) 'isn't all about you', and 'do you ever think of anyone but yourself?' Which is so unfair. I think about Aunt Ed all the time, but I almost don't want to because, when I do, there is a horrible dark Aunt Ed shaped gap where she used to be in my head. I can't seem to get past this to the Aunt Ed I remember.

After the funeral I'm going to stay with Gran and Uncle Brian for a few days because they feel it would be better for Susan to have another child in the house. I don't suppose it will be better for Susan to have me in the house. We don't even like each other. Why do adults automatically assume that because you're a child you will have lots in common with all other children?

It is amazing that although Aunt Ed was so special and lovely there is hardly anybody at her funeral. Grandpa's funeral was much more popular.

'Why aren't there any people, Gran?'

Gran says, 'It's just family.'

'But where is Aunt Ed's family? You're not her mum.'

'She was a charity child, Bonnie. *Dr Barnardo's.*'

'A charity child?'

'Now don't start.'

'A charity child? No mum and dad? No brothers and sisters, cousins or aunts?'

Mum says, 'Ed never wanted it discussed.'

'No presents from her mum and dad on her birthday? Nothing for Christmas?'

'Bonnie, not now. If you keep on, you're going to upset everyone,' my mum says.

'But aren't we supposed to be upset?'

'You weren't much bothered at your grandpa's funeral. Now stow it. This isn't easy for any of us.' Gran grabs my hand and marches me towards the church porch.

After the service, as we leave the church the sun comes out. Aunt Ed would have liked that. Dad and Uncle Brian help two other men carry the coffin to where a grave has been dug. They could have managed the coffin and Aunt Ed between them – she was so slim and little.

The coffin is lowered into the ground. Mum tries to take my hand but I take a step away from her. I count the mourners; Mum, Dad, Gran, Uncle Brian; Mrs Lewis – Aunt Ed's cleaner, and Martin Rossiter – Uncle Brian's manager. Eight mourners including me.

The vicar says, 'Ashes to ashes, dust to dust', and Uncle Brian and my dad step forward and drop pink roses down onto the coffin. I wish I'd had a pink rose to drop or a bunch of sweet peas. Aunt Ed would have preferred sweet peas – I'd never ever heard her say she liked roses. Mrs Lewis, the cleaner, blows her nose and gives Uncle Brian a watery smile which he doesn't notice because he is responding to Martin Rossiter who is squeezing his shoulder sympathetically. I wonder if Mrs Lewis will have an affair with Uncle Brian now that he doesn't have a wife anymore.

'What's going on in that head of yours, Bonnie?' Gran asks.

I take a deep breath and go for it. 'I was wondering what dress Aunt Ed is wearing.'

Gran does not reply with 'God give me patience' or 'I'll swing for this child'. She takes a handkerchief out of her coat pocket (one of my birthday handkerchiefs – I recognise the embroidered 'S' in the corner) and blows her nose, but in a ladylike manner.

'And that matters to you?' She puts her handkerchief back in her pocket.

'Yes, it does. It would matter to Aunt Ed as well.'

'And supposing I chose the wrong dress?'

My voice doesn't come out quite right because suddenly I have an image of Aunt Ed walking away from me towards the boating lake in Small Heath Park, the skirt of her dress lifting in the breeze. 'As long as you didn't choose a dressing gown.'

Gran clicks her tongue behind her teeth. 'I found one with cherry red buttons. Susan called it a shift dress. She said it was the latest fashion and her mum would like to be buried in it.'

I nod. 'Good choice, Gran. And matching shoes?'

'No, we didn't put her in the red shoes. The heel was broken. Black winkle-pickers.'

'I wish I'd seen her.'

'I didn't think at the time but I can see now it might have been a good idea.'

'Did Susan see her?'

'No. She didn't want to. Hush now.'

There is no party. Aunt Ed would have been very disappointed. She'd have called Uncle Brian 'a cheapskate'.

'We'll disperse now,' Gran says and so we do disperse.

Dad is driving Mum home. They both kiss me goodbye but I have no sense of them caring about how I feel. I sit in the back of Uncle Brian's car, my gran sits in the front with him, and we drive to his house in absolute silence. I think about it really being 'his house' now, nothing to do with Aunt Ed. I remember when Aunt Ed showed me Uncle Brian's bedroom; the shelves of books. Will he change everything? Fill their lounge with shelving? Get rid of the cushions and rose pink lamp shades? A couple of times Gran looks over her shoulder to check on me but she doesn't speak. The drive seems to take forever. By the time we arrive it is growing dark.

As we slow down in the front of the house Uncle Brian says, 'That's odd; I didn't leave a light on.'

He swerves into their driveway and parks haphazardly. Gran is knocked forward against the dashboard.

'Steady on, Brian. Whatever's the matter?'

'Susan must be home.'

'Surely not? I expect she's got Lucy with her.'

'Lucy's parents wouldn't leave two eleven-year-olds on their own.'

Uncle Brian leaps out of the car and sprints towards the house. Gran turns to me. 'Run Bonnie.'

'Why, Gran?'

'Just do it.'

I chase after Uncle Brian. He's unlocked the front door. 'Susan, Susan!' he bellows and takes the stairs two at a time.

I follow. My foot is on the top stair as he barges into Susan's bedroom. Within a second he races out and into Aunt Ed's room. I notice the bathroom door is ajar and the light is on. I push the door open. Downstairs Gran is stepping into the hall.

'Shall I come up, Brian?'

In the bathroom I stand completely still. I have stepped into a nightmare – I grab hold of the wash basin to steady myself. Uncle Brian rushes in behind me and pushes me out of the way. Susan lies in the bath. Water laps around her neck and shoulders. The water is

186

bright red but darker close to her body.

I say, 'Susan, what have you done?'

Uncle Brian makes a groaning noise. Without moving her head Susan looks at him.

'Dad,' she says.

Her face is very pale, even the freckles across her cheeks and the bridge of her nose have faded. Her eyelids are like two pink sea shells half covering her eyes.

Gran rushes in, pushing past a frozen Uncle Brian.

'Susan,' her voice is like an animal's roar.

'Let me help, Gran.'

'Get out of here.' She grips my shoulder and sort of runs me back out onto the landing. She kicks the bathroom door shut against me but it swings open again. They don't notice. Both are bent forward over the bath.

Uncle Brian holds Susan under her armpits, raising her a few inches. I hear the water running away down the drain, that snorting noise it makes. Gran covers Susan with a bath towel. Ignoring me she goes into Aunt Ed's bedroom and begins opening drawers in her dressing table.

'These will do,' she says pulling out two narrow belts. She hurries back into the bathroom. 'Brian, hold her arms above her head. Bonnie… '

'Yes, Gran.'

'Telephone 999. We need an ambulance. An emergency. Tell them to hurry. You know the address.'

'Yes, Gran.'

'Do it now. Use the extension in Ed's bedroom.'

When I get back to the bathroom Susan is wrapped in fluffy white towels but still lying in the now empty bath. She appears to be asleep. Only her arms aren't covered by towels, they are positioned above her head. It looks like she's wearing red rubber bands around her wrists. Above each elbow one of Aunt Ed's belts is tied.

Uncle Brian goes in the ambulance with Susan. I can see Gran wants to go as well but someone has to stay with me. She rings my mum and dad then makes me beans on toast. While I eat, she drinks cup after cup of tea.

'I can't stop shaking.' She holds out her hands and stares at them as if they don't belong to her.

'Will Susan be all right?'

'I think so.'

I wonder if she knows that I've wanted Susan dead. I think about Susan being dead as I eat – am I disappointed or relieved when she says 'I think so'?

We wait for my dad to come, for Uncle Brian to telephone from the hospital. We sit in the lounge. Gran switches on one side lamp and we have the light from the hall. It is chilly in the room but neither of us knows how to switch on the *Richmond* gas fire. Gran looks ill and very tired. One hand lying in her lap keeps clenching and unclenching.

We still wear our clothes from the funeral. Gran's dress is new – she'd bought it especially, for the first time choosing some other colour than black or grey. It is navy blue with pale green polka dots the size of sixpences. Now it is creased and stained. Susan's blood has dried a rusty brown.

'I'm cold, Gran.'

Very slowly she turns her face in my direction. Her eyes don't quite meet mine as if I've recalled her from somewhere far away.

'You're right – it is cold in here.'

She goes out into the hall and stands thinking. She looks up the stairs, puts one hand on the banisters then seems to change her mind, turning away and going over to the hall cupboard.

'You're not averse to one of Ed's coats, are you?' she calls out.

'No, Gran.'

It is the camel coat Aunt Ed wore for what she called 'local shopping'. Mum would have kept it for best.

'Just tuck this round you – you'll soon warm up.'

'What about you, Gran? Shall I fetch you a cardigan from the blue room.'

She sits down again. 'No, don't go upstairs. I'll hang on for the moment. I've got my liberty bodice to keep me snug.'

She almost smiles. I wonder if that were a joke or if my gran does wear a liberty bodice. Outside we hear a car slowing down. Dad's car. I recognise the tick-tick of the indicators. I start to wriggle from under the coat but quick as a flash Gran is out of her chair and has laid her hand on my shoulder, pushing me gently back into the armchair.

188

'Bonnie don't,' she says.

I understand. Don't rush forward. Don't start crying. Don't cause a scene. She leaves the lounge before she can see my eyes fill up and by the time she returns I've concentrated so hard on what Janet Page – Girl Groom would do in my situation that my tears have evaporated. Behind Gran comes Dad and behind him comes Mum. This is the first time ever that my mum has been to Uncle Brian's and Aunt Ed's house and it seems like a very strange thing, an out of its rightful place strange thing. I know Dad visited but he's never been here when I've been here either. They're still wearing their clothes from the funeral, although Mum has changed her hat for a headscarf.

'Bonnie, are you ok?' She strokes back my fringe as if checking to see whether I have a temperature.

'She's been a tower of strength,' Gran says.

'Well done, darling.' Mum kisses the top of my head. 'Is there any news from the hospital?'

'Not yet.'

Dad says, 'It's bloody freezing in here.' He twitches a dial on the side of the *Richmond*; the flames appear, the logs glow. As he straightens up, he looks around the room, frowning. 'Mother, why the devil are the two of you sitting in the dark?'

He switches on the table lamp and two more side lights, stares angrily up at the chandelier as if tempted to switch that on as well. He shrugs irritably. 'Susan will be all right. She'll probably have to spend some time in hospital. They keep suicides in.'

'It wasn't suicide,' Gran says.

'Have it your own way – suicide, attempted suicide, an accident.' His voice is harsh and nasty.

'That's enough from you, boyo.' Gran is beginning to look better, there is colour coming back to her face, I can feel forces mustering. 'I'll make a pot of tea. Eileen, do you want to give me a hand?'

Mum follows her into the kitchen and shuts the door.

Dad ignores me. He strides over to the picture window and opens the Venetian blind. Outside it is night. I look at the mantel clock. Twenty past twelve.

'The epitome of style.'

'What, Dad?'

189

'These blinds. How Ed described them. The epitome of style.'

He doesn't look round at me. Stays where he is opening and closing the blinds.

'You know Bonnie – she made everything appear better than it really was. She had a knack. Not much of a knack to have, but a rare one.'

I let Aunt Ed's coat slide down on to the carpet and get to my feet. I stand next to Dad and tweak the hem of his suit jacket. He takes my hand and we both lean forward, peering through the metal slats. At first the sky seems thoroughly inky black but as my eyes grow used to the black I can pick out stars.

Behind us the telephone rings. The kitchen door flies open and my gran shoots across the hall and has picked up the receiver before either of us can take a step.

'Brian?' she shouts, then, 'Good. Wonderful news. Tell her, her granny says she's been a bloody fool and I hope they *do* tell her off.'

Mum is framed in the doorway holding a large dark brown tea pot.

'Good news?'

'The best news. The little critter's out of danger.'

'Thank heavens. Ken, isn't that marvellous?'

'Where did you find that tea pot?' Dad asks.

'At the back of the larder shelf. The other one looked far too good to use.'

Dad lunges for the tea pot.

'Leave it Ken, you'll burn yourself,' Gran shouts.

'Give me the bloody handle.'

'Don't be stupid,' Mum says but then suddenly she lets go and the teapot falls between them, hot tea splashing the wall, the carpet.

'Have you taken leave of your senses?' Gran pushes my dad away and barges between them into the kitchen. I hear her running water into the washing up bowl.

'Ed only ever used the best,' my dad yells. Not really at Gran or Mum, more just yelling at everything.

Then he rushes upstairs and into Aunt Ed's bedroom. Mum takes a tea towel and presses it into the carpet, soaking up excess tea; Gran wipes the walls with a damp cloth. From upstairs comes a sound that doesn't stop.

'Bonnie, go back into the lounge and put the television on,' Gran says. 'The two of us will clear this up.'

'There's nothing on television at this time of night.'

'Then curl up on the sofa and try to sleep.'

TWENTY-NINE

Summer

Gran and her friend Hilda were in the garden, sitting on the Bristows' memorial bench. In front of them cups, saucers and a plate of biscuits were set out on a white metal table. They were playing cards. I heard their laughter which made me hesitate at the top of the flight of steps that led down onto the lawn.

'Stop skulking up there, Bonnie,' Gran called out. 'Did you bring the chocolate gingers I asked you to get?'

'I did.'

I'd spoilt nothing. Both women smiled at me. Gran's glance was approving. I'd worn bright colours that I know she likes, although not on herself.

'No trousers today?'

'I don't only wear trousers.'

'I thought you did.'

Hilda began to collect up the cards.

'Please don't mind me. Carry on with your game.'

'No. We've had three games and Shirley's trounced me, three-nil.'

'You're going to be lucky in love, Hilda,' Gran told her, which set them laughing again. Hilda put the pack of cards in her handbag, waved and said, 'Be good.' Although she has a walking stick, I've realised that she uses it more to poke at things than to lean on.

Gran looked, well – wonderful. In fact she looked better than I ever remember seeing her look in my whole life. Her hair, which is pure white, had been beautifully styled into a short feathery cut.

'Gran,' I exclaimed, 'you're wearing make-up.'

'Just a little. What do you think?' She looked up at me, doubt in her eyes.

'You look like a million dollars.' We beamed at each other and, as a rule, my grandmother doesn't beam. 'Why ever haven't you worn make-up before?'

'Your grandpa didn't approve, then the boys didn't approve and so I got out of the habit. I've always used *Ponds Cold Cream* though. Susan took me to the hairdressers this morning and then did my face. She loves make-up, just like her mother.'

Gran watched me carefully for a reaction. If anything my smile widened.

'She's done a magnificent job. Your hair looks terrific. You look ten years younger.'

'They say eighty is the new seventy, and I'm in my eighties for another two weeks.'

'I haven't forgotten.'

'I'd never imagine you would forget.'

'It's lovely out here.'

'It is.'

Gran folded her hands in her lap and surveyed the fields stretching away, right as far as the blue horizon. I sat down next to her. I folded my hands in my lap. I too surveyed the fields and wondered why I so rarely took the time to just do nothing.

'Hilda and I are off to Scarborough next weekend.'

I glanced sideways at my grandmother. She'd lifted her face up to the sun and her eyes were closed; she was trying not to smile.

'What, just the two of you?'

'Susan and Geoff are taking us. Geoff is her partner.'

'I thought they were married.'

'No, that was Peter. This is Geoff. He's very nice. Peter was very nice too.'

'Do they allow you to take off for a weekend?'

Gran opened her eyes; they were bright with amusement. 'This is a Residential Home, Bonnie, not Alcatraz.'

It was late afternoon – we were back in her bedroom. Gran sat in the armchair watching the news with the sound turned down to inaudible.

'Why must it always be about war? I could do with a good, meaty murder followed by a good, meaty murder trial.'

'Surely not?'

'Don't tell me "surely not". Break open the *Cadbury's Dairy Box*,

193

please.'

I broke them open and picked out an orange cream for her. I've started bringing in my own cushion for the white plastic chair. It has a rather stylish, sage green linen cover that matches the leaf pattern in the room's curtains. I left the box near her on the window sill and returned to Gran's *Family Circle* magazine which isn't a magazine I'd ever normally read but on each visit I'd found it full of enthralling information. That afternoon I was in the process of cutting out a recipe for Summer Vegetarian Lasagne.

'Is Jay a vegetarian?'

'Not quite. Can't resist bacon... or sausages... or lamb chops.'

'The boys loved my shoulder of lamb. Have you finished vandalising my magazine?'

I liked the way she referred to my dad and Uncle Brian as 'the boys'. It brought them to life again as those two handsome young men I chose to remember.

'Yes.' I folded up the cutting and slipped it into my shoulder bag. 'Gran?'

'Not more questions?'

'Just the one. Do you remember that time we saw Dad and Aunt Ed in the park together? We were on our way home from the jumble sale where I bought the stuffed seagull?'

She nodded.

'I followed them.'

'I thought you might.'

You and Mum were in the scullery. Mum wanted all our jumble sale purchases; your china, my woollens, even the crocodile skin handbag – checked, scoured, aired before they found a permanent place within our house. I remember hearing Mum's voice and thinking 'she's putting her foot down' – you sounded almost defensive.

'But they're perfectly fresh Eileen.'

'How can they possibly be perfectly fresh?'

I opened our front door, slipped out, and closed it quietly behind me. Fortunately no sign of the Mallabys. I crossed the road and entered the park by the small iron gate that the park gardeners use, pushing through the shrubbery to come out half way along the avenue of trees where we'd seen my dad and Aunt Ed. I didn't go stealthily; I marched along looking to left and right as I imagined a person who just liked walking in the park might do. I thought if they see me, I'll make up a perfectly reasonable excuse. I had no idea what that excuse would be but was certain it would arrive on my tongue when needed.

I thought they'd be either on the island or near the lake but it was the end of the season and the boat house was locked up. I had to think about where I would take Aunt Ed just supposing I wanted her all to myself. There was a small, grassy hollow almost surrounded by shrubs. From there you could see right down to the lake and as far as Tennyson Road but nobody could really see you.

That's where I found them. They didn't notice me but then why should they? They were concentrating on each other. Nothing much was happening. They weren't having sex or anything like that. Although at the time I couldn't have put it into words, I remember how shocked I was, because I didn't quite recognise them. They looked too young to be my dad and my aunty. These two people were nothing to do with the Benson family. We were forgotten. We didn't exist.

Dad stripped off his vest and tossed it towards Aunt Ed. He lit a cigarette. She is smiling at him. In a pretend American drawl she says, 'What are you waiting for, big boy?'

Dad's smile broadened. 'You,' he said. 'Always you, Edina.'

I looked at Gran. I wished she wouldn't sit so very still, it was unnerving.

'That's quite romantic, isn't it, Gran?'

Immediately she adopted an amused expression as if some smart remark was just begging to be set free but then surprisingly she said, 'Well yes two people loving each other is romantic.'

'And Aunt Ed being so ill. Surely it wasn't wrong of her to want to seize the moment?'

'Ed had been seizing moments, often other people's moments, long before she became ill, and to put the record straight her name was Edna, plain and simple – the Edina was your father's nonsense.'

'But Gran, the thing I don't understand was that Mum didn't really love my dad yet she was jealous, whereas Uncle Brian loved Aunt Ed passionately but never showed anything but good humour.'

'You don't need to love someone for jealousy to be involved, you should know that. Often it's what the person or situation represents.'

Gran began to pat the chair arm with the palm of her hand, a sure sign that she was running out of patience with me. 'I'm meeting Hilda in the conservatory in twenty minutes for a sherry. I haven't the time or the inclination to go into this now.'

She stood up, stretched, shuffled steadily across to her wardrobe, glanced at herself in the long mirror and pulled a face, before opening the wardrobe door. 'Anyway your Uncle Brian wasn't passionately in love with Ed.'

'Of course he was.'

'Now my damn cardigan was in here somewhere... I'd say he was attracted to her glamour more than anything.' Her next few words came out slightly muffled as her head disappeared into the tightly packed dresses, blouses and cardigans. Gran had never had so many clothes. 'Of course his affections lay with Martin Rossiter.'

'His affections lay where?' Gran's magazine slipped out of my hand, down onto the lino floor.

Gran emerged from the wardrobe clutching a bright red cardigan. She was laughing. 'Martin Rossiter. Honestly Bonnie, you think you're so clever but you never spotted that?'

'Uncle Brian's office manager? The man who sold dad the car for fifty pounds and who was always ringing with a problem at the factory. Gran, you can't wear red with navy blue and white, you'll look like a Union Jack.'

'I can wear whatever I want and that's the Martin Rossiter I'm talking about. I don't suppose there was another one in the Birmingham motor trade during the nineteen-sixties. Bonnie, your aunt and uncle slept in separate rooms. Brian condoned an affair she had with his brother that lasted almost up till her death – did you never ask yourself why?'

'I accepted that they were both in love with her and Uncle Brian was exceptionally... tolerant.'

'Well more fool you. How tolerant would you be in those circumstances?'

'You're telling me that Uncle Brian was a homosexual? Did my dad know?'

'Of course he did.'

'And Mum?'

'I'm not sure.' Gran looked keenly at me. 'You don't have a problem with Brian being gay, do you?'

I felt a sudden urge to re-enact one of my mum's embarrassed

196

chicken movements. My face felt hot. A scarlet cheeked, middle aged woman stared back at me from Gran's wardrobe mirror. I heard my grandmother say, 'In your own time, Bonnie.'

THIRTY

Summer Now

I dreamt I was beneath the surface of the sea, my bare feet half hidden under a fine silt of sand and broken shells. Shoals of tiny luminous orange and turquoise fish swept past as if set on urgent missions of their communal own. The sea was lit by a yellow light. I thought, *far above the sun must be shining.*

In front of me and to my right appeared a cloud of inky darkness. Susan emerged from the cloud, approaching me quite quickly as if the cloud had breathed in and then expelled her. Her hands were thrust deep into the pockets of a droopy cardigan she'd never have worn in real life.

'I take long walks by the river,' she said in a dreamy voice, again nothing like her own, much more how I'd imagine Virginia Woolf might have spoken just before filling her pockets with large stones and walking into the River Ouse.

I clearly remember what I wore (nothing changes); fawn trousers and a white shirt, the sleeves rolled neatly to above my elbows. In one tanned hand I held a notebook, in the other a pen – I shot questions at Susan as if I were an ace reporter. I couldn't hear what I was asking only her answers. The word *love* kept coming up which made me uneasy. Even in my dream I recalled my grandmother telling me, *love's not a word to bandy about.*

'They only loved *her*,' Susan said. 'She only loved *them*. No love left for me.'

She swayed forward so her face came close to mine. 'No love left for you either, Bonnie.'

Her face was greenish white. She hardly looked like Susan. Finally she said, 'I'm sorry. My breath's almost gone and I can't feel my legs anymore. I have to sit down.' She made no attempt to sit.

198

I was exasperated with this changed, compliant cousin. Suddenly I saw Gran although I sensed she'd been near us for some time. She sat on our scullery stool, hunched into her black overcoat watching us. Her surprisingly bright brown eyes connected with mine as if willing me to behave better, to show some emotion she privately doubted I was capable of.

I made a feeble waving gesture with my hands; a half apology implying that reluctantly I must now make my way alone back up to the surface. The notebook and pen floated away. I stopped meeting Gran's gaze, ignored Susan as she sank down onto the sand. I looked upwards. Gracefully I shot one arm out and began to swim away from them. I can't swim.

It's morning. The smell of toast arrives before Jay and the breakfast tray.

'In a low key way this trip is quite exciting,' she says as she walks into the bedroom. Jay has not been Joanna for at least three decades. She no longer wears her hair in ringlets either; in fact these days she denies ever having them.

'My hair was very curly, Bonnie that was all.'

'But I remember ringlets. Like corkscrews.'

'Then you remember wrongly.'

Her hair *is* curly. She wears it short. Jokingly we call her hair style an 'elfin cap', although due to its extreme volume we should really liken it to a 'mob cap'. The colour is pepper and salt although the sun still searches out and finds threads of red-gold.

She puts the tray down on the bed. From under the plate of toast she takes a paper serviette and blots my eyes.

'Cheer up. I hope you're not going to spend the weekend crying.'

'For me this is an emotional experience.'

'Everything's an emotional experience with you. Now what should I wear? The cerise taffeta or my shantung silk?'

Which makes me laugh.

'That's better,' she says. 'Will your grandmother be shocked when she finds out your "Jay" is me?'

I shake my head. 'I don't think so.'

I take Aunt Ed's tiny, glass swan's head with me. Even with all I now know about my aunt, I can't bring myself to leave it behind or

199

worse, throw it away. It's my good-luck talisman. For years it travelled wrapped in Jay's blue chiffon scarf but that finally disintegrated. Now the swan's head lies snug and safe in a velvet pouch.

We wear jeans and t-shirts. In the side pocket of my rucksack I have a present for my grandmother.

'Bonnie, there's nothing I need.'

'You don't have to "need" a birthday present.'

It is a photograph of me with Jay, our arms linked. We are standing on a beach, the sea sparkling behind us. I won't mind if Gran adds it to the pile in her top drawer of Benson family photographs.

We stay at the *Holiday Inn* near Birmingham New Street Station. That first day we explore the city centre, both of us marvelling at the amount of change. I can't quite explain the impact of being back somewhere so intrinsically familiar yet altered. I'm smiling while at the same time being close to tears. I drink in voices, my ears tuned for what Aunt Ed always scornfully called the Brummy whine. When I do catch that particular high, nasal intonation my pulse actually quickens with pleasure. Later, in a restaurant sited in the middle of a new retail development with a fountain and Mexican band playing in the background, I say this to Jay.

'You're mad. I hate that whine. It's awful.'

'It's how all my family spoke. Me too.'

'Surely not your Aunt Ed?'

'When she was angry she sounded more of a Brummy than my gran.'

'But I don't remember you having an accent.'

'I hardly said two words to you at school.'

'Or perhaps I liked you so much I didn't notice – or care.' She studies the menu. 'Do you remember kissing me on the cheek in the playground with my mum watching and thinking "What's that strange little girl up to with my daughter"?'

This is a romantic foolish question that still seems to bear asking and answering many more times before I die.

'Of course I do.'

On Sunday morning after an early breakfast we set off from the town centre. Birmingham is only just beginning to stir after a hectic Saturday night. Outside *Starbucks* the staff are sluggishly arranging tables and chairs in expectation of another fine day. We walk down Edgbaston Street then right onto the Digbeth Road. I've bought a map in the hotel because the roads whose names were very much part of my childhood have become unrecognisable.

'Now, this should lead into… ' but no, it doesn't.

Hand in hand we walk between ramshackle buildings, warehouses, shuttered shops, houses that look as if they've been boarded up for years.

'Coventry Road,' I say, almost to myself.

'Bit deserted. Wish we'd driven,' Jay says as we pass under the soot blackened bridge of Bordesley Station. Across the bridge a pockmarked sign proclaims 'You are entering Peugeot Country'. No, we are leaving it.

So many streets of shabby Victorian houses have disappeared beneath major roads and roundabouts. At one point we find ourselves outside a king-sized *McDonalds*, our only view a gigantic complex road system of fast moving traffic. It is impossible to cross. Jay consults the map while I buy chips.

'Should we eat *McDonald's* chips?'

'We do today,' I say firmly.

Off we go again. Arthur Street. Bolton Road. There are branches and leaves scattered across the pavements from a tornado earlier in the week. I think, 'Gran would enjoy a good tornado.' We walk parallel to a motorway. Once we turn around and Jay takes photographs of the Birmingham skyline, the cluster of tall buildings rising out of a flattened alien landscape.

At one point I lose heart. As a child with far shorter legs I could never remember feeling so weary. I don't remember the smothered quiet either – as if the many new wide roads have effectively separated the heart of the city from its limbs.

'It's bloody miles,' Jay complains as we turn into Cookseye Road. 'You must have been a sturdy little girl walking everywhere.'

'I was. Dad only used our car for family outings and we had hardly any of those.'

We stand forlornly on a mini-roundabout. My memory box supplies no such thing. And then suddenly I spot them, the tall wrought iron gates of Small Heath Park. There is Waverley Road still curved around its outer edge. I smile with relief and recognition.

Waverley Road, Golden Hillock Road. Later we find the slightly posher Byron Road where Gran's friend Miss Venables lived. Not posh anymore. Only half the houses are still standing. The back fences have fallen inwards and we stare into neglected gardens.

In Waverley Road there are surprisingly few cars, surprisingly few people. I expect, while not really expecting, to see them all – Dad, Mum, Gran, even my grandfather. Mrs Mallaby perched on her front wall, Mrs Brown hurrying into her house, her eternally sad face averted. And perhaps just arriving in one of their many sleek new cars are my aunt, uncle and Susan, all three of them looking glamorous and sophisticated. There is Uncle Brian, urbane and suited as Cary Grant, Aunt Ed, a curvaceous Gina Lollobrigida, and Susan. Who would she be?

Remembered places when re-visited often appear to have shrunk. Small Heath Park hasn't shrunk at all. If anything it seems bigger. The grass stretches into a misty distance; a hundred yards away a football match is in progress, men in muddy black shorts and red pullovers. Apart from the footballers and a woman with a long-haired Alsatian, the park is deserted. I'd remembered the lake as a small one, a large pond really, but I have to take three different photographs to capture its entire width. The central island of birch trees and rhododendrons, appears to have crept nearer to the main bank. There are literally hundreds of Canada Geese squawking at us self-importantly as if we are the interlopers. Where are the ducks and swans, the jetty and the rowing boats?

On a slight incline looking down over the lake we spread out a blanket. This might be the exact spot chosen for our family picnic all those years ago. I have the unsettling feeling again, as if time can be flipped backwards; a photograph for each year – ah yes, here's one of the Benson family in apparent good humour.

'They're coming,' Jay says.

Yes. First a girl and boy, ages sixteen and eighteen. Behind them, walking slowly, a short stocky man with thinning brown hair, maybe Peter or Geoff. On his arm leans an elderly woman in a tweed coat – my grandmother's friend Hilda.

'Gangway,' someone shouts.

Along the tarmac path encircling the lake a wheelchair is

powering through the ranks of geese. In her early fifties I thought my grandmother ancient, somehow now at ninety she doesn't look so bad. She's half her original size; a tiny, white-haired, pale skinned old lady in a scarlet coat, black boucle wool collar turned up to frame her face. My cousin Susan pushes the chair, jogging behind in track suit and blindingly white trainers. She is the grown-up version of the child – who rode her bike everywhere, who pushed me down the stairs, who tried to kill herself when she was eleven, who loved her mother in spite of. She's shrieking with excitement, her untidy grey-brown hair flies.

'Susan, be careful,' the man warns.

Jay and I, we get to our feet and wave wildly.

'Why it's Bonnie,' my gran says.

'Go Bonnie.' Jay pushes me.

I hesitate. Jay slaps me on the back and I start running towards them. The geese rise several feet into the air. There is the rushing sound of their flapping wings. They are a moving, changing cloud between us. The effect is like interference on our old television screen, the image of Gran and Susan disappears, re-appears. I take a deep breath and plunge straight into the cloud.

Acknowledgements

A big thank you to Sarah Waters whose advice and support with this novel have been invaluable; to Clare Summerskill for vital input in the final draft; and to Adele Ward, my publisher, who took on *Always you, Edina* over a jolly cup of tea at the West Hill Cafe in Hastings.

About the Author

VG Lee is an author and a stand-up comedian. She was born in Birmingham but has gradually worked her way southwards and now lives and writes in Hastings, East Sussex. She has published three novels; *The Comedienne*, Diva Books, 2001; *The Woman in Beige*, Diva Books, 2003; *Diary of a Provincial Lesbian*, Onlywomen Press, 2005; and a collection of short stories, *As You Step Outside*, Tollington Press, 2008.

Her work has appeared in *Chroma, Magma, Poetry Review* and *Mslexia*; and her short stories have been published in *Boys & Girls* and *Men & Women*, two anthologies from Glasshouse Books.

In 2009, to celebrate her sixtieth year, she decided to become a stand-up comedian and perform at sixty venues. Sixty venues became ninety and she was a runner-up in the prestigious 'New Act of the Year 2010' at the Hackney Empire. She has appeared twice at the Edinburgh Festival.